Adrian Day and Martyn Bilton are two young journalists adrift in the *New Globe* – a newspaper so grotesquely large that it has a supplement listing all the other supplements. While Adrian, editor of the prestigious 'Me & My Pen' slot, knuckles down to endless lifestyle features about fatuous celebrities, Bilton is the thorn in the side of this over-inflated world.

For Bilton is an old-fashioned Marxist, a man of principles who writes about things that matter – or so he claims. What is certain is that he is impressively rude, frequently drunk, and that his career is going absolutely nowhere.

But then, after The Incident (involving a cup of coffee, the prime minister, and the exploitation of the working class), an explosion of hype blows Bilton out of the cutting edge of lifestyle journalism and on to a much larger stage . . .

Bilton is that unusual thing, a satirical comic novel crammed with hit-and-run jokes and hilarious reversals, which is both immediately engaging and deeply, seriously funny.

Andrew Martin is a former Spectator Young Writer of the Year. He works as a freelance journalist, and has contributed to the *Guardian, Daily Telegraph* and *Independent on Sunday*. He is currently a Contributing Editor to the Evening Standard's *ES* Magazine, where he also writes the Tube Talk column.

Bilton

'Enormously **funny**, genuinely moving
and even a little scary.'
Jon Ronson

'Genuinely **funny**.'
Joseph Connolly

'A very **funny** début.'
Tim Lott, *The Times*

'Both sour and **funny** about the current state of journalism.'
Lynn Barber, *Observer*

'**Funny** and accurate in its attack on the witlessness of most
British newspapers.'
Sunday Express

'**Funny** and readable.'
Evening Standard

'A brilliantly **funny** and accomplished first novel.'
Spectator

'Remarkably **funny**.'
Daily Telegraph

'Sharp, **funny**, and occasionally savage.'
Sussex Latest

'A lively, genuinely **funny** début.'
Yorkshire Post

'**Funny**.'
Independent on Sunday

BILTON

Andrew Martin

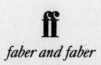

faber and faber

First published in 1998
by Faber and Faber Limited
3 Queen Square London WC1N 3AU
Open market paperback edition published in 1999
This paperback edition published in 1999

Typeset by Faber and Faber Ltd
Printed in England by Mackays of Chatham plc, Chatham, Kent

© Andrew Martin, 1998

Andrew Martin is hereby identified as author of this work in accordance
with Section 77 of the Copyright, Designs and Patents Act 1988

A CIP record for this book
is available from the British Library

ISBN 0–571–19565–2

10 9 8 7 6 5 4 3 2 1

Chapter One

(Four months before the incident)

The lifts at Globe Newspapers were incredibly quick, but on the other hand they made you feel sick. On the tenth floor the doors opened with a sucking sound to reveal June Brown.

'Adrian Day?' she said.

'Er yeah,' I replied suavely.

I followed June Brown down a wide, white corridor with oil paintings. We passed an open door, and I fleetingly noticed a small man standing still with his hands in his trouser pockets and saying, 'Fuck, fuck, fuck, fuck, fuck.'

The oil paintings were intensifying now, and statuettes were starting to appear. There was a peculiar inside-out quality to Globe House in that the nearer you got to its editorial heart the less it seemed like a newspaper office and the more it seemed like some sort of rambling country house.

'How *is* Mr Piper this morning?' I asked June Brown as we pounded on.

'Stressed out,' she said, flatly.

It had been a silly question; the product of sheer nerves. I had read so much in the media magazines about the man June Brown personally assisted that the prospect of seeing him incarnate was very intimidating.

Harry Piper was a journalist of the old school, or, to put it another way, an alcoholic. Yet he was also a master of lifestyle features, with a whole string of lifestyle regulars to his name, starting with 'Just My Cup of Tea', in which celebrities talked about whether they put the milk in first or whatever. Now, as

Head of Lifestyle at *The New Globe,* he outranked the News Editor, was on an almost equal footing with the Head of Advertising, and was right at the top of the tree that I was trying to climb.

Back then, *The New Globe* was, of course, the most widely read and, in its paper format, physically the biggest newspaper in the country. It was the first paper to introduce a supplement giving a listing of all the other supplements and providing a précis of their contents. Every edition ran to three-quarters of a million words, and it was the boast of 'Little' Willie Meltchitt, the peculiarly styled Chief Editor in Chief, that he never read a word of it. 'I don't have time,' he'd blithely say. A rotating team of trainees with firsts provided a verbal digest of its contents as that volatile man-mountain took his morning coffee.

But now June Brown had disappeared.

I walked a cautious couple of paces, looked through an open door to my left and there was Harry Piper. June Brown, standing by his side, gave vent to a ragged raucous cackle and then peeled away to the back of the room as I approached.

Harry Piper rising to greet me had the paradoxical effect of making me want to collapse with nerves. He was short and quite squat, with a lot of shaggy grey hair and a red-grey, actually rather handsome face. He was in his late fifties; his suit was green tweed. The room which he shared with June was large and light, red-carpeted, oak-wainscoted. There was a standard lamp, and an old leather armchair that had had a skin graft. On a bookcase were four boxes of Midnight Raider chocolates, and a rugby ball (I'd read that Piper used to like to fool around with one of these when he'd just been to see Little Willie).

On the wall behind Piper was a painting of a bottle of wine, which I guessed was his equivalent of having a picture of his younger self. Piper, as everyone knew, had been on the waggon these past ten years, apart from the lunch which he gave on the day of his promotion to Lifestyle Head, which had lasted – so it was said – for over three days.

'How's life on *The Sunday Thinker*?' enquired Piper after the opening formalities. (His accent contained just a hint of the original Scottish.)

'Difficult,' I said. 'There's no money; readership's way down.'

Piper nodded.

'How would *you* straighten things out there?'

'How would *I* straighten things out there?'

I held forth – confusedly – for a while and then, trying to be bold, asked Piper what *he* would do.

'Difficult. I suppose I'd sack all the existing staff and then . . . close it down, I guess. But there's some good stuff in there.'

Piper put his feet on the desk. He didn't *seem* particularly stressed out.

'Little Willie loves that thing you edit, you know.'

'"Me and My Pen"?'

'He told me it had, and I quote, "the true brilliance of all truly brilliant ideas". It was *your* idea, wasn't it?'

'Yes,' I said.

Piper looked at me, expecting more.

'I thought it up in the bath,' I said.

'What was the inspiration behind it?'

This was a curious question; I decided to be honest.

'There was no inspiration . . . not as such. I was just thinking about some of the other lifestyle regulars I'd seen in the papers – "Me and My Personal Computer", "Me and My Desk", etc. – and then it came to me: "Me and My Pen".'

'Brilliant,' said Harry Piper. 'Celebrities talk about their pens. Sheer brilliance. And I expect you get a lot of juicy ads around that slot.'

'We get a lot of ads for pens around there,' I said.

'Yes,' said Piper, nodding, 'I'll bet. Now we're prepared to pay good money for you to leave *The Sunday Thinker* and come to us, and when I say good money, I mean . . .'

Two things happened at this point: June Brown approached Piper's desk with coffee, and Piper smiled at her knowingly as he scribbled on a scrap of paper, which he then slid across the desk to me. On the piece of paper was a figure that was almost exactly three times my present income on the struggling *Sunday Thinker*.

My father had told me always to negotiate in situations like this, and I tried to summon up some fragments of appropriate phraseology. 'Is that your final offer?' I said, with a sort of gasp.

Piper looked surprised.

'To be pedantic,' he said, 'it's my *first* offer, but it might as well be my final one because I'm not going to change it.'

'Then I accept,' I said.

'Good,' said Piper. 'Now what about your job title?'

I thought hard. Even though I had come up with the idea of 'Me and My Pen', I was not, as Piper seemed to imagine, in charge of the feature on *The Sunday Thinker*. Instead, management had carved out for me the role of part-time editorial assistant, which essentially boiled down to emptying the bins. But I also got a chance to suggest appropriate celebrities for the slot, so my job had a kind of circular quality in that my suggestions formed by far the largest component of the rubbish in the bins that I then emptied.

Harry Piper was tired of waiting.

'How about Editorial Executive, brackets "Me and My Pen"?'

'Okay,' I said, 'fine.'

'Right. Now when can you start?'

'Well, obviously I have to give notice to *The Sunday Thinker*, and . . .'

'Tomorrow suit you?'

'Tomorrow,' I said; 'that's pretty soon. But no. Tomorrow it is then.'

'Good,' said Harry Piper again, 'and by the way, I like your negotiating style. Decisive, and yet always tending towards agreement with the other party. Now just before you go, I want to get a couple of things clear: you'll be in Lifestyle, and you'll be working alongside Hailey Young, a real hotshot.'

'"What I Did Yesterday"?'

'You know your stuff, that's good. Between you and me, we're having a few problems with that feature. It's a good idea but lacking authenticity. Hailey's interviewees are tending to talk about what they did the day *before* yesterday, or even, in extreme cases, what they did last week. One guy, some pop star, even told her what he was going to do *tomorrow*. No bloody use at all. I want to get that feature kicked into line, and I'm going to need your help. That's not to say that I'm slagging Hailey off. She's a wonderful girl, brilliant writer, full of ideas, hard-working, charming, a delight to have around. You'll also be working closely with another guy we've just taken on: Bilton.'

Harry Piper paused, looked a little lost for a second, then smiled absurdly and said, 'Okay?'

Evidently that was it.

'I have a question,' I said, as June came to take me away. '"Pen" was my idea, sure, but don't you think *The Sunday Thinker* is going to be pretty angry about having its feature stolen?'

'We shaft them all the time,' said Piper, briskly verifying the

5

presence of fags in his tweed jacket pocket, 'and they shaft us all the time. It's a sort of gentleman's agreement. Oh, one last thing: what do you think of our Prime Minister?'

'Mr Lazenby?' I said stupidly. 'Well, I don't mind . . .'

Harry Piper was suddenly scowling at me. The fact was that I didn't mind Mr Lazenby as much as everybody else seemed to at that time, but I decided to change tack.

'. . . I don't mind admitting that I think he's losing his touch,' I said.

Harry Piper's scowl was modified into a sort of semi-comical parody of a shrewd expression. He leant forward and began repeatedly drumming his fingers on the table.

'June will show you the Floor,' he said, '. . . familiarisation.'

The lift took us down to the lobby with the merest twinkle; barely enough time for June Brown to hand me a copy of that day's *Globe* in its transparent carrier bag.

Then the doors melted open and June led me across the high, cool *Globe* lobby, which was basically an enormous white marble box. Except for the slowly revolving blue and brown globe suspended from the ceiling, a tiny reception and a tiny receptionist, it was completely empty. Originally, of course, it had been quite full: containing a *large* reception desk, a security booth, a permanent exhibition celebrating the history of journalism, some statues, a fountain, and a bar that served fashionable types of coffee. But then the top brass at *Globe* had commissioned a redesign by the famous Japanese minimalist, I. No, who had paid some removal men to take everything out of the lobby, and then sent in an invoice for a million pounds plus expenses.

Recessed around the top of the lobby was the famous champagne balcony and, sure enough, some people were already drinking champagne there and looking down on us. I felt dazed and elated: finally on the verge of the big time, on the verge, I felt sure, of the champagne.

I'd always wanted to be a journalist.

My father and I loved newspapers. Every Sunday morning back home in Yorkshire, my father would cook one of his 'specials' – a breakfast comprising eggs, bacon, black pudding, fried tomatoes, sausages and other unhealthy ingredients depending upon seasonal availability – then we'd sit down and read the papers in silence for five hours. Very sociable we were. My great-grandfather would sometimes be present (if all attempts to dissuade him had failed), perusing the absurd freesheet *The Sunday Brightener*.

Every week he read out the tongue-twister on page ten. He was surprisingly good at this, especially considering the state of his teeth, which were both false and suffering from decay. As he slitheringly got to grips with some new piece of alliterative garbage, my father would smile, put down his newspaper and give me a thrillingly grown-up, complicit smile: 'Listen to the old fool' was the message he seemed to be conveying. Once, aged about twelve, I was sufficiently emboldened by one of his smiles, and my ready comprehension of a number of difficult pieces, to put aside my own paper – from the very earliest age it would have been a 'quality' of some sort – and say, 'For fuck's sake, great-grandad, do shut up.' After being hit very hard on the side of my head by my father, I trudged disconsolately upstairs with some motoring supplement or other, which I cast aside in favour of the *Beano*; a conscious regression to a safer world. But I was soon back on newspapers.

In my late teens, I wrote seventeen letters to our perfectly good local newspaper, *The Yorkshire Spotlight*. The first sixteen were condemnatory, attacking its parochialism, the prose style of its astrologer, the excessive space given to rugby and pigeons, the misuse of semicolons and, much to my shame, the soft-focus picture of the TV reviewer, Daphne Bridges. (I'd seen her in the street and she looked nothing like that.) The seventeenth was a request for a job. 'I have always enjoyed your newspaper immensely,' I wrote. I never got a reply, so I wrote back informing the editor that I didn't want a job on his little paper and reiterating, with swear words, many of the points I had made in my first sixteen communications.

Five stressful freelance years later, I found my first ever staff job as Junior Interviewer on *The View from Here* in which celebrities were asked what they'd watched on television in the previous week. I found that I had a knack for eliciting/ inventing interesting quotes from them, and *The Sunday Thinker* had actually poached me from *View* within six weeks of my starting there.

By now June had stopped half-way across the lobby and was talking to someone else. Again the laugh. Of course, I didn't *know* June Brown, but there was something rather rude about the way she seemed to have a great time with everyone but me.

I looked through the transparent plastic at the *Globe*'s headline: 'LAZENBY DENIES BALLS-UP', I read. I stared at a picture of Philip Lazenby denying a balls-up, and glanced further down the page: 'Ethnic Russians riot in Estonia'. Now that was interesting because I had thought, up to that point, that Estonia was somewhere in a fairy story. I didn't actually read the article, though, because June Brown – poker face restored – was now leading me on to the Editorial Floor.

The editorial floor was a single, hideously distended office. You were aware of vistas and horizons. The desks were arranged in clusters across a dingily carpeted space full of swarming, gesticulating, jabbering journalists. There were dark, tunnel-like alcoves off the main floor into which men in suits would swoop, and from which blabbering, shrugging teams of executives – awesome meetings on the move – raucously emerged. You didn't want to go too near to them in case you were asked to do something or got swirled into the argument.

In the middle of the floor stood a big scaffolding gantry on which a gang of men were doing restorative work to the building. Objectively, their operation was big-scale – roaring oxy-acetylene torches, several wardrobe-sized banks of electronic monitoring equipment, an electrical buggy or control module of some sort – but they were just a flickering distraction, such was the scale of the journalistic operations.

June led me across the floor, and we homed in on the most comprehensively weird-looking person I'd ever seen. He was tall, cadaverous and concave, with a long, coffin-shaped face, powdery white skin, and large, piercing violet eyes rammed deep into blue-dusted sockets. His poignantly dandruff-flecked hair was black except for a jagged lightning flash of a russet colour (I knew at once that his hair wasn't dyed, but just naturally defective), and shaped like some sort of medieval haystack or something. He had a great white cliff of a nose and fat, purplish lips behind which his teeth were large and perfectly square. He wore an ancient, mildewed black jacket and a shapeless shirt with the texture of an old winceyette blanket. Apart from a general air of etiolated adolescence, the hint of overbite in his jaw, and the slight sense that he'd been buried under peat for roughly seven thousand years, you might have said that Martyn Bilton was good-looking. Eventually, a lot of people *would* say that.

He was staring at a screen and, even while we stood over

9

him, he continued to type faster than I'd ever seen anyone type before.

'Bilton,' said June, 'stop it!'

Martyn Bilton laid his long, white hands quiveringly on either side of his keyboard, sighed and lifted his head.

'Adrian Day – Bilton,' said June. Or the other way round.

Bilton looked sceptically at my outstretched hand out of the corner of his eye for probably five seconds and then perfunctorily shook it. You can usually read the message in a handshake, and his said, 'Go away.' I formed the idea that he didn't like people looking at him. He seemed like a man – or a boy, really – who was sorry to be mired in his own strange looks.

'You on "Tit and Tat"?' he said. It took me a second to work out that he was referring to 'Royal Tittle Tattle', the royal gossip column presided over by the formidable fading beauty Roz Newbold. Its potent combination of sycophancy and downright lies had earned it a daily front-page slot, and it was where most young recruits to *The New Globe* began work.

'No,' I said.

Bilton wasn't remotely interested, yet nor was he taking the piss. I liked that. He had a deep, dark voice; accentless.

'Which department are *you* in?' I asked.

Bilton looked at his amazingly horrible black plastic watch and sighed.

'"Comment and Analysis",' he said, 'political stuff.'

'Martyn Bilton,' I mused. 'Haven't I seen your name on some gardening features? I seem to remember a piece by you on the new move towards smaller cucumbers.'

He gave me a fuck-off look.

'I have a roving brief,' he growled.

'Bilton,' said June, 'I'd like you to show Adrian around the office. Tell him what's what, and so on.'

'Can't,' said Bilton. 'I'm on a deadline.'

But June had already gone.

'What does she think I am, a fucking tour guide?' said Bilton to himself, but he stood up and, in doing so, evidently swayed too close to me. He swayed quickly away again.

'You've got five minutes,' he said.

The people Bilton knew tended to be gofers, tea ladies, security guards and the like. He didn't introduce me to the bigwigs so much as point them out from a distance of about three hundred yards.

We approached a blank little desk in what was, amazingly, a quiet corner of the office.

'You've heard of "The World of Roger Warburton"?' said Bilton, referring in a bored tone to *The New Globe*'s most famous column. 'This is where it's produced.'

To the naked eye, the world of Roger Warburton consisted of a telephone, an ashtray, and a copy of the *Pics 'N' News* tabloid. Then a shambolic, greasy-haired, middle-aged man sidled up to the desk. He sat down, sighed, pushed his hair out of his eyes, moved the ashtray slightly to the left and picked up the paper. He began to read.

'Roger Warburton?' I whispered reverently to Bilton.

He nodded.

Bilton and I watched as Warburton took a packet of Polo mints from his pocket, removed one and placed it absent-mindedly into his mouth. He then reached into his mouth with thumb and forefinger and extracted a small piece of Polo wrapping which he had inadvertently placed upon his tongue along with the sweet. He began flicking through the newspaper. Eventually, arriving at the crossword, he removed a pen from the inside pocket of his jacket, and scrawled in the margin of the newspaper to test the flow of ink. He scribbled irritatedly for a while – obviously the pen didn't work. The phone rang, and Roger Warburton answered it. 'World of

Roger Warburton,' he said into the receiver, still scribbling, quite furiously now, with the pen. He listened for a while. 'Yeah,' he said, 'you've obviously got the wrong number. This is the "World of Roger Warburton", as I said before.'

He put the phone, and the pen, down and began staring blankly ahead, occasionally scratching his upper thigh. Then Roger Warburton got up and slowly walked away.

'Seven hundred and fifty thousand pounds a year,' said Bilton simply.

'What does it say at the top of his page?' I asked rhetorically, '"He's got his ear to the ground, his finger on the pulse and his nose to the grindstone . . ."?'

'Yeah,' said Bilton, 'and his brains in his arse.'

'You don't really rate him then?'

But Bilton had walked on.

'Ads,' he said, dismissing, say, three hundred people with a wave of his hand.

'But I thought this was the Editorial Floor. The advertising department shouldn't be here,' I said plaintively.

'I do hope you're not going to start running around shouting "Hold the front page",' said Bilton, who was now craning to look into the far distance; then he changed direction.

'This is news,' he went on, indicating a smoke-clouded area. The personnel of the newsdesk all looked more or less the same: male, sallow and hirsute. Cool dudes.

'Where's our man in Moscow?' one of them was shouting at someone passing by. 'Can't raise him. Where the fuck is he?'

'Our man in Moscow is in Paris,' said the passer-by calmly. 'He's helping our man in Brussels write a biography of our man in Peking. Who is in London. Our man in Stockholm is in Moscow, if that's any use.'

'Christ!' said the news man.

How I would love to have been 'our man in Moscow'. The situation there had, of course, been particularly interesting for the last two years – ever since the collapse of Western bridge building, and since General Zubarov's coup against the other General whose name nobody had been able to pronounce, and which I had in any case forgotten. But maybe 'Me and My Pen' would provide a springboard for writing about the niceties of international diplomacy.

'"Comment and Analysis",' said Bilton, pointing at some other desks occupied by milder-looking people. We walked towards them and my eye caught a sentence being typed on a screen by a young reporter.

'According to opinion polls . . .' he wrote; he stopped for a second and then resumed, '. . . Mr Lazenby has plumbed a new low.' An older man appeared behind the writer's seat, looked at the screen for a while, leant towards the keyboard and replaced the word 'plumbed' with 'plummeted to'.

'You're not at university now, you know,' he said, almost gently, to the young man.

Regarding Lazenby, *The New Globe* was at this point in time – well into his second term – veering from ambivalent support to definite hostility. The paper had been one of the few to express any real enthusiasm for the muted rallying cry, 'Together in the marketplace', which had secured him his first term seven years before. Back then, Lazenby had been new and glamorous – although a big factor in his first victory (according to subsequent research) was that he looked a bit like the little one in The Monkees.

Actually, Lazenby was personally kind and intensely, in fact rather boringly, eager to learn about the everyday problems of ordinary folk – an eagerness which the ordinary folk in question often found quite overwhelming. He was also brilliantly intelligent, at least on paper, with his double first, doctorate, fellowship of All Souls, Harvard stint and a string of books about something he called Inward Economics.

With his pretty, brown face, bouncy dome of brown hair, and down-pointing moist brown eyes, women wanted to mother him and men wanted to smother him. He was shy and rather surprisingly dandyish, with his trademark high collars creating a slightly Elizabethan effect, and his habitual chalk-striped blue suits taken sharply in at the waist, so that he somehow looked like a Prime Minister in a musical comedy; or simply a dancer. He was, in sum, a hyperactive, meticulous, genial, honourable, dapper and tedious man whose walk was a scuttle and whose voice was a rapid rustling whisper.

Lazenby's early years were successful; his daily popularity ratings in the permanent polls were uniformly high. The economy boomed; he complicatedly sorted out the local government thing; did much good work transport-wise. Then, at the start of his second term, the boom started to falter, and that unfortunate episode in the Bois de Boulogne cost him his personable deputy, Michael 'Beezer' Burnside, who'd been so good at presenting the crabbed and drily technocratic policies in an interesting light. Before standing for Parliament, Lazenby had taken the standard Media for Politicians course at King's, but he couldn't relax in an interview, in spite of (it was said) a course of hypnosis to help the problem. He was quite incapable of spontaneity.

And then he walked into the quagmire of Social Dynamics.

Lazenby had begun as a humane, enterprising, but conventional enough manager of the free market, but a year after his second election victory he surprisingly announced that he had a 'guiding light' after all. 'And that guiding light,' he fatally intoned, 'is Social Dynamics.'

14

The first initiative under that banner was Lazenby's policy of Fostering the Good Heartedness Of Relatives and Neighbours (FOGHORN), but as this involved little more than subsidised bus travel for people willing to fill in a very long form it wasn't much of a clue as to the meaning of Social Dynamics. But the full-blown Initiatives followed shortly afterwards.

So what *was* Social Dynamics?

Well, in a nutshell, it wasn't possible to put it in a nutshell, but, crassly distilled, as far as I know, it came down to something like this . . .

Individuals (amalgamated into one of an ever-changing series of semi-formal collective bodies) or businesses or voluntary organisations would be financially rewarded through an incredibly complex network of tax breaks or Community Payback Vouchers, or any one of a number of other financial incentives, for any act deemed to be 'socially useful'. Any acts deemed to be socially useful and which also promised 'significantly to increase', or to be 'potentially capable of significantly increasing generative capacity' . . . well, they earned double.

An act was deemed to be socially useful if, in the eyes of the regulatory, locally elected Community Forums and their advisers, it promoted (normally) any three of the following: individual responsibility; a spirit of community; an increase in generative capacity or a reduction in public spending, and all of these criteria were unified in one over-arching principle, which stated that for an act to be socially useful it had to be adjudged Socially Dynamic.

Which brought everything back to square one.

It was all regulated by Professor Chivers's famous Interlocking Sliding Scales, out of which, of course, a whole new branch of mathematics emerged which eventually led to the squaring of the circle.

Why was the policy so very irritating? Well, it was billed as being bold and radical, but if you examined the small print, which nobody could ever be bothered to do, it appeared hedged about with self-defeating contradictions, recondite in the extreme and ideologically ambiguous. Was it left wing or right wing? Lazenby himself proudly announced, with the alienating gleam of the pioneering zealot, that it was 'both, either or neither'.

On the one hand, there was the word 'community', pietistically repeated at every turn, which seemed to imply egalitarian intent. Yet, on the other hand, the profit motive appeared to be at the heart of Social Dynamics. It was, you might say, like one of those trick drawings of a staircase which at first glance looks plausible enough, but which then takes on the appearance of something quite unclimbable.

When Little Willie Meltchitt, fuming about the state of the country from his customary vantage point of a yacht moored off Mustique, said that Social Dynamics was the work of a 'schizophrenic chameleon with an identity crisis standing in a hall of mirrors', many people knew exactly what he meant. Or very nearly.

And then, of course, there was always Zubarov in the background, relentlessly expanding in all directions around Russia. Whereas Philip Lazenby was a decent, pleasant man who wanted to do the best he could by everybody, Zubarov was just a guy who liked blowing people up, and never the twain could meet. At the time of my arrival at *The New Globe*, Lazenby was already leading the international response to Zubarov with his 'guaranteed two-for-one concession ratios' in talks, his 'rolling symbolic borders' and 'phased deadline renewals', and other pieces of diplomatic sophistry, which he combined with periodic bouts of shrill sabre-rattling.

But Social Dynamics was the big issue back then. Only a

week after I arrived at the newspaper, the editor, Jack Christie, put his name to the famous Unanimous Editorial, in which every national newspaper editor (bar one) had called for Lazenby to abandon the 'madness' of that policy. (The exception being Bill Draper, editor of the downmarket *Daily Thunderball*, who maintained, perhaps because he was related by marriage to Lazenby's beautiful wife, Eglantine, that Lazenby was 'doing a wonderful job, and is the best man we've got'.)

As I emerged from my dreamy contemplation of the computer screen, I realised that Bilton had disappeared.

I turned around to see him sit down at his desk, take a swig of some sort of rehydrated soup from a little plastic bucket and start typing. He seemed completely wrapped up in himself; *committed*. I looked at all the reference books around him, squinting at the tome by his elbow. The title was impressively generic: *Thought and the Human Instinct, Volume 2*. (I later discovered that this was simply a book that Bilton had brought in to read in his lunch hour. And that he was not in fact writing a article for the heavyweight 'Comment and Analysis' section, but rather completing a small, hard-won commission from the Travel Editor about what to with your budgerigar when you went on holiday.)

He was writing with the same absurd intensity; indeed, he accelerated as I came close.

'Tour's over,' he said, above the noise of his rattling, bouncing keyboard. 'If there's anything you need, feel free to ask someone else. See you around.'

Now this really was quite offensive; I walked silently away, and then Bilton tapped me on the shoulder. 'I'm very busy,' he said, 'that's all it is. I hope you don't get sacked too quickly. It really is best not to ask me.'

He paused.

'I'm usually away – on stories and so on.'

And then he looked resolutely in another direction before stalking off.

Well, at least you couldn't accuse him of being false and oleaginous. I rather liked him actually. The truth is that Bilton fitted my romantic notion of the ideal journalist. He was obviously a martyr to words, and he represented, to me, a chink of light in this bureaucracy.

Chapter Two

I attempted to resign from *The Sunday Thinker* by phoning up the features editor. I thought I would do the decent thing and tell him in person that I was shafting him. But his phone was never answered.

A couple of days after I started at *The New Globe*, I was reading the front page when I happened to notice a new line of small print underneath the logo: 'Incorporating *The Sunday Thinker*', I read. Well, that explains a lot, I thought.

In my first week at *The New Globe*, I and a small team of assistants got 'Pen' up and running, and I became the main contributor to a weekly column called 'Fripperies'. This column was the result of intensive market research which revealed that there was a large group of *New Globe* readers who had, quite literally, more money than sense, and were so overburdened with cash that they would buy almost anything simply to get rid of the damn stuff. I reviewed a self-cleaning cleaning brush ('cleans itself as it cleans the floor'), a range of stainless-steel avocado stands, and a very complicated device called a 'sandwich aligner'. Basically, anything that was a waste of money came within my purview.

I was installed at a desk in the heart of Piper's Lifestyle empire. Hailey Young sat next to me. She was very tall, upper class, stand-offish to the likes of me. I noticed with dismay that she had received a personal letter from Little Willie. It was pinned up on her notice board. '"What I Did Yesterday",' he had written, 'has the true brilliance of all truly brilliant ideas.'

Bilton was a couple of desks away, although his appearances in the office were, indeed, intermittent. He never talked to anyone when he came in – 'good morning' wasn't his style – and worked in seclusion most of the day. The only person he had regular conversations with was a man always known simply as Timm, *The New Globe*'s stylish, bullet-headed, crew-cut, multi-millionaire cartoonist. They exchanged books, and exchanged looks, too, when anyone said anything crass or right wing. Timm, despite being a millionaire, appeared to share Bilton's interest in old-fashioned socialism.

Bilton came in one morning and put a book on Timm's desk. *Socialist Register*, it was called. 'There's some good stuff in there from way back,' he said, nodding at the book.

At the end of the day, Timm would sometimes walk up to Bilton and say, simply, 'Pint?' which always made me strangely jealous. Once, I noticed a bundle of doodles of Bilton at work by Timm. They looked like sketches by Mervyn Peake of some tower-bound fiend.

Timm was a pretty good cartoonist, actually. He went big on Lazenby's relative smallness. In Timm's cartoons Lazenby was often followed around by the irate 'Little Old Lady' – a sort of woman on the Clapham omnibus – who was, of course, depicted as being not quite as little as Lazenby. Timm captured Philip Lazenby with one wavy line which somehow took account of the bouncy hair, the beseeching brown eyes, the buckled shoes and pernickety tailoring; and he honed this line by watching Lazenby on television around the clock.

It was while I was watching the TV screen over Timm's shoulder that I saw Lazenby's disastrous 'I say this' rejoinder during that celebrated Prime Minister's Question Time. It was a week after his first big set-back in the Social Dynamic-related 'Keeping Community Local' programmes – his party (by now, of course, semi-officially rechristened the Social

Dynamic Party) had just lost three seats in by-elections.

That perennial thorn in Lazenby's side and the leader of the Left Rump, Robert Downer, asked the fatal question. It was simple and brilliant.

'Are trees Socially Dynamic?'

Prolonged screams of laughter. The contradictory statements on this matter over the preceding weeks – concerning a number of tree-planting proposals by do-gooding businessmen in search of tax breaks – had reached a farcical intensity.

Lazenby stood up, smiling. His tie knot was beautiful; sumptuously fat and lazily off-centre to just the right degree. He was smiling. He balanced in his hand a great floppy ream of paper.

'I quite understand the honourable gentleman's confusion. He is, after all, confused on most points.'

Some laughter; not much.

'The answer to the question is that, yes, trees are Socially Dynamic . . .'

Some rapid, favourable muttering from Lazenby's side.

'. . . Sometimes.'

During the ensuing ten minutes of guffawing, Lazenby sat down, rapidly reading his papers with legs tightly crossed.

Eventually he stood up again.

'Unfortunately the world is not the simple place that the honourable member for . . .'

The laughter was rising again. Lazenby stood up, sat down, stood up again.

'. . . would dearly like it to be. He insists on using the word "tree", which is a crude portmanteau term. Oak trees, for example, are Socially Dynamic, and – and – I would have thought that was obvious. As for beech trees, ash trees and elms . . .'

He was drowned out momentarily here, too.

'Beech trees, ash trees and elms . . .' croaked Lazenby, unprecedentedly rattled, and the rest of his sentence was inaudible.

'. . . To put forward the proposition – which I have not, incidentally, just done – that a particular field of endeavour is not Socially Dynamic . . .' Lazenby was saying when I could hear him again, '. . . is not for one minute to deny that it may well not be, or rather, may well actually *be* dynamic *socially*. Now the distinction might be made in the following terms . . .'

Lazenby was looking down at his papers, and Timm turned to me and shook his head. We conferred in amused tones for a while and then I looked back at the television screen just in time to see Lazenby, with the Commons wailing and howling all around him in a manner that had not been seen for years, in the middle of his fatal peroration, the one that came in response to cries about the Unanimous Editorial.

'The papers say resign, of course they do,' Lazenby shouted, 'the television pundits say resign, and there are voices in my own party – I admit it – saying resign. To all of those individuals, to all those people who don't have the stomach for the introduction of a bold new political initiative, to every last one of these sniping, carping, doing-down, pettifogging profits of doom, I say this . . .'

As Philip Lazenby riffled feverishly amongst his papers in search of precisely what he *was* going to say next, as the hiatus stretched from seconds to minutes in a House made suddenly silent by horror and unprecedented, elemental human sympathy for a man in trouble, as Lazenby checked his pockets, and then all too clearly urged his embarrassed Chancellor sitting alongside him to do the same, and as the same embarrassed Chancellor looked at Lazenby, and visibly mouthed the words, 'Just make something up,' I glanced back at Timm. He was packing away his pencils.

'I'm a satirist,' he muttered, 'and this is beyond satire.'
Bilton had his head down. He was working.

By this time, I'd found out more about Bilton (everyone called him Bilton), mainly from Timm. He was twenty-six; one year older than me. He'd been born in shady circumstances in Greenwich; his mother had given him up for adoption, and he was pinballed around middle-class foster homes, first in Greenwich, then in the gloomier parts of the Home Counties. He was connected with *The New Globe* in some highly ambiguous way, and that was how the editor liked it. He wandered the corridors doing odd bits of writing (at which he was very good), and some rewriting of the work of less intelligent but better-dressed people. Bilton wore a range of mildewed coats which he was able to pick up cheaply on account of the fact that they were falling apart and stank. He always wrote at his desk with an unnecessary pen in his mouth, and he was bloody clever, having wrested a good degree from the not very good south of England university to which he'd been consigned.

We didn't talk for a while after my first day, but one empty morning I approached him again.

'What are you writing at the moment?' I asked. 'Comment or analysis?'

He looked at me directly. 'Are you being funny?' he said.

'Actually,' I said, 'I was wondering whether you'd like to have lunch.'

'Don't do lunch,' he mumbled.

I'd been warned that Bilton had political objections to almost everything smacking of cronyism. His detractors called him sanctimonious.

'So, you're saying no?'

Bilton sighed, yanked open a drawer, pulled out a bent diary and flipped through numerous empty pages. Eventually, he stopped. 'Tuesday after next,' he said, 'one o'clock. The Ink Spotte. Now if you don't mind . . .'

And he curled up over his keyboard like a clever schoolchild trying to prevent a yobbish classmate from copying.

The Ink Spotte was located in a leafy square just round the corner from the towering late-post-modern folly housing *The New Globe*, but that ridiculous building was invisible from its windows. I walked to the pub on a windy but sunny spring day – a limbering-up, good-things-on-the-way type of day.

The Ink Spotte, with its lingering summer afternoon sunbeams, its blackened, bare bricks, its bay windows of twisted glass through which bright, blurred window-box flowers swayed and swooned, was to become very familiar to Bilton and me – a haven away from the pressure of work. I spied Bilton sitting in the corner of the saloon bar, underneath a stuffed squirrel in a box.

He wore a dusty, blue corduroy jacket and a stiff green shirt which looked to be about a hundred and ten per cent polyester. He also wore a food-clouded tie on which large blue specks merged queasily with green and orange specks. The tie civilised his wild, gothic features. But only slightly. We ordered wild boar sausages and beer.

'These sausages are good,' I said, when we were half-way through them and into our second beers.

Bilton suddenly stopped eating, and, with his mouth open, he looked at me assessingly for a while before resuming his meal. Eventually I asked Bilton whether he'd actually written a leader, which was, after all, the main point of being on 'Comment and Analysis'.

'Written?' he said, as though it was a ridiculously nebulous term. 'I've had *influence*, if that's what you mean.'

I told him about my novels. I'd written three, none of which had had any impact outside my own immediate bedroom. Had he tried any creative writing?

'I've written a novel,' he said warily.

'What was it about?'

'It examined the fate of the West through the metaphorical prism of a man who works in a shoe shop in Hull.'

'Sounds good,' I said. 'What happens in it?'

'What do you mean what happens?' said Bilton, combining – none too pleasantly – a sneer with sausage mastication.

'What's the story?'

'Jesus,' he muttered. 'There's this man. He's a tramp. Then he gets a job in a shoe shop in Hull. He gets ripped off; doesn't like having to arse-lick to the public. So he walks out and takes up where he left off as a dosser.'

I nodded.

'Interesting. How does the guy – the tramp – actually get a job in a shoe shop? I mean, does he have any experience of working in retail?'

Bilton laid down his knife and fork.

'It's very hard to respond to a point which is, with all due respect, so incredibly simple-minded.'

'All right,' I said. 'Sure. But I mean, *I* couldn't get a job in a shoe shop. You need the right references, experience of cash handling, not to mention some knowledge of shoes and . . .'

'It's a fucking political allegory,' said Bilton. 'All right?'

'And was it published?'

'It was considered. Some publishers hung on to it for a while.'

'How long?'

'A day,' he said. 'That was the longest.'

'I think it's *who* you know, isn't it?'

'What?' he said impatiently. 'The novel's dead. It was a nineteenth-century thing. Forget it.'

'So what is worth pursuing?'

'In literature nothing,' he said briskly. 'Try politics.'

'Presumably, for that, one would have to join a political party?'

'It's not a matter of parties,' he said, 'it's gone way beyond that. It's gone beyond democracy. That's just who's got the smartest fucking haircut, or something.' (In that case, I couldn't help thinking, it was jolly lucky for Bilton that things *had* gone beyond democracy.)

'Look,' he said, 'let's cut the crap. I need pieces for "Downbeat".'

'Ah,' I said.

Now this was nice of him. I was untested as a serious writer at *The New Globe*, and I admired 'Downbeat'. It was Bilton's brainchild and took up most of his working week. It was designed as an antidote to all the cheerful, optimistic pieces which were the stock in trade of *The New Globe*'s various lifestyle sections. The feature had begun shortly after I arrived at the paper, and the first one consisted of an interview by Bilton with a man from Nottingham who suffered from a very rare condition known as Rapidly Ageing Hair: he had started receding when he was six, and was completely bald by the age of nine. He was a complete social cripple, of course: a recluse. It was a fascinating piece. Bilton wrote well, in a limpid, Orwellian way, and with a lot of humanity.

'Downbeat' had even, against all odds, found a constituency amongst some of the *Globe*'s humbler advertisers, and the spaces around it were usually taken up by organisations like The Samaritans and Mental Health Helpline.

'I'd love to write for "Downbeat",' I said, 'but I don't have any ideas at the moment that are sufficiently, you know . . . down.'

'Not down,' said Bilton, 'just real. Are you interested in pigeons?'

'No,' I said.

'I want you to go up to Blackpool and write about the North of England Annual Pigeon Fair. Of course a lot of people are just breeding pigeons for the social kudos of it now that it's so trendy.'

'I know,' I said eagerly. 'It's massive in Notting Hill.'

'Notting Hill?' said Bilton. 'Fucking *Nothing* Hill, that's what I call it. Here we've got another piece of working-class culture that's become a fashion. Why? I want you to get to the bottom of that.'

I was interested now. 'Some people say the pigeon boom represents a return to making your own entertainment. You know, a reaction against media saturation.'

'I don't want you to get to the bottom of it *now*,' said Bilton, glancing crossly at his watch. 'But you might bear in mind that Little Willie Meltchitt has been promoting pigeon racing and pigeon breeding flat out for three years. When he started there was one pigeon item a week in *The New Globe*.'

'Oh, I think I remember that . . .'

'"Nelson's Column" it was called. By an old guy called Nelson Hill. He'd thrashed out a deal in which he was paid, literally, peanuts, which he fed to his birds, and then when they started "Pigeon Pull Out" they chucked him off staff because his face didn't fit. Typical bloody *Globe* behaviour. Anyway a few years ago Meltchitt shrewdly acquired, for about four pounds I think it was, the world rights to televise pigeon races, and the broadcasts start next year.'

'But how can pigeon racing be made suitable for television?'

'It can't,' said Bilton, 'which is why I want you to slag the whole deal off as a grotesque commercialisation of an important piece of working-class culture.'

I gulped, metaphorically speaking.

'Wouldn't Little Willie just sack me on the spot for using his own paper to slag him off?'

Bilton shrugged.

'I can't afford to worry about that. If he's going to make working people pay through the nose for something they invented he's got to expect trouble. And if you get any funny little stories about what endearing creatures pigeons are, for God's sake leave them out. I want a big piece about pigeons but I'm not interested in having any fucking stuff about *pigeons* in it. I'm interested in ordinary people; I'm interested in facts; I'm interested in hard-headed analysis.'

And he banged the table very hard.

'Oh, and one other thing,' said Bilton, stopping to retrieve the ashtray that had bounced on to the floor, 'Lazenby breeds pigeons.'

'Right,' I said. 'I'd forgotten that.'

'In lifestyle terms he majors on the clothes, pipe-smoking, cricket, tennis and sailing. But he's Honorary President of the British Pigeon Club, and every year for the past four years he's opened the Fair. Sure-fire PR coup. This year, though, the way his ratings are going, I think he might have some trouble.'

I nodded.

As our lunch ended I was certain of one thing: Bilton was either brilliantly clever or extremely stupid. He was very interested in politics and seemed to have set his heart on becoming some sort of dictator. The hallmark of his political position, it slowly became apparent, was a refusal to go into detail, and a fusing together, preferably under the influence of beer, of the extreme left, the extreme right, and the extreme centre – although he actually professed a strict Marxism, of which, of course, there had long since ceased to be very much about.

But I liked him. He made me laugh and I was happy to be his straight man.

Chapter Three

(Three months before the incident)

The stunted train approached Blackpool warily, through fields dotted with perfunctory sheep and malfunctioning electronic billboards. The tower – seeming to rise incongruously from fields – appeared, perplexingly, first to the left of the carriage and then to the right. Ultimately it disappeared altogether, except presumably to the driver bearing down upon it. In the complex of bunker-like pubs and dance halls at its base twenty thousand pigeons awaited.

The train was packed with pigeon men. Many of them smoked pipes and had little pigeon boxes on their knees, containing creatures deemed too sensitive, I supposed, for the dark traumas of the guard's van.

We pulled into the station and a porter drove a little rattling baggage waggon alongside to receive the crates of pigeons. I climbed into a station cab which wound through wet streets of rain-shadowed pebble-dash. A few small-scale amusements were tentatively open: a man looped the loop on a bicycle within a transparent bubble; a bouncy castle, moored to a lamp-post in a car park, bounced in the breeze.

I climbed out of the cab and gazed at the creaking tower; young police and old pigeon men milled around me. I went through the ancient, grating turnstile, was searched by two security guards and ushered towards Ballroom Three, an enormous brown hall with ornate plaster work and gargantuan chandeliers.

The ballroom, which smelt like an old barn, was about

three-quarters full although the Fair hadn't officially started. The birds made a sound like twenty thousand little engines being revved. In the centre of the ballroom was a grid of trestle tables on which rows of pigeon boxes were piled, and alongside one wall were more trestle tables covered with white tablecloths dotted with small, stiff pennants announcing 'food'. All along the opposite wall was a recessed bar whose security grille was lowered; behind it, uniformed homunculi complacently polished glasses. Around the halls were televisions – supplied by Globe Newspapers' TV arm – showing slow-motion, silent film of a pigeon in flight and details of forthcoming televised pigeon races.

Neat men in white coats with very sharp pencils in their pockets moved amongst the pigeon boxes. They were the judges, limbering up, getting ready to inspect some birds for beauty, others for racing potential. Most of the pigeon men were clustered around a stage which was bristling with trophies. Some held tremulous pigeons in big tattooed hands – like the beginning of a squeeze in eternal freeze-frame. In amongst the gnarled, dun-coloured blokes were younger people, cool dudes. Leather-jacketed guys with hand-held video cameras wandered amidst the throng, and many interviews were taking place.

'So my best bird took a sharp right in a Channel fog and ended up in the bloody Hook of Holland,' an enormous, baronial-looking man in a bristly jumper was saying.

'And I expect you had a good laugh about that,' said the reporter, who was wearing leather trousers.

'You're not a pigeon man yourself, are you?' said the moustachioed man.

I spotted a TV producer that I knew slightly. As I walked towards him I remembered that his name was Dan Argent. He looked pretty harassed; kept hauling his long silky hair out

31

of his eyes. It turned out he was involved in the planning of the race broadcasts

'How,' I asked, 'are you going to make pigeon racing suitable for television, given that the races go on for hours, and given that you won't be able to keep track of the birds in flight?'

'Well, you know, we'll have the start, with lots of cameras at the liberation point as it's called, and then it's straight into thirteen hours, or whatever, of expert analysis.'

'Expert analysis of what, though?'

'Yeah,' said Dan Argent, 'well, we're working on that.'

I collared a Yorkshireman who was called Ray.

'There's one bloke at our club,' said Ray, ruefully, '. . . he's not been profiled, not even on radio, and I'll tell you, he's *that* pissed off . . .'

'How many times have *you* been profiled?'

'Lost count. Ask my agent. They've made a whole series about me: "The Bird Man of Halifax". Following me to races, following me to the *bathroom*. Bloody daft. It's good money, mind you.'

I was talking to Ray and making notes when six men in suits filed onstage from a rear door. My eye fell naturally on the third of them. He had wavy, grey hair, a thin face, a predatory nose, and a frightening blue stare. Beside him – beneath him, in fact – was the Prime Minister. As Mr Lazenby beamed out at us, he appeared to be struck on the ankle by an elderly woman who was still sweeping the stage. (The Little Old Lady! How Timm would have loved to see that!) She was remonstrating with the Prime Minister as the Lady Mayoress of Blackpool joined the Lazenby entourage on stage.

Lazenby, having shaken off the dilatory sweeper, moved towards the microphone with his complicated, mincing walk. He was shuffling his cue cards all the while, like a magician without any tricks. He humbly lowered the level of the microphone, and stood there, adjusting his beautiful suit and arching his feet in his buckled loafers. He was waiting for the background bustle to die down, but it didn't, so he started anyway.

'You know,' he began, 'even Social Dynamics has its boring moments, and it really is quite amazing how often I'll be sitting in a meeting, or even amongst friends in an informal think-tank, and my mind will go back to all the birds I had in my youth.'

A big, dirty laugh, which Mr Lazenby, of course, had not intended. He stepped back from the mike wearing a stiff, twisted grin while the tall bodyguard concealed his titters by simply turning his back on the audience. Eventually – after shuffling his cards for a couple of minutes and making a little note on one of them with a maroon and gold fountain pen – Lazenby was able to continue.

'. . . I was lucky, as a young boy, to fall under the tutelage of that legendary pigeon man, U.A. Stanion . . .'

'Never heard of him,' Ray whispered in my ear.

'. . . and he it was who very kindly helped me set up my loft at the bottom of the garden, in which I had sixteen blues of excellent racing stock. Now I shall never forget that hot summer morning when, just eleven years old, I packed my birds into my wicker basket, propped it on the back of my bike and set off for my first practice release. Eleven miles I bicycled, through the undulating cornfields of Oxfordshire which rippled in the breeze like a silently surging sea of light. Shirt tail flapping behind me, nervous and elated, speeding over green-tinged shadows of oak and . . .'

'Yeah, yeah, yeah,' a man near to me boomingly drawled.

The metal screen protecting the bar was rattling upwards and there was a move towards the beer. Some of the judges had started making their rounds in earnest, and the volume of talk was increasing.

'Can you imagine my delight – my delirious excitement – when all the birds were sitting on the roof of our house when I returned home?' Lazenby continued more loudly. 'And shortly afterwards I began racing competitively, my fascination with these amazing creatures increasing daily. You know, so much about pigeons is mysterious. Why do they avoid water at all costs during flight? Why does the cock harry the hen so brutally towards the nest after mating? What, precisely, is the extent of a pigeon's field of vision? Why are some birds so inexplicably lazy, and why, why and why again do all pigeons hop three times on their right leg before every meal time . . .'

'Rubbish!' someone shouted.

'They don't do that!' shouted someone else.

'You've just made that up!' shouted a third.

A fairly loud disco soundtrack was now accompanying the television footage of birds in flight.

'. . . And above all why,' Lazenby was almost shouting, 'do the birds come home? How do they navigate? That is the greatest mystery at all and, although I am no scientist, I was fortunate enough at university to be able to participate in some of the experiments on pigeon brains conducted by Professor Morris . . .'

'Shame!' someone shouted.

The hubbub was very loud now.

'The lads aren't wearing it,' said Ray, 'they've had enough, they want to get on with the Fair.'

'. . . Which brings me,' Lazenby agonisingly continued, 'to the most important part of my business today, which is, of course . . .'

A tannoy crackled into life.

'Will the owner of the car, registration number . . .'

(The distortion was excruciating).

'. . . kindly remove it because it is blocking the car-park entrance. Thank you.'

And now Lazenby was sadly leaving the stage with his little entourage. He had declared the Fair open and nobody had actually noticed. I turned back to Ray, who'd been joined by his friend Don. Don was eating a sandwich. He had a badge on his lapel with a picture of a pigeon on it.

'This'll be big news,' I said, 'pigeon men snub Lazenby.'

Don was shaking his head.

'Lazenby's a man who's interested in pigeons . . .'

'*Maybe*,' qualified Ray.

'But he's not a pigeon man,' continued Don.

'Not a *pigeon* man,' said Ray.

'You see,' said Don, 'he's just using the pigeon fancy to get back some popularity. That's become very clear today.'

'Has it?' I said, making a note.

'To be honest,' continued Don, 'we didn't want Lazenby at all this year. We wanted that children's TV presenter who's really into pigeons – Tommy Snuggles.'

Ray was nodding.

'Someone with a bit of *weight* behind 'em.'

'Someone who makes a bit of sense when they open their mouth,' said Don. 'Instead of yapping on about bloody Social Dynamics.'

'What do you two think is the real appeal of pigeons?'

'Money?' suggested Ray. 'Prize money's going up all the time, which is good, but it's ruining the social life in the club.'

'They're also fantastic creatures,' said Don. 'Complex, characterful, delicious in pies.'

'We could go on all day about that,' said Ray.

*

'What do you think is the real appeal of pigeons?' I asked Tommy Snuggles, who was standing before a stack of caged, grey, puffed-out, puttering birds. He was wearing his trade-mark rainbow-coloured jumper and eating a cake.

'I think it's the authenticity of the thing, you know. It's been going for God knows how long, and you're doing things in a time-honoured fashion. It's slow; it's hard work; there's no quick fix. I personally find that pigeon racing is a great anti-dote to all the bullshit of the media world, speaking of which, would you mind giving my new kids' gardening show, *Round and Round the Garden with Tommy Snuggles*, a mention. It starts Tuesday, 4.30 p.m., Channel 26.'

(I liked Tommy Snuggles; there was a kind of honesty about him.)

I also glimpsed Gene Loader of the doomy beat group Sui-cide Pact, but his agent wouldn't let me get near him.

'When Gene's with his pigeons he doesn't do interviews,' said the agent. 'He just likes talking to them and mixing with the pigeon men on an equal footing. A lot of them don't even know who he is.'

I rather doubted that; for Gene's pigeons had been dyed black to fit in with his image.

I concluded my business at the Fair by talking to a man called John Harding. He was wearing a T-shirt and a flat cap and smoked a twisted little roll-up. He had one boxed pigeon on his knee. He was a dream from the 'Downbeat' point of view, going on about how commercialisation was wrecking the sport and doubling the price of maple peas, which, appar-ently, pigeons got through a lot of; and about how the con-stant coverage was making even the keenest pigeon men bored with their own sport.

'Why *do* they come back?' I asked him, by way of a final question.

We both looked at his little bird, hopping forlornly in its tiny box.

'Beats me,' said John Harding.

At seven o'clock, the Fair ended, and I took a cab to my hotel. Bilton had further endeared himself to me by insisting that I stay the night in Blackpool, and I'd checked into a hotel called the Beachside Palace, which was essentially a two-up-two-down about a mile from the sea and almost entirely obscured by a large sign saying 'Beachside Palace'. Underneath this sign, 'tea making facilities' and 'hot and cold running water' were stridently advertised.

Ten minutes later I was taking advantage of both of these luxuries – i.e. drinking tea in the bath while reading *Blackpool Now*. (Headline: 'PIGEON MEN GIVE LAZENBY THE BIRD'.) For a local paper, it was good, with surprisingly extensive foreign coverage. I read a long piece about the death of three British peace-keepers at the hands of Russian soldiers in the Protected Republic of the Ukraine. They had been defending territory in the western Ukraine. It was primarily a Catholic area, its citizens not keen on Russians. I tried to remember this. It was the sort of knowledge that was fairly surplus to requirements on 'Me and My Pen', but essential, I imagined, if you wanted to be our man in Moscow. The article concluded by blaming Philip Lazenby for the deaths. He hadn't, it seemed, made it sufficiently clear to Zubarov that he wasn't supposed to kill British soldiers.

I was still in the bath when my mobile trilled. It was one of Piper's gofers. I was to write a short news piece on Lazenby's embarrassment at the Fair, to be filed by phone in just under one minute's time. I was to write the 'Downbeat' piece as planned, delivering it the next day.

37

Chapter Four

The newsdesk – I discovered over breakfast the following morning – had changed every word of my two paragraphs. ('Don't worry,' said the news editor, 'we often do a lot more than that to a piece.') At three o'clock I nervously placed the 'Downbeat' feature on Bilton's desk, but he was out. At five o'clock he called me from a cab with a surprising invitation: round to his place for dinner. I was to bring the article with me.

Bilton inhabited a thin, falling-down terraced house next to an expanse of spooky scrubland in a grimy part of East London. Oh, what the hell: it was Leytonstone. There was a dismal Sunday-ish feel about the place. Rain fell.

'It's not a bad place,' I lied, as Bilton held the door open and unleashed a fusty waft from the interior.

The place smelt of old Oxo. When I had entered – which I did nervously – Bilton turned and plodded down a long hall containing a collapsed bicycle and a horizontal wardrobe. I followed him into a cold kitchen which was dirty but quite neat, or at least spartan. The wallpaper was peeling off the walls; the formica was peeling off the table. The bulb was the lowest wattage I had ever seen. It seemed to give off darkness, somehow. There was no microwave, just a battered, yellow gas cooker.

'I'm cooking dinner,' said Bilton. He brandished a tinned pie.

'That'll be nice,' I said. 'This is for you.'

I handed him my article. He stood very still and read it. He was wearing an imitation leather jacket and a purple shirt. When he'd finished, he slowly raised his head.

I could hardly wait for his verdict. I was especially concerned that he might think I'd not been hard enough on Little Willie.

'Well,' I said, 'what do you think?'

'It's okay,' he said, 'in parts.'

'Do you think I'll need to rewrite it?'

'No,' he said thoughtfully.

'Will you be able to use it?'

'Should think so, although we've got a couple in hand. Nice piece about a guy who drank himself to death on an oil rig; another about a woman who's digging her own grave in a Welsh churchyard.'

'Literally?'

'Literally.'

'My piece . . .' I said, 'I thought it might be a bit up for "Downbeat".'

Bilton shrugged.

'It's a bit gratuitously optimistic in parts, but you've minimised the cute stuff, and there is analysis there.'

I felt a sudden surge of exhilaration. There was analysis there. Bilton did like it, although, obviously, it wouldn't be his style to actually say so.

'You're a communist, aren't you?' I said.

'It's not a crime, is it?'

We didn't speak for a while. Bilton poured some horrible white wine into cups for both of us.

Then I said, 'If you were to sum up communism in one sentence, what would you say?'

'That's a request of quite mind-boggling fatuousness,' said Bilton calmly, 'but if forced I would say it's about liberating the individual.'

'I see,' I said, 'the exact opposite of what you're doing to that pie.'

(Bilton's tin opener didn't seem to be working.)

'Do you have anything else to drink?' I said, after a while.

'I can do you some water,' said Bilton.

Normally this would have been an offer guaranteed to depress me, but I was discovering that I enjoyed Bilton's company to the extent that I was overcome with burbling levity.

'Do you know what I've always thought about communism?' I asked, inspecting the sink.

'Something platitudinous?' Bilton said, now holding his ear to the tin and shaking it.

I ignored this.

'I've always thought it was closely akin to religion. That it is, in fact, a type of religion in itself, with an almost mystical inner core which is completely unsusceptible to objective analysis.'

I had read up a bit on communism, and this was a direct quote from somebody or other.

Bilton just kept working on the tin. He was now straining to remove the tin opener from the small hole in which it had become wedged, and from which a small amount of the pie was oozing.

'It's all about liberating people from the fear of economic failure,' he continued, 'and the fear of losing social status, both of which dominate everybody's thoughts all the time. It's about removing the fear of living life as it is meant to be lived. Through other people, and not through money. There's more to it than people today have got the capacity to imagine. It's set out pretty well in here'.

He temporarily abandoned his pie and fished out a paperback from the top of a small pile of papers on the bread bin. He lobbed the book across to me: *Das Kapital, Volume 1*, by Karl Marx.

'Borrow it if you like. Try this as well.' He tossed a second book at me. 'The correct mode of behaviour for a communist today,' he went on, 'given the completely apolitical nature of our society, is simply this: to be a thorn in everybody's side.'

The second book was simply entitled *Why You Should Be a Communist*. It was by seven people. I glanced at a sentence at random: 'The global struggle of the working class can/should today be viewed and taken account of in the light not only of a modification in the synthesisation of elemental Leninism – as referred to in the preceding chapter – but also in the light of the new contextualisation of the work of the early anarcho-syndicalists with reference to a new analysis of the fragmentation of the "spaces between individual con- sciousnesses", as propounded by Professor Sturgeon and Leonard Tangye, whose work on molecular proliferation in society may yet . . .'

The sentence was threatening to encoil me like a boa con- strictor; I rapidly replaced the book.

'What do you think of Social Dynamism?' I said.

'I prefer not to talk about such disgusting things while food is being prepared.'

'Come on, though. Really.'

'It's fiddling in the wind,' said Bilton distractedly (he was reaching for a tea towel), 'pissing while Rome burns.'

'Ineffectual, then?'

'Irrelevant,' said Bilton, who was now wrenching at a shard of tin with his fingers wrapped in the tea towel. A few moments before he had, with what seemed to me misplaced optimism, set the oven to preheat.

'How did you actually become a communist, Bilton?'

'When I was about twelve, I met a man in the street selling a communist newspaper. The headline caught my eye – "Fight!" it said, and I liked the sound of that. We got talking, and he asked me if I'd be willing to set up a revolutionary cell in Dulwich, which is where I lived at the time.'

'Wow!'

'It seemed like a good idea,' Bilton continued, 'and I managed to get a couple of people together.'

'What did the cell achieve?'

'Nothing,' said Bilton.

I tried to recall something I'd heard about communism.

'Didn't Marx say, "From each according to his abilities to each according to his needs"? Well, what I'd like to know is . . .'

'That was Proudhon,' said Bilton, 'not Marx.'

'Oh,' I said. 'Well . . .'

But now I'd forgotten what I wanted to know.

'Want to hear some music?' said Bilton.

'Sure,' I said, and Bilton, putting down his tin, walked across to a small, dirty CD player.

'What are you going to play?' I asked.

'K.C. and the Sunshine Band,' he said, picking up a disc.

'Never heard of them,' I said.

'Before your time,' said Bilton. 'In fact, they were before their own time. This song – it's called "Queen of Clubs" – says more about life under late capitalism than any so-called symphony by any so-called composer.'

The music started. There were some lyrics; and then Bilton held one wavering finger in the air as if to say, pay particular attention to this next part. A terrible sort of scream came from the singer, which Bilton savoured with eyes closed and intent nodding of the head in the aftermath. When the song stopped, Bilton stopped the machine.

'Do you want to hear it again?' he asked.

'Okay,' I said, and changed the subject. 'Tell me, how do you get on with your housemates?'

I had heard that Bilton shared the house. It was an odd concept: Bilton with people.

'Perfectly okay,' he said. 'They're women, you see, and they go out with . . . you know . . . men. So they're not around much.'

'And they don't complain, at all . . .?'

'About what?' said Bilton, lobbing a tea bag casually in the general direction of a gaping plastic dustbin, as the singer from K.C. and the Sunshine Band (presumably K.C. himself) started his deafening scream again. The tea bag splattered against the wall and slumped sadly down to the skirting board, leaving a thin brown film.

'I mind my business; they mind theirs,' said Bilton, now resuming his struggle with the tin.

'Do you cook a lot of stuff?' I said.

'Tomato soup I do a lot of,' he said, now beginning to sweat at the temples as he wrestled with the tin. 'Baked beans, too. I do sardines. I like them on toast. Tuna, too. I like that with bread. Keep it simple, you know.'

'But it's all tinned stuff, right?'

He stopped and considered.

'You could say that's a leitmotiv of a lot of my dishes, yeah. That they come out of a tin. Never thought of that.'

There was a second stack of books, mouldering on the floor in the corner of the room. I looked at some of the titles. There was *Socialism in Detail* (very thick), *Karl Marx: The Man and His Work*, *The Struggle for Liberation* by somebody with an extremely foreign name, *Rosa Luxemburg: A Life in Politics*, and *How to Improve Your Herbaceous Border* by Miss T. Eppingham-Winsley.

'What's this doing here?' I said, brandishing the latter work.

'Oh, Piper was going to give it to some moron to review. I

said, "Hang on, give it here: might as well get it done properly."'

'It's funny that you should write so much about gardening,' I said. 'I mean, it's not as though you've actually got a garden or anything.'

I was now gazing out of his kitchen window. There was a sort of area with dustbins.

'I do it all from first principles,' said Bilton incomprehensibly.

He was now holding down the tinned pie on the floor with his foot, and yanking at it with a pair of pliers he'd found in the cupboard under the sink. I was beginning to get rather hungry.

'How long does that pie take to cook?' I asked.

Bilton interrupted his exertions, lifted up the can and squinted at the small print on the label.

'Cooking time, twenty-five minutes,' he read.

'And what's the opening time: two hours?'

He battled on.

'Bilton,' I said, 'I don't understand why you are a journalist. I mean, you're not exactly on the watchamacallit front line of the class struggle, are you?'

'Ideally, I'd be a bricklayer. But you do what you can,' he panted. 'Karl Marx was a journalist in his early days.'

'Yes,' I said, 'but he didn't write about gardening . . . did he?'

'He wrote about the social conditions of ordinary people, and that's what I'm trying to do. Anyway gardening's harmless. I don't mind writing the odd piece about it, and I'm doing my bit politically with The Group.'

He began ferreting around in his pantry.

'What's The Group?'

'A collection of like-minded people.'

'And what's your aim?'

'The complete overthrow of world capitalism, amongst

other things. But the immediate priority is to get a regular meeting place in the Leytonstone–Mile End area. At the moment we're just hammering out tactics. You know, are we going to set ourselves up as a revolutionary élite along Leninist lines? Or is it going to be more of a Rosa Luxemburg-type thing? . . . How do you fancy a boiled egg?' he said, sending the pie, still in its tin, skittering into the bin.

During the next hour, over four boiled eggs and cream crackers – the entire contents, as far as I could see, of Bilton's larder – Bilton explained a lot about his politics (leaving me none the wiser) and we discussed the uncomfortable developments in Russia. Bilton was sure there would be a war. 'It's what capitalist countries do,' he said, 'and they're both capitalist countries now.'

Bilton had a soft spot for Russia, of course, for old times' sake. He seemed to have a sneaking admiration for General Zubarov, too.

'He's a nationalist, which is no bloody use to anybody. But he's expressing a frustration with Western materialism which is valid. It's got nothing to offer; we all know that.'

I suggested that a few of its trappings wouldn't go amiss in this kitchen.

'I was quite sympathetic,' said Bilton, ignoring me, 'when Zubarov announced his plan to throw that load of cheeseburgers from the Russian McDonald's into the Black Sea. Anyway,' he went on, scrutinising his watch, 'you must be off now. The number three goes right past the door. There'll be one along in five minutes.'

I wasn't in the least offended by this. Bilton was beginning to open up with me, I reflected, as I waited in the faltering rain for the number three. And my piece appeared in 'Downbeat' the following Thursday.

*

Over the next fortnight, Bilton and I went to the Ink Spotte several times. In his company, one drank tumultuously, the beers forming a queue at one's elbow. The real average wage in Britain, 1979–91; the crisis of something called Fordism; the global failure of something called hyper-liberalism; trade unionism in South-East Asia – Bilton held forth on them all. And he told me his theories about journalism, which he believed was nothing more than the celebration of multi-millionaires.

'There's this cult of being a multi-millionaire,' he'd say; 'it's like one of those games you used to play at school. When you get to be a multi-millionaire, that's it: you're home and dry.'

He had no interest in the women's movement, environmentalism, or the socio-political implications of the Internet. He was, as he admitted, purely concerned with the elemental struggle between capital and labour, and in this he was, of course, peddling a very unfashionable line. You'd have been hard-pressed indeed to find anybody even in the Left Rump who had any time for Bilton's politics.

Chapter Five

(The month before the incident)

In early June, Bilton left *The New Globe*. His resignation, which I observed from the portals of an adjacent gents' lavatory, took place during an exchange with Piper, suspiciously hard on the heels of a pub lunch.

Harry Piper stopped Bilton in the corridor. Bilton was carrying a printout.

'Martyn,' he said, 'how are you?'

'All right,' conceded Bilton.

'What are you working on?'

Bilton held the printout before him and, in an ironical, orator's voice, began to read: 'By our meteorological correspondent.' He pointed silently at himself. 'May got off to a fairly sunny start and continued to be quite sunny throughout, although, on the whole, temperatures were not unusually high. Rainfall, too, was pretty much . . .'

'All right, all right,' said Piper, holding up his hands. 'Martyn, you're not going to like what I have to say.'

'I already don't like it,' said Bilton, in whom insubordination was tolerated to a surprising degree.

'I'd like you to join the "Royal Tittle Tattle" team on Tuesday.'

The alliteration made the request all the more contemptibly absurd, and Bilton's response was entirely predictable. 'Bog off,' he said simply. 'In my opinion the royal family should be removed from their palaces, charged with offences against the people and, after a fair trial, executed.'

'Bilton,' said Piper, 'I'm afraid you have no choice in the matter, I'm *telling* you to work on "Royal Tittle Tattle".'

'Yes,' said Bilton, 'and I'm telling you to fuck off.'

And with that, he battered through some double doors conveniently placed for dramatic effect, and marched into the uncertain world of the freelance.

The day before Bilton left *The New Globe*, I had moved into his house. The two elusive women who had shared with him had moved out – 'They wanted to live somewhere else,' said Bilton with a shrug – and I was glad to resolve my own tenuous position in the South London back bedroom of a friend of a friend.

Bilton's domestic habits, observed at close quarters, provided few new shocks. By day, he hardly emerged from the book-stacked bedroom – as bland and depressing as a library stockroom – in which he clattered away on a grimy, primitive word processor, before faxing or even physically delivering his articles. He was the only person I knew who wasn't 'modemed-up'.

We both worked very hard, I at the office and Bilton at home, next to his clanking, oil-leaking fan. The end of his working day, and the start of his drinking evening, was announced by the playing, much too loud, of 'Queen of Clubs'.

Bilton was a skilled journalist. Before joining *The New Globe* he'd worked on several local newspapers and, following his resignation, he picked up a fair number of commissions from national newspapers, which was surprising considering his absence of conventional charm and the obscure thing he had against lunch. But I don't think he made much more than a subsistence wage and he wasted a great deal of time writing unpublishable political essays and working on his emphatically uncommissioned, amazingly boring masterwork, which he could never decide whether to call 'The Death of Ideology', or '*On* the Death of Ideology'. In a way his life was depressingly predictable: a curious mixture of austerity and beer.

Aside from my responsibilities on 'Pen' and 'Fripperies', I was given a new role as editorial consultant on a new slot I'd invented called 'My Favourite Word'. ('What I like about this one,' Piper had said, 'is that it's short. It won't take up much space.')

On 15 June, I was attempting to solve an irritating little problem that had arisen on 'Word' – the first two celebrity respondents had both chosen 'glockenspiel' – when I was distracted by gleeful shouts from the newsdesk.

'I don't believe this one!' someone yelled. It was Eamon Clough, number two on the newsdesk, who was, if anything, even more sallow and hirsute than his colleagues.

Everybody broke off from their own shouting and looked at Eamon.

'You know that conference in Athens?'

'What to do about Zubarov?' said someone.

'Yeah. You know that Lazenby said he was going to get rid of all his advisers, go in there alone and take the Various Nations and shake them by the scruff of their necks? He was going to get a clear strategy on the latest Russian incursions into the Ukraine, and cabinet press made a big thing of saying he was going to do it "in his own inimitable fashion", right?'

People nodded; they knew what he meant.

'Well, get this. Lazenby's walking in there. He's got the fucking pigskin briefcase or whatever, which is bulging, and then, under the other arm, he's got all these papers just loose, and he's walking up the steps to the conference centre, and he's wearing those ridiculous new shoes . . .'

'QC loafers,' someone said. 'Black suede, gold buckle,

whereas his other ones had silver; we did that three-thousand-worder on them last week.'

'Well, one of them comes off as Lazenby's going up the steps and he stumbles and these papers go flying, blowing away in the breeze. And our man Finch just grabs one of them and it says at the top "spontaneous and improvised speech, page forty-five", and then Finch grabs more pages, and they've all got these little stage directions all over the place, like: "Hit table (quite) hard" with the word "quite" in brackets. I mean, this is so bloody priceless, and look at the picture . . .'

A picture of Lazenby tottering on one leg amidst an upwardly swirling spiral of papers was, I now noticed, displayed on the screens of everyone on the picture desk.

'Hey!' shouted someone else on news. 'There's only one headline. "Lame Duck", yeah?'

Eamon Clough smacked fist into palm.

'Good one, Nick! But not exceptional . . .'

I loved watching the newsdesk brainstorm as they came up with headlines.

'Lance,' Eamon went on, 'any thoughts?'

The little old guy called Lance was the headline genius. He did nothing else all day but think up headlines and get coffees for people. He looked at Eamon and shook his head.

'How about something about Lazenby not using his loafer?' said someone without much conviction.

'Nah,' said Eamon.

The man called Nick spoke again.

'Why not just – very simple – "Blown Away"?'

'I *love* that, Nick,' said Clough.

Nick beamed.

'. . . But it's not right.'

Nick stopped beaming.

Then Lance spoke.

'The picture's so fantastic,' he said, 'that we don't need a headline. We just run that shot full bleed on the front with this caption underneath in forty point.'

And he handed a piece of paper to Eamon.

'At the Athens Conference today,' Eamon read, 'Mr Lazenby went about solving the problem of Zubarov in his own inimitable fashion.'

'Bingo, Lance,' said Eamon, and dashed across to the subs desk.

Everything subsided for a while; Lance was thanked and went to get the coffees.

Then Eamon came back from the subs shouting.

'Nick,' he roared, 'get one of the professors on the phone. One thousand words: how much longer can this farce go on? Then get some international guy. New shame for Lazenby's baby.' He was referring, of course, to the fact that Lazenby had been largely instrumental in founding the Various Nations . . .

Ever since it had been decided, in the wake of the many years of conflicts over conflicts, that the term United Nations was putting it a bit strongly and that the term Various Nations more honestly reflected the real situation between the participating powers, *The New Globe* had made the new organisation a target. Its brief was even more nebulous than the UN's had been, the paper argued. It could do something about refugees and inter-ethnic strife in the trouble spots around Russia but nothing against Zubarov's nationalist guerrillas. The idea of bringing in rotating prime ministers to chair the perpetually squabbling nations was especially derided. It struck *The New Globe* – meaning, of course, that it struck Little Willie Meltchitt – as desperate;

reminiscent of the bureaucratic excesses of the European Community.

The farcical attempts to protect the republics of the old CIS against Zubarov's machinations and interventions, and the decision to designate them 'Protected Republics' had been remorselessly satirised. Lazenby was, at this time, the unhappy chairman of the Various Nations; thus neatly uniting two targets.

The *Globe* had recently moved decisively against Lazenby for other reasons. Unemployment and inflation were showing sharp rises, and environmental issues were blowing big again. Lazenby's relentless fiscal juggling, and his continued toying with the already nebulous criteria for Social Dynamism ('introducing, we believe, a new and valuable fluidity to the determinants of generative capacity at the local level') were dismissed on all sides.

In fact, *Pics 'N' News* printed a calender on its front page every day for four weeks between June and July, under the heading 'Countdown for Lazenby'. ('We're so convinced that the Prime Minister is doomed that we're prepared to put money on it. *Pics 'N' News* will donate a substantial sum to charity if Philip Lazenby is still in office after thirty days.')

When the excitement on the newsdesk had died down, I telephoned the well-known anchor man who had chosen 'glockenspiel', and asked him whether he could think of another word that he liked as much.

'I quite like spatchcock,' he grudgingly admitted.

Now came the hard part.

'We need a few sentences on *why* you like that word; nothing too elaborate; I'll write them down as you talk.'

There was a lengthy pause.

'No,' said the anchor man, 'I couldn't do that.'

I wasn't sure about 'My Favourite Word'. It wasn't panning

out. And, even though it was only half past four, I went to the Ink Spotte and drank beer, following the familiar curve from depression to optimism and inexorably back to depression.

Chapter Six

(The incident)

On 21 July, Bilton stalked into the kitchen wearing his suit. It was black and, as he always pointed out, had been tailor-made. The trouble is that it hadn't been tailor-made for *him*. It was too small, and when he sat down, the narrow trousers left a white mark around his calf. He resembled a Dickensian criminal. 'I am going to do some writing,' he said, looking down his nose, both literally and metaphorically, at my seethingly multi-coloured breakfast cereal. 'I can meet you at lunchtime.'

'Okay,' I said, 'see you in reception at one.'

Twelve thirty on the day of that fateful lunch found me sitting in the office looking at a fax just in from the not particularly famous actor James Xavier. It was his response to the 'Me and My Pen' questionnaire. I remember quite clearly that a busker in the street three storeys below was playing an irritating little tune on a piccolo; the sun had just juddered out from behind a cloud, and the Venetian blind in the office was up. I could feel a headache coming on.

The fax, frankly, depressed me. The first five entries read as follows:

1. *What is your favourite pen?* A biro.
2. *Where did you purchase your favourite pen?* Can't remember.
3. *What attracted you to the pen?* I needed something to write with at the time.
4. *What important documents have you signed with the pen?* Various.

5. *Are there any special memories connected with the pen?* No.

Obviously, by compiling this questionnaire I was wasting my life, but on occasions like this the thought came home to me with nauseating intensity. I had been trying hard to fulfil the brief given me by Harry Piper, 'to get people to talk movingly and thought-provokingly about their writing implements', and it had proved quite impossible. How I wished I was chronicling the tense summit between Zubarov and the new leader of Belarus in Kiev. I made a note to look up the name of the latter; then I called Xavier. After thirty-five minutes of desperate prompting the situation was like this:

1. *What is your favourite pen?* A Bic biro.
2. *Where did you purchase your favourite pen?* God knows.
3. *What attracted you to the pen?* The price (cheap).
4. *What important documents have you signed with your pen?* Does this questionnaire count?!
5. *Are there any special memories connected with the pen?* No.

He had been most adamant on that last point. 'What do you want me to do?' he said. 'Lie?' I put the copy through to the sub-editors. At least, I reasoned, it was a true reflection of Xavier's very dull personality. I was glad to have a few days' holiday coming up.

It was one o'clock.

Bilton stood next to the security desk as I clattered towards him in my metal-tipped shoes. Every footstep echoed around the four walls for a good twenty seconds, so there was a small interlude of rattling footsteps as we stood face to face waiting to talk.

'Hi,' I said.

Bilton inclined his head ever so slightly. He had shaved equivocally; he was sweating. On top of his suit he wore his brown, stifling, summer coat which – and here was the consummate detail of the master slob – featured a large, dusty footprint on the back.

'Fancy a drink?' I said.

He sniffed. 'Yeah.'

'What have you been up to?' I said as we approached the lobby doors.

'Writing,' he muttered. He was swaying slightly, like a television mast in a breeze.

'Where?' I said.

'Mile End library, then in the pub next door.'

'What time did you go to the pub?'

'What time?' said Bilton, in a shocked tone. 'Opening time.'

I wondered what he'd been writing. He was doing a lot of work on *The Sunday Paper*'s 'My Favourite Thing' slot, an incredibly broad-ranging feature in which celebrities could discuss anything that could legitimately be described as a 'thing'.

'Don't you find that if you sit in a pub with a notebook you look a bit of a lunatic?' I asked.

Bilton looked at me with his glittering, violet eyes, and sent his skinny hand crawling through his strange, circular hair.

'I don't follow you,' he said.

At the Ink Spotte, there was the usual flurry of round buying, and then we were sitting at the corner table with three empty glasses apiece in front of us. The place was packed.

'Hello, Lenin,' said the small, cockney barman as Bilton went up for the fourth round. (He'd overheard many of Bilton's monologues in the past.)

'Two pints of bitter,' grunted Bilton, who returned unsteadily. I was going a bit that way myself, and felt reckless.

'Come on, Bilton, be honest: communism is completely played out – even the reaction against communism is played out. Hasn't the time come to look beyond it to something else? I mean, it's dead, isn't it?'

'What do you think you are?' said Bilton. 'Head of the school fucking debating society?'

'Well,' I said, 'Philip Lazenby says that old-style socialism is dead, and that he's the new alternative of the socially dynamic centre right/left. I think he's got some good ideas. The Community Forums – they're a good idea. Getting ordinary people to get together for a chat from time to time.'

Bilton stared at me with contempt.

'With a cup of tea.'

Bilton still stared.

'And a piece of cake, possibly . . . I mean a lot of people on the so-called left have come round to all this, and no wonder. All that old stuff: capital and labour. It's quaint now, that's what it is. Quaint. Since I've got to know you I've been reading some history. The Militant Tendency. What the hell sort of name is that? It's hard to know which is worse – the militant bit or the tendency. The General, Municipal and Boilermakers' Union. I mean – come off it. And surely Boilermakers are part of General, so why refer to them specifically? Anyway, I think Philip Lazenby's right when he says we must face the challenges of today with the ideas of tomorrow, or whatever it was that he actually said.'

'Jesus,' said Bilton.

'Come on,' I said, 'over to you. What do you say?'

Bilton said nothing. I did five minutes of moody silence, then bought the next drink, which meant that Bilton bought the one after that, and so on.

'Same again, Trotsky?' enquired the little barman, cheerily enough, some rounds later.

Bilton nodded, teetering backwards slightly. The drinks were placed on the bar, and Bilton simply picked them up and zigzagged back towards our table.

'Oi, Karl Marx,' shouted the now indignant barman. 'Don't you ever say thank you?'

Bilton stopped in the middle of the floor, swivelled saggingly around – displacing a good deal of beer – and then resumed his erratic progress towards our table. The barman angrily flipped his glass cloth over his shoulder, lifted up the barflap and scurried towards us. He wasn't a tough-looking guy, but it was alarming to see him at large like this, suddenly unconfined by beer pumps.

'You've been coming in here for a bloody year,' he said, drawing level with Bilton, 'and never once have you said thank you, please, excuse me, good morning or good night. I don't have to serve you, you know. I've got a right not to. And I'll tell you something else. I've listened to your opinions, and I think they're shit.'

There was a silence.

'Have you finished?' said Bilton.

'I don't think I have, actually. I mean, who the fuck are you? Some kind of bleeding intellectual. I've been working here five years and I've never in my life . . .'

'Your life?' said Bilton. He'd been staring at a beermat, but now he looked at the little guy. 'How much do you earn?'

'You what?' snapped the bantamweight. 'I don't earn a lot,' he continued with surprising, and rather touching, dignity, 'but I'm happy with my life, and I'm not trying to be something I'm not.'

'I see,' said Bilton, 'everything's fine. Tell me, are you an adherent of Dr Pangloss?'

'Dr fucking who?'

'Not heard of Dr Pangloss? He said that everything was for

the best –' Bilton took a great sloshing gulp from his beer –
'in all possible worlds.'

'I beg your pardon?' said the barman, who'd gone white.

'I'm only asking,' said Bilton, who then took another sip of
beer. 'I'm quite interested. I mean, where do you live?'

He turned around to face the barman for the first time.

'Let me guess. You've got a house. Or a flat. I don't
bloody know. A small, cosy place with the emphasis on small
. . . and the emphasis on squalid. Your boss – the geezer who
owns this whole chain of rip-off hostelries – he lives in a castle, and I know that for a fact because he likes to give interviews in it only about every day. Do you know how he's got
that castle?' Bilton aimed a stabbing finger at the barman.
'You.'

'He's got it because he's worked his way up,' said the barman.

'That's right,' said Bilton, 'you've taken your trousers
down, bent over and he's worked his way up your fucking . . .'

'Bilton,' I said, 'stop it! You're in danger of going too far.'

'Apologise,' gasped the barman. 'Apologise. If you don't
you're going to get your head smashed in by my brother!'

Bilton looked down at the little man – he really was about
four foot ten – with genuine astonishment, but I went one
stage further and laughed out loud, a laugh which I quickly
stoppered.

'Hello,' said an enormous paint-spattered decorator, 'I'm
Terry's brother. I know I don't look like him but that's
because I was adopted.'

And so saying he kicked the back of Bilton's legs, which
naturally buckled, sending him crashing to the floor, back of
the head first.

'That didn't hurt me at all,' said Bilton, in an admirably
defiant if rather childish way. But he shrewdly remained lying

down, with the big guy's boot hovering just above his forehead.

'Are you going to attack my little brother again?' said the big guy, boot poised.

'What do you mean "again"?' said Bilton.

'It's all right, Lee,' said the little barman. 'He's learnt his lesson.'

The big brother swiftly pulled his boot back, as if he was going to deliver the kick anyway and, having secured a look from Bilton that might have passed for fear (although I thought it was simply panic, for Bilton was brave), snarlingly withdrew. Bilton sullenly regained his feet and trudged towards the door.

I apologised to the barman.

'Not your fault, mate,' he said, and even gave me a handwritten receipt for my expenses claim.

I suppose that at this point, I imagined the worst of the day to be over.

Running out of the front door of the Ink Spotte, I found Bilton leaning against a lamp-post and reading a newspaper. As I came up to him, he slung it almost playfully into a litter bin and bounded on down the street. He approached a telephone box and opened the door. What the hell was he doing now?

'Phone yourself a whore, mate, I would!' he shouted at the man inside, who, turning round, revealed himself to be the happily married and, for good measure, homosexual gardening editor of *The New Globe*.

'Don't mind him, he's pissed,' I assured the gardening editor as I scampered after Bilton. I felt as though I was in a dream as I caught up with him in Spanish Joe's, a sort of smoke-filled shack clinging to the base of the New Globe building. He was serenely sipping a coffee.

'You're pissed,' I panted as I sat down opposite him. 'Do you realise who that was in the phone box?'

'Have you got a cigarette?' said Bilton.

'Why did you *do* that?' I asked, although I had a shrewd idea. Bilton never had sex himself, and he took a pretty firm line with those who did.

'Did you see him looking at the cards in the phone box? Sex slavery is one of the more disgusting aspects of capitalism. I don't normally take solo direct action but I do make an exception in certain cases . . .'

'Like when you're pissed,' I said. 'I'm off back to work.'

I was all over the place as I walked down the street, and suddenly there was Bilton, on my right, now on my left, toting his plastic coffee cup, and singing gently to himself as he often did. I remember the words: 'Here comes the sound of a tempest now / In a 'lectric storm will the trouble be born.'

I tried to shake Bilton off, even, at one point, breaking into a shambolic trot, but somehow we both ended up on a small marble bench in the gigantic lobby of Globe Newspapers. I had never noticed this bench before but it certainly came in handy, I gratefully reflected, when you were drunk out of your mind, borne dangerously aloft upon a surging tide of beer. I stared upwards at the Globe's globe. The world whirled. I wondered whether it was true that a high-spirited executive had once been sacked for leaping from the champagne balcony on to this rotating ornament and then shouting, 'Stop the world, I want to get off!' I didn't fancy walking upstairs to my office; I didn't much fancy standing up, as a matter of fact. I began to feel sick. Bilton was burping absent-mindedly in between slugs from his plastic cup, while I fumbled in my pocket for the receipt which I would present in my expenses claim: 'Fourteen pints of bitter,' the barman had baldly written, and I had specifically asked him just to put down 'lunch'.

I now indicated to Bilton – rendered pop-eyed by another gaseous surge – that I really had to get back to work.

'Right. Thanks for buying me lunch,' he slurred. 'I think I'll get something to eat now.'

He stood up.

'You've got a footprint on the back of your coat,' I said.

'That,' said Bilton, 'is as may be.'

Just then I noticed, clumping towards us, Walter, the square-headed senior security guard at Globe Newspapers.

'Prime Minister's coming,' he said, as if it happened every day (which, in fact, it almost did at Globe Newspapers). 'So come on, hop it.'

He flusteredly ushered us in some direction or other, Bilton proceeding with a reluctantly compliant shuffle, still clutching his coffee cup, and now pantingly singing, random extracts from 'Queen of Clubs' over and over again.

The lobby doors were then flung open with medieval flamboyance by the bibulous, gnomic-liveried gentlemen in charge of them. These phoney art deco doors of greenish massy brass were as tall as three men, and through them walked a person who was as tall as one man: Philip Lazenby, Prime Minister of Great Britain and Northern Ireland. But only just. Many assumed that this was his last week in power, such was the scale of the foreign and domestic crises swirling about him.

Viewed this close, he looked quite foreshortened, like somebody in a hall of mirrors. You couldn't believe there was so little of him. His suit was magnificent, of course, but he lacked, as he trippingly clacked across the polished stone floor, the swagger that the true dandy ought to have. As he squeakily sashayed towards Bilton and me, Lazenby splayed some of his little pointed fingers in front of his mouth to cover a tiny yawn, during which his eyes became crazy, wonky slits. In his hands were his habitual cue cards, which he was absent-mindedly shuffling, not even looking at them.

The following events are so well known that they hardly bear any repetition.

Lazenby and his entourage hung around the security desk, straightening their jackets and some of them actually clearing their throats. Suddenly, from the door across the lobby, emerged the not so much business-like as bus-like figure of Little Willie Meltchitt, attended by twittering flunkies. Little Willie had, of course, frequently condemned Lazenby, but he was always personally jovial towards important people and, as he approached Lazenby from the corner of the lobby, he began miming a series of cricket shots – a few jabbed forward defensives followed by one explosive hook – in humorous acknowledgement of Lazenby's interest in the sport. With each stroke Meltchitt's twisted, uncomfortable smile approached its gruesome limit. Lazenby, to do him credit, did look rather embarrassed as the man-mountain rolled and flailed towards him.

I've often thought about how I would definitively describe the incident. I think present tense is best.

Lazenby moves forward. The handshake. It's one of those extra-special handshakes with sincerity enhanced by the free hand coming in on top of the two joined hands. Then Little Willie lifts up one of his hands and points to the door from which he has just emerged. The two entourages coalesce and approach. 'Over here, lads,' hisses Walter, at which point I move to the left to avoid the Lazenby entourage, and Bilton does not.

Still clutching his coffee cup, Bilton gives me a look of unprecedented cheerfulness and shrugs; I note the flare of strange energy in his eyes. He then turns away from me and takes one staggering step towards the approaching, scuttling, twinkle-toed figure of Lazenby.

'Excuse me,' says Bilton. 'Mr Lazenby? Can I have a word, please? It really won't take a minute.'

Mr Lazenby stops and Bilton pitches the contents of his coffee cup at his face.

It's as simple as that really. What follows – Bilton's ragged, mad shouts of 'You're a disgrace, man, a disgrace, a fucking disgrace!' and the two simultaneous, rib-cracking body charges upon him by Lazenby's detectives, the outraged howling of Walter, the raucous laughter of a man, never subsequently identified in order to be fired, in the champagne balcony – is chaotic and immaterial. Although it is interesting, if you watch the film, to note that, as the bodyguards begin to beatup Bilton, Lazenby, ignoring the fine spray of coffee about his beautiful collar, lifts both his hands to his temples and delicately cradles his face with his fingers, and when he looks up again, there is, or so it seems to me, a new light in those mild eyes. For this was the incident. The straw had broken the camel's back, and nothing would ever be the same again.

I was given the afternoon off by a frowning Harry Piper. He didn't attempt to discipline me. Clearly, he could smell the alcohol on my breath; but then, thoroughgoing bastard though he could be, Piper had a soft spot for pub visitees.

After an uneasy night, I awoke to find a photograph of Bilton on the front pages of all the newspapers that lay on the doormat in the hall. He had secured a black eye: a preposterous, parodically perfect circle. I couldn't take this and went back to bed. When I woke up a second time I read the newspapers' neutral accounts of the incident as a news story.

I turned the television on and saw Bilton. He was standing on shimmering tarmac outside the police station from which he'd just been released, Philip Lazenby, the reporter's voice-over informed me, had insisted that no charges be brought.

Bilton was holding a press conference in the sun. He looked – as everybody who holds a press conference seems to look – as though he'd done it hundreds of times before. He stood with his coat over his arm – attesting, it seemed to me, to a new-found confidence – before a squad of sweating hacks.

'What I did,' he said, moving his head from left to right, 'was a political act. It was a gesture of the contempt in which I, an ordinary citizen of this country, hold the government of Philip Lazenby. The coffee cup was hurled on behalf of the poor, on behalf of the sick, on behalf of the unemployed, and on behalf of the workers.'

(I think it was at this precise point that I clearly formulated the idea: Bilton has gone mad.)

'You're saying it was a political act?' said one sweaty reporter.

'Are you deaf?' said Bilton. 'That's exactly what I said, and that is precisely what it was. It is time that the people of this country were made aware that behind all the shifts in strategy and presentation, there is one common political denominator to the actions of every British government, no matter what its rhetoric of social concern: the protection of the interests of capital, and an attack upon the interests of labour. Mr Lazenby would not want to *be* ninety-nine per cent of the people he governs, because they are too poor, or too poorly educated or their lives are just too miserable. Yet he dares to pretend that the problems of society can be confronted by the so-called "hands-off fine tuning" of Social D . . . I'm sorry but I just can't bring myself to say the word.'

'Are you a member of a political party?' asked the same reporter.

'I am not a member of a political party; I am a member of a group.'

'A pop group?'

'No. A group dedicated to the overthrow of capitalism throughout the world.'

'By violence?'

'By violence, or peacefully if need be. As the Black Panthers said, *By any means necessary.*'

'What are your tactics, Mr Bilton?'

'Given that our endeavours are obviously of considerable interest to the forces of reaction, I think that is rather a naïve question.'

'Do you regret what you did to Mr Lazenby?' asked another hack.

'There's a twinge of regret,' said Bilton. 'After all, it was a very good cup of coffee.'

'Will you be taking any action about the black eye?'

'TCP,' said Bilton, gravely.

'I mean, will you be taking any legal action?'

'Fat chance of me winning if I did,' snorted Bilton.

A journalist who'd been standing proprietorially at his shoulder now stepped in front of Bilton, neatly blocking him out. 'This press conference is now concluded, gentlemen, thank you very much for your time.'

Bilton, I subsequently found out, went on to a restaurant with this journalist, and allowed him to buy him a big lunch, thus departing from the habit of a lifetime. The hack worked for the mid-market, slightly left-leaning tabloid *Here and Now*, and Bilton gave him the story of his life; or at least *a* story of his life. A long profile would appear the following day under the leaden headline 'An Angry Young Man Speaks

Out', alongside a picture of Bilton mooching about near some sort of breaker's yard.

After the lunch, Bilton was taken back to the offices of this newspaper, and waited while the reporter composed the piece, which, Bilton later told me, took seven minutes. He was then presented with proofs of both the profile and the following day's leader.

Sitting across the kitchen table in his falling-apart dressing gown – he had uncharacteristically bathed – and doling out whisky with K.C. screaming triumphantly in the background, Bilton invited me to read the proofs out. He was euphoric: frighteningly, utterly changed.

'It's crude stuff,' he said, 'but it does the job.'

'Martyn Bilton is twenty-six years old . . .' the profile began. 'He was born into a poor South London family, at least so he assumes, for he has never seen his mother.'

'Except when I was born,' Bilton chipped in. 'I would have seen her then, obviously, but I can't remember about that. Carry on.'

I carried on reading. 'He grew up with foster parents, worked hard at school, and now makes his living by free-lance journalism. It's a tough job, and he works around the clock for very little money. He lives in rented accommoda-tion in a poor part of London, encountering grinding poverty, unemployment and the extremes of human suffer-ing every day.'

'In the Cock and Flower,' explained Bilton, referring to our local pub.

The next sentence was in bold. 'Yesterday, Martyn Bilton snapped . . .'

'I can't read this rubbish,' I said.

'Try the leader,' said Bilton.

'Yesterday,' I read, 'Martyn Bilton had an opportunity which a lot of people in Britain would dearly like for themselves – a chance to say something to our increasingly self-absorbed and over-intellectual Prime Minister. His words were simple and effective, and hundreds of phone calls prove they've struck a chord with our readers. He called Philip Lazenby "a disgrace". We agree with that judgement.'

This last bit was underlined.

'Very few people can even understand what this government is doing on the domestic front,' the leader went on. 'Meanwhile, the economy deteriorates, and unemployment and inflation soar. Abroad, Philip Lazenby has brought humiliation on Britain by his complete inability to decide what to do about General Zubarov. Everywhere, the story is the same: confusion, indecision, and embarrassment.

'Martyn Bilton is a man of the left, a man of the *hard* left. His views, to us, seemed outmoded and confused . . .'

'Hang on,' said Bilton, 'I spent an hour explaining my position to those guys. I gave them a fucking *diagram* . . .'

'This paper cannot condone violence of any sort. But if yesterday's events provoke Philip Lazenby into a change of direction, this intense, thoughtful young man will deserve our thanks. More than that. Martyn Bilton will be a national hero.'

'Bollocks,' I said simply, putting the paper down.

'It *is* bollocks,' Bilton was good enough to agree, 'but something real is happening now. It's going to be interesting.'

He was the happiest I had ever seen him. He was so cheerful that he almost smiled. And no wonder. I had, to my mounting irritation, taken eleven telephone messages for him during the day, and the list of media solicitations lay on the kitchen table between us now, to be responded to in the morning.

*

That evening, Bilton appeared in the kitchen wearing his best – i.e. his least greasy – jacket, and an actual hat.

'What do you think of the hat?' he said, which was almost the first question he had ever asked me. It was a sort of twisted Panama with food stains.

'It goes with the coat,' I said, 'in the sense that it is very dirty.'

'Right,' he said jauntily. 'I'm off out.'

'Where are you going?'

'Partying.'

'Partying?' I said. 'You can't go partying, you don't know anyone.'

'I'm going to an opening,' he said. 'A TV producer wants to meet me there to discuss a programme idea.'

And he almost winked at me with his bad eye.

A few hours later Philip Lazenby was being interviewed on TV by Rupert Granger, the aggressive current affairs inquisitor.

'. . . He called you . . . what was it now . . . a disgrace?'

'He was shouting hysterically, making no sense.'

'Is that the phrase he used, though, "a disgrace"?'

'I really have no idea.'

'Is there any truth in that? Do you think you actually are a disgrace in any sense? I mean, does it ever cross your mind?'

'Mr Granger, are we here to have a serious debate, or to discuss the actions of a young hothead who is very lucky not to be facing serious charges at this moment.'

'All right,' said Granger. 'Let's turn to what I suppose I must call your economic policy.'

He paused. Lazenby crossed his legs; then uncrossed them; then recrossed them again.

'Now, in your mini-budget you're putting up taxes and reducing benefits for many people . . .'

'Yes,' said Lazenby, 'but we are also putting *up* benefits and *reducing* taxes for many people.'

'It's a somewhat confusing policy, isn't it?'

'It may confuse *you*, Mr Granger.'

'All of your policies are confusing. Social Dynamics, for example: it's all twisted up like bloody barley sugar, isn't it?'

'Barley sugar?' said Lazenby, trying to smile. 'At heart it's very simple, surely. A series of Initiatives designed to boost the individual aspects of collective endeavour, or rather the collective aspects of . . . no, sorry, I was right the first time.'

'You can refer to your notes if you like,' said Granger sarcastically.

'That's really quite all right, thank you,' said Lazenby nervously. 'The overall aim of Social Dynamics is surely very clear. It is to make the entire system of taxation a lot more . . . well, socially dynamic. But should you be in any doubt, Rupert, I urge you to do a little reading yourself. My book, *Social Dynamics, a Three Minute Guide*, is available in any bookshop, after all.'

'Do you seriously think I can spare three minutes to read that?' said Granger with apparent fury. 'As I understand it, the take-up on Social Dynamics is fifty per cent short of target – people just aren't interested – while the budget is running way out of control. Which raises the question: is Social Dynamics socially dynamic?'

'It is, yes, it absolutely is. I know it's your job to be sceptical, Rupert . . .'

'No,' said Granger, 'it's my job to be intelligent.'

'. . . But Social Dynamics is very definitely the way forward for modern Britain; allowing for choice, flexibility and freedom, and yet also a certain necessary degree of social nurturing within the market context. Take our latest Initiative: Building Bridges in the Community.'

'Do you mean that you will be literally building bridges in the community?'

'In some cases, yes, Building Bridges in the Community will actually involve building bridges in the community. But it's also about . . . Well, take a lollipop man. You might give him some luncheon vouchers on a use-or-return basis and then . . .'

Granger was yawning like a basking shark.

'It's all about motivating local community workers,' Lazenby went on, 'and boosting the income of local businesses . . . within a mutually dependent, er . . .'

'Yeah,' drawled Granger. 'Well, I get the drift . . .'

'As I said in Edinburgh last week,' Lazenby continued with enthusiasm, 'while speaking at the launch of the third new "Hand in Hand with Money in Hand" programme – and here I *would* like to look at my notes if you don't mind . . .'

But Granger just steamrollered on. 'We come now to the foreign situation . . .'

Lazenby looked up from his notes, astonished.

'. . . It's getting out of hand, isn't it?' continued Granger. 'Zubarov's guerrillas are walking all over the Protected Republics, are they not?'

'We have undertaken, along with our allies, to reach a position of concord concerning the territorial integrity of the Protected Republics and that will be achieved.'

'*Will* you protect them?'

'We will reach a position.'

'When?'

'In time.'

'I'm going to keep asking "When?" until you give me an answer.'

'Look, it is not always possible, when talking about time, to quantify it in terms of seconds, minutes, hours, days or years or anything like that.'

'But you unconditionally promised to protect the Ukraine, which Zubarov has just reinvaded.'

71

'But how . . .'

'You made a promise.'

'Well, of course, absolutely, but I mean there are promises and there are promises. Of course I don't mean that literally. Did I say that? What I mean is that, although I know what you're going to say, I . . .'

Lazenby had simply seized up. This was unprecedented. He seemed to be struggling to breathe.

'Did I hear you correctly there, Mr Lazenby? Did you say, "There are promises and there are promises"?'

Lazenby gasped.

'No, I . . .'

'Ones to be kept and ones to be broken, do you mean?'

'Our fundamental aim, our fundamental *promise,* is to . . .'

This all came out in an appalling rush.

'Do you admit that you broke a promise?'

'No. Well, yes, I suppose I've got to be honest, I . . .'

With exquisite timing, the closing theme tune – incongruously serene strings – blotted out Lazenby's desperate explanations, and the camera angle changed to show a long shot of Granger and Lazenby in silhouette: Lazenby small, fumbling to collect his papers, Granger long-legged, stretching and now actually putting out his hands and cracking his knuckles. Lazenby had been decisively worsted. Again.

Just then Bilton walked in.

'What was the opening like?'

'Not a bad drop of red,' he said, wobbling towards the lavatory. 'The white was complete muck. They had some interesting bottled beer. Dutch, or maybe . . .'

'I mean the art,' I said.

'Oh,' he said, '*that*. Self-indulgent bourgeois crap.'

Bilton always said that about art.

Chapter Seven

Hot light streamed through my bedroom curtains; birds scuffled on the window-sill. I was dazed, partly through just having woken up, and partly through Bilton.

The mobile gave out its fluttering call very early. It was an over-excited Harry Piper.

'Okay,' he said, 'I want you to write us a profile of your friend Bilton. Nobody talked of anything else at conference this morning. There's some embarrassment that the thing happened on our premises. But Little Willie is very keen on Bilton now, and, between you and me, we're thinking of asking him to darken our door again.'

'Take him back on staff?'

'Exactly. That sort of animus, that sort of balls, is just what we're looking for in a communist – a columnist, I mean. His views are so bracingly simple. I mean, *communism* . . . Everyone had forgotten about all that stuff and now . . . Well, no one actually *wants* communism – it's obvious crap – but they want Bilton. The elemental simplicity of what he's saying after all that academic Social Dynamic stuff is just so refreshing. It's refreshed even me . . . Well, almost. And he's immediately focused all the resentment against Lazenby that's been building up, and causing this major downward plunge of his in the perma polls . . .'

'I'd like to see him do an *upward* plunge,' I said.

'Just shut up and get on with the profile, all right? *Qui est* Martyn Bilton? Who is this guy who doesn't care about popularity, who thinks everything's terrible – I mean what exactly is so terrible about everything? Get to the bottom of his philosophy, his politics, his spirituality if any, his clothes, and any personal grooming tips, although I suspect they're going to be pretty unorthodox in this case.

'And I want some *vox pop* in there too. You know what the herd does when the leader isn't strong? It turns. Is this what's happening? Get out there. Get opinions. Don't just talk to Bilton. Incidentally, he's not contracted to *Here and Now*, is he?'

I had no time to answer.

'So look, take a couple of days off work and nail the guy down. Oh, and incidentally, I've got a nice headline: "The Last Communist". Can't be many of them left these days.'

'What about China?' I said.

'What?'

'You've got nearly two billion people there who . . .'

'Look, don't waste my time with facts. Just get on with the fucking piece.'

'And what about "Pen"?'

'Fuck "Pen".'

The next call was from Channel 12. They wanted to talk to Bilton about 'money', and left it at that.

Over breakfast, I tried to work out my attitude to Bilton's overnight fame. Funnily enough, I felt pretty tolerant and good-natured about it. This is wild, I thought, let's see what happens. There seemed little chance of Bilton gravitating to that rarefied world of continuous fluke that some media folk seemed to inhabit. He wasn't slick like that. He would fuck up in time. And besides, I genuinely liked the guy.

It was, looking back, a rather tenuous position.

Bilton's newly acquired agent (she'd introduced herself to him at the art gallery the night before) was called Carol

Crane. She was handsome rather than pretty, quite big, with a vague outline to her body, and very determined. Her mother was the famous novelist Simone Crane.

Carol Crane lived in Camden and therefore dressed entirely in black; her Camden office, though, was entirely white, and stylish in a minimalistic, completely impractical sort of way. Bilton and I sat on extremely thin, low, buttock-scrunching, wrought-iron milking-stool-type seats which were apparently what everyone was sitting on in Camden that year, chairs having been deemed *passé*. Carol, to be fair, sat on one too. She opened a great big black logbook, and began talking about Bilton as though he were not present.

'Now Martyn Bilton,' she said, 'is a very in-demand quantity across the media, having been involved in a particular . . .'

'Incident,' I prompted.

'. . . incident, which received major national coverage. He is now "on the map", and our job is to keep him there. He is a person of considerable integrity, both personal and political, and will not do just anything . . .'

Bilton nodded gravely. He was wearing his unsuitable suit.

'He is an excellent writer, whereas many people with his degree of fame are not; he is a good speaker, and would do well on radio. His appearance is highly – let us say – distinctive, making TV work a definite option. And speaking of TV work, I've had a call from the producer of *Singalong*, the celebrity karaoke show on Channel 6. They'd like Bilton to appear on the show next Tuesday, singing along to some old hits of a left-wing bent, if they can find any.'

Bilton flicked to the appropriate page in his diary, and began writing.

'. . . an offer which we obviously have to reject if we have any hope of building Martyn Bilton up as a person with credibility.'

'Right,' said Bilton, hastily crossing out the diary entry.

'We also have another, more interesting television offer, by which I mean the coffee advert . . .'

'The what?' I blurted out.

Carol Crane frowned at me.

'A television producer friend of mine has been wanting for years to make an anarchic, wild instant-coffee advert. He has approached me with the idea of creating just such an ad around the Martyn Bilton persona. The theme would be that this particular coffee is "too good to throw away". Now, basically, Martyn is going to be accused of selling out if he does this, thus endangering the integrity which is his main asset. My conclusion here – and I've thought about it a lot – is that Martyn Bilton should refuse to do the advert.'

I thought she was going to continue speaking; and so, evidently, did Bilton.

'Fine,' he said, 'that's fine by me.'

He looked bloody miserable, though.

'Just out of interest,' said Bilton, 'what sort of fee was this director talking about?'

'Oh, something in the region of fifty grand,' said Carol. 'That would be the usual thing.'

Bilton nodded.

There was a silence that continued for a while.

I looked at Bilton.

'I have a suggestion,' he said, putting his hand into the air like a schoolchild. 'How about if I do the advert and worry about the consequences later? We're talking about integrity, but that's a completely meaningless concept in the context of mass exploitation, environmental vandalism, and all the other evils inherent in late capitalism. Plus, I'm a long way behind with my rent.'

'Right,' said Carol. 'I'll get a major, pre-emptive damage-limitation exercise under way. No problem.'

So that was decided. And we moved on.

'Bilton,' said Carol, now addressing him directly: 'on the writing front, have you considered doing a sort of autobiography?'

'I don't approve of autobiography. It's a smug medium, quintessentially middle class.'

'Sure, but just tell me something about your early life.'

'My mother abandoned me when I was six months old, and I never knew who she was; I never knew my father either. I had a miserable upbringing with foster parents, and most of them are dead as well.'

'Excellent,' said Carol, 'great material for a book. You could call it *The Making of a Radical*.'

She looked at Bilton and slowly reached for a futuristic jug of water.

'Can I tell you something, Martyn?' said Carol. 'In all honesty. You stand to do very well out of all this. You're a lone wolf, a square peg in a round hole, a potential icon, a symbol of excitement for a fatigued and enervated society. Let's face it, you're a rebel, and there hasn't been one of those for a very long time. You could be just the catalyst that Britain – and when I say Britain I mean the British media – needs. I'm really, really excited about the possibilities here, and I don't say that to just anyone that I take on.'

She paused to drink her water.

'Well, I *do*,' she continued, putting down her glass, 'but this time I mean it. To be honest with you, I see a new word in the English language.'

She extended her arms towards the ceiling in an incongruously little-girlish gesture, sending heavy bangles falling to her elbows: 'Biltonesque!'

Carol kept her hands in the air and looked at Bilton quite sexily.

'Ridiculous,' said Bilton, but there was none of his usual casual vehemence in the word.

'Okay,' said Carol, grinning, 'Biltonish, Biltonate, Biltonite, Biltonic – to describe awkwardness, cussedness, bloody-mindedness, adherence to principle. You know, the last time I saw this sort of potential in a client was with Josh Peters.'

Bilton and I looked blankly at her.

'World tiddly-winks champion,' explained Carol. 'Young, good-looking, articulate. Superhumanly gifted at tiddly-winks. I was going to use him to put the game on the map. The books, articles and merchandising we had lined up, you would not believe!'

'What happened?' I asked with some trepidation.

'Josh developed a condition in his right hand; some sort of nerve trouble that marred his technique. It's too painful for me to go into details, but, basically, he could tiddle but he couldn't wink.'

She looked profoundly sad for, literally, a second.

'I hope you're going to let me buy you lunch?' she said.

We transferred to a sun-filled restaurant: mellow wood, richly upholstered lemon-yellow chairs; suspiciously pretty abstracts. Bilton was being interviewed outside the entrance by the roving team from Channel 11's *Spotted in the Street* slot.

'Carol,' I said, as we waited for Bilton, 'do you personally have any sympathy with Bilton's political position?'

'I've always had a lot of time for communism,' she said glibly, 'although I wouldn't want to see it put into practice again. God forbid. But I quite like the idea of it. I like the image, if you like – very straightforward. The red worked really well. And I admire people like Bilton who've stuck with it. That takes guts. Funnily enough, I've always said that communism might have benefited from better representation, of the sort that I myself might have been able to supply. Oh, I know that must sound pretty stupid . . .'

'Not at all,' I said, as Bilton loped toward us, 'makes a lot of sense.'

'How was it?' said Carol to Bilton.

'Frustrating,' said Bilton. 'I wanted to make some points about my protest. They wanted to know the colour of my underpants.'

'Well, that's a thing they're very big on,' said Carol, 'underpants and so on. It's actually one of the biggest programmes going out in the immediately pre-dawn zone.'

A waiter came and handed out menus. He gave Bilton a special nod. 'Good afternoon, Mr Bilton,' he said.

'Now,' said Carol, clasping her bangled hands in a praying gesture, 'your TV appearance tonight, Martyn. *The Celia Stein Show*, which is on Channel 19. She's pretty light, flirtatious, and I thought we might get in a few lines about some personal details.'

'Actually,' said Bilton, who'd been rummaging ominously in his knackered satchel, 'I was hoping to discuss something I'm calling "The Assimilation of the Culture of Rebellion by the Forces of Modern Capitalism".'

He produced a handwritten document two centimetres thick.

'It's to show that I'm aware of what's going on here.'

'I see,' said Carol. 'Could I take a look?'

Bilton passed it across the table.

'Now I'm going to take this back to my office and read it very, very carefully –' Carol glanced anxiously at the front page – 'footnotes and all. I don't want you to do anything with it until I've been through every word. Is that understood?'

'I will not go on the show,' said Bilton, 'unless I can discuss matters of weight.'

'Just do your best,' said Carol, with a tense smile. 'Shall we order?'

The wine waiter appeared.

'Drinks for you?'

'I'll have a beer,' said Bilton.

'We have German, Belgian, Italian, Spanish, French, Finnish, Icelandic, Chinese, Mexican, Argentinian, Patagonian and Indonesian beers, sir, not to mention a full range from Britain and America.'

'I'll have whichever's biggest,' said Bilton.

'Ha ha!' pealed Carol, clapping her hands. 'Biltonesque!'

In the cab, the driver, having been told to proceed to Channel 19's westerly redoubt, half turned towards Bilton and me.

'One of you going on TV?'

I pointed at Bilton.

'Him,' I said.

'You got an act, then?' he said, turning his head back towards the direction we were going in. Bilton put two fingers up at him, a gesture clearly visible in the rear-view mirror. The driver didn't seem to have noticed, but I felt sorry for him and decided to elaborate.

'He's the guy who threw the coffee at Lazenby.'

'That right?' said the driver. 'I take me hat off to you, mate.'

He *was* wearing a hat, funnily enough – a sort of pork-pie affair – and he duly lifted it, nodding to Bilton in the mirror.

'You're some kind of left-winger, aren't you? I'm not left-wing; I'm a taxi driver. But my old grandad, he was a communist. In a trade union. Always going off to meetings – the whole bit. Calling everybody comrade. Wound me gran up something terrible – I mean, he called her comrade as well – but I had a lot of respect for him even though I was only about four at the time.'

'Your grandad sounds like a good man,' said Bilton, embarrassingly.

We pulled up outside the automatic glass doors of Channel 19's shabby skyscraper, and Bilton paid the cabbie.

'I notice you haven't tipped me,' the cabbie observed. 'Quite right. My grandad was against tipping: called it the patronising charity of the boss class. I'll always remember that. Good luck to you, mate. No – good luck to you, *comrade*! Eh?'

'Right,' said Bilton, 'definitely.'

On the pavement outside the peeling tower, I looked at Bilton. A thought had occurred to me.

'Bilton,' I said, 'you're not going to become an arsehole, are you? I mean, it's there for the taking – if you want to be one.'

He just looked away and shook his head, more in bewilderment than denial.

'Value judgements,' he sighed.

Having been directed by a receptionist, we battered through the floppy rubberised doors of a certain studio E. A small suntanned woman called Melanie gave me a cup of tea which had been made by a computer. I was then shown to a plastic chair in a black ante-room, while Bilton was taken to make-up by a depressed-looking make-up artist.

A TV set was in front of me, tuned to news. Inflation was up again. The latest education reforms proposed by Lazenby had caused an unprecedented outbreak of agreement between teachers, pupils and parents. A spokesperson for the school janitors had also fiercely denounced them. Zubarov had made a speech slagging off the Estonian government in a threatening way. He 'dared' the Various Nations to send a peace-keeping force there.

By the time Bilton returned, a small drinks party had assembled itself around me, for the friends, agents and hangers-on of Celia Stein's other guests. Bilton's face had, effectively, been painted brown. His odd quiff was unnaturally parted somewhere between the centre and the left. The black eye – already fading to a mustard colour – had been accentuated slightly. ('I asked them to do that,' said Bilton shamelessly. 'If the State gives you a black eye, you let people know about it.') Someone had actually gone out and bought him a new shirt, and the shocking effect of this unaccustomed smoothness about Bilton's chest was to make his face seem crumpled. His suit had simply received a light sponging by a team from costumes.

'Would you say my hair was normal to greasy?' said Bilton, accepting gin and tonic from a roving waiter.

'It's certainly greasy,' I said. 'I don't know about normal. Why do you ask?'

'They washed it for me,' he mused, 'and gave me some of the shampoo to take home.'

He took from his pocket a small bottle containing a liquid whose fluorescent purple hue belied the words on the label: 'Simply Natural'.

'Your hair looks okay,' I said cautiously.

Bilton shrugged.

'I'm not bothered what it looks like. I'm not here to impress anyone. Most of this lot –' he gestured at the showbiz crowd at the other end of the room, experienced minglers all – 'pure fucking vanity. Nothing to say except "look at me".'

Celia Stein, the elegant, cat-like, leather-skirted hostess, approached us.

'Okay, boys? We're going through now, Martyn.'

Bilton followed her round the corner.

I watched the interview on a monitor in the hospitality room. Bilton was Celia's third guest. She got under way with one of her famously elliptical openers.

'Well now,' she said to Bilton, 'you're a strange one. What's that poor old PM ever done to you? He's out there, minding his own business, and you come along and sock him with a cup of coffee.'

The audience laughed; some applauded.

Bilton's face appeared in daunting close-up. His eyes furtively swivelled to the bottom left-hand corner of the screen.

'Is that a question?' he said.

'Why did you *do* it?' Celia reiterated, good-naturedly.

'It was a political action; it explains itself.'

'And what have you achieved by it?'

Bilton essayed a weird trembling smile; the smile of a novice smiler.

'I'm on this show. You're paying me decent money. I seem to have become moderately famous. Isn't that what everyone's supposed to aspire to?'

'Your aims are purely selfish, then?'

'Ha!'

'You find that amusing?'

'You bet,' said Bilton.

'Would you care to elaborate?'

'Would you care to elaborate,' repeated Bilton disorientatingly. 'Minister, could I press you on that point. Part of the thing that I'm tired of is all this fatuous TV talk. But look: by reaping the rewards of the incident in which I was involved, I'm illuminating the inherent illogic and injustice of the system by which we live.'

'Naff off!' shouted a member of the live studio audience.

'Do you have a girlfriend, Martyn?' said Celia.

'If I had a girlfriend,' sighed Bilton, 'what would that make me? A boyfriend. The boyfriend. It would be laughable.'

'I don't know,' said Celia, 'if you smartened yourself up a bit – got a slightly less strange suit – you wouldn't be too bad.'

'This is pure hypothesis,' said Bilton.

'By the way,' said Celia, 'how's the eye the bodyguard gave you?'

She made as if to touch it. 'Looks nasty,' she said.

'I'm seeing double through it at the moment,' improvised Bilton. 'Which means that, in effect, I'm seeing treble.'

'But come on,' said Celia, sitting back in her chair, 'have you never had a relationship with a woman in your life?'

'I've told you, it's just not my type of . . .'

'Never been chatted up?'

Bilton stared at the floor. A frown was forming. Just for a moment, I thought he might be about to tell the truth. During a heavy session at the Ink Spotte, he had mentioned to me a party he'd been to at which a woman – a nurse – had said to him, 'I really wish you were a patient in my hospital.' Now it was possible to take this in two ways of course, but Bilton, who was quite without vanity in these matters, had seemed convinced of her benevolence.

'Do you believe in love at first sight?' asked Celia, this being one of her well-known stand-by questions.

'I don't believe in love, full stop,' replied Bilton, grateful to be back in condemnatory mode, 'and I don't believe in a lot of other things that I'm supposed to.'

'Such as?'

'Democracy.'

'Go on.'

'Freedom. God. Rock music. Family values. Father Christmas. The institution of marriage, and the Right Honourable Philip Lazenby, MP.'

There was applause here.

'So,' said Celia, 'your philosophy, Martyn Bilton . . . What would you have us be thinking of at this very moment?'

'Good grief,' said Bilton rudely, 'is English your first language? All right. Look. Just change everything in this country so that people are not taking on board all this media crap but thinking for themselves and living their own lives. All this celebrity rubbish, this lifestyle garbage, worship of multi-millionaires – let's get rid of it. Let's get working people running this country, instead of mealy-mouthed politicians in the pockets of businessmen. Get people agitating, and being on the street and moving the goalposts, and actually doing politics for themselves again . . .'

'I'm interested in the phrase "lifestyle garbage",' interrupted Celia. 'Do you include this programme in that?'

'Yes.'

'Then why are you on it?'

'I'm here to tell you that your show's garbage.'

Partial, but heartfelt, applause here; a genuine *frisson* of excitement.

'Your policies,' said Celia, 'they don't seem very specific.'

'Well, if you want specific instances, let's take world poverty. Number one . . .'

A distracted look flashed across Celia's face, and she suddenly said, 'Martyn Bilton! Ain't the guy a hoot! Come on, let's hear it!'

As she leant forward and shook Bilton's hand it was clear to me that Celia Stein had achieved the note of triumphant epiphany on which chat-show encounters are supposed to conclude.

Sure enough, the audience applauded.

'What are you drinking?' said Celia Stein, in a patronising, but really quite sexy mucking-in-with-the-lads sort of way. 'Beer?'

'Yes please,' I said.

Bilton nodded sternly. 'I'm on for one,' he said.

We had been whisked through the too-warm evening to a smart, dark, continental-style bar with statuesque male waiters and music blaring. Celia bought the beers ('Don't worry; they're on expenses') while Bilton visited the gents'.

Celia leant across to me. We were underneath a circling fan, which made her fringe look as though it couldn't decide where it wanted to be.

'Do you know Bilton well?'

'I'm his best friend,' I said, 'and, no, I don't know him at all well. Nobody does.'

'What about his family?'

'What family? He was given up for adoption at the age of none.'

'At birth?' breathed Celia. 'Wow, he must be really screwed up.'

Disloyally, I said nothing. I suppose I didn't know it at the time, but I was irritated that Celia was taking an interest in Bilton that went above and beyond the call of duty.

When Bilton returned, Celia started gazing admiringly at him. 'Are you a totally political animal?' she asked.

'To be honest, I find that a rather naïve question,' said Bilton.

'What do you mean by that?'

'We're all totally political animals. But some of us are aware of the fact. You don't know anything about dialectical materialism, I suppose?'

She smiled, bit her lip; she was alarmingly successful at looking cute when she wanted to.

'That's Marxism?'

An idea had crystallised: I liked Celia Stein. I liked the way she measured the beat of the juke-box music with a minimal foot tap, effortlessly adapting to each new song.

'That's Marxism?' she said to Bilton, a second time.

'Look,' he said, not, of course, deigning to answer so basic a question. Fishing around in his musty, mould-spotted jacket, he produced a crumpled brochure. 'This is a seminar. It's taking place next Tuesday. Go there and you'll learn something.'

I looked at the piece of paper, now on the table.

'Perspectives on the Politics of Ambiguity', read the heading. 'Number eleven in a series of fourteen lectures'.

Celia reacted with commendable speed. 'I'd love to go, but I'm doing something every Tuesday for the next two years.'

'Pity,' said Bilton. 'I give these out to anybody I know who's got a brain.'

He stopped here for a second, and I noticed a small signal of regret in his boggling, star-like eyes. He then shamefacedly fumbled one of the pamphlets in my direction.

My irritation was increasing.

'Let me get this straight,' said Celia. 'Do you really believe that the State should just . . . own . . . everything?'

'There would be common ownership,' said Bilton. 'What you fail to understand is that the State will eventually dissolve away of its own accord.'

'How?'

'Anyone want another beer?' I said hastily. 'Or shall we go somewhere else?'

We went somewhere else – to a little club in Soho dedicated

to the young literary élite, and which I'd never heard of.

The club was inside an elegant Georgian house, with walls of an old-fashioned green, on which played the giant, candle-made, rearing shadows of media types carrying wine between deals, and between meals. There were no chairs, but everyone had a *chaise longue* to themselves. Even Bilton and I had one each, next to a fireplace big enough to stand up in, and full of pale blue dried flowers which wavered in the warm turbulence from an open sash window. Bilton cut a peculiar figure: stiffly supine, silent, his thin nose reflected hugely on the walls.

'Come on, Bilton,' cackled Celia Stein, setting down a couple of bottles of wine. 'Lounge.'

'Where's that?' I said, realising too late that she meant it as an injunction to the man of the moment.

Celia kicked off her shoes and rolled on to her own recliner. She lay there and looked at Bilton. She grinned.

'Bilton,' she said, looking straight up at the ceiling with an expression of hilarity on her face, 'I suppose you were in the old communist party, before it imploded?'

'Do me a favour,' said Bilton, revealing thereby some arcane prejudice never to be explained. 'I've established a little grouping with some like-minded friends, or should I say comrades. It's called The Group.'

'How many people are involved?'

Bilton appeared to think for a while.

'Two,' he said.

Celia snorted. She was laughing.

'I mean two besides me,' said Bilton, crossly. 'Three in all.'

'What are their names, the other people in the group?'

'What's that got to do with anything?'

'Sorry,' said Celia.

Silence.

'They're called Allan and Michael,' said Bilton, eventually. 'They're brothers.'

'What do they work as?'

'Why do you assume they've got jobs?' said Bilton. 'Plenty of people haven't, you know.'

'Okay,' said Celia, 'fair enough. Silly middle-class assumption.'

'Actually,' said Bilton, 'Allan is a barrister, and Michael is probably the only Marxist merchant banker you're ever likely to meet.'

'Surely it's a sell-out for him to do that job?' said Celia.

'It's a hard one to call,' said Bilton, surprisingly. 'He's also an expert on fine champagnes, but, as he always says, "Why travel steerage on the *Titanic*?" Or maybe it was someone else who said that.'

Celia, still horizontal, was shaking her head with incredulity when a tall dandy with swept-back, golden hair and a shirt that reminded me of the eighteenth century approached. I recognised him as Rupert Granger, the ruthless TV inquisitor, although he looked rather different – fatter, basically – without his trademark black suit. Granger gave Celia a despairing what-are-you-doing-with-these-losers type of look and kissed her on the mouth.

'Hey, Celia,' he said. 'Caught the show. Fucking excellent; best one of the series. And that dude at the end: the guy that attacked Lazenby. The guy is fucking cool.'

'Well, there he is.' Celia pointed at Bilton, who was staring at the fireplace, pretending to be far away.

'Rupert Granger,' said Rupert Granger to Bilton. 'Like to shake the hand of the man that did that to Lazenby.'

Bilton put out his hand, nodding peculiarly to himself all the while.

'Bilton,' said Celia, in the tone of a mother coaxing her

child to be sociable, 'you should do a little networking here. Rupert might like to have you on his new late-night show. It's called *Fifteen Minutes*.'

'You've seen the show?' asked Granger, cautiously.

'Yeah,' said Bilton.

'Do you like it?'

Bilton hesitated.

'Let's just say I'll go on it if you want me to.'

Fifteen Minutes was Granger's late-night interview slot: intense encounters with anyone who could be called political, from the Prime Minister, who, of course, Granger had demolished only the day before, all the way down to . . . well, to the likes of Bilton.

'Isn't he wonderful?' said Celia Stein. 'And he looks cute with that pout. Bilton here is a communist, Rupert. That's why he did what he did to Lazenby. It was political, you see.'

Granger was nodding shrewdly; surveying Bilton with his searing eyes.

'My producer will call you,' he said. Then he pointed towards me with a forefinger extended, thumb raised, gun shooting point. To Celia he moved his raised palm in front of his face from right to left. A goodbye gimmick for everyone, and then he was gone.

At eleven o'clock, Celia left, inevitably, to meet her boyfriend. It was a melancholy moment for me. Bilton was blank.

Bilton and I left the club, and mooched around in Leicester Square. The just-cleaned cobbles steamed as we queued at a van for tea.

'Tea,' said Bilton to the man in the van.

'Sugar?' said the man.

'One,' said Bilton.

'Large or small?' said the man.

'What – large or small *sugar*?'

'Very funny,' said the man. 'Hey, I know you! You're the . . . with the . . . eh! I thought you drunk coffee, though! Here, pal. On me and it's a large one.'

He handed Bilton a tea.

Next, we stared listlessly at a screen inside the window of a burger bar, showing obsessive intercutting between shots of Moscow and London. Then there was footage of Lazenby addressing a gathering in some village hall somewhere; he banged on a trestle table with his fist. The table wobbled.

Later, Bilton and I took the last train back to Leytonstone. Bilton, spurning a nightcap, retreated quickly into his own grease-smeared bedchamber. Away from the glitz, I felt more at ease with him, and I made a rare visit into his inner sanctum to say goodnight just after brushing my teeth. He was sitting in bed, spooning baked beans from a can, with a big, boring-looking book propped in front of him.

I noticed something for the first time.

'What's that enormous sort of three-dimensional, mouldy brown patch on your wall?' I asked him.

'What?' said Bilton, distractedly. He turned a page of his socialistic tract, then put it aside and walked across the bed on his knees towards the wall. He inspected the brown lump, briefly, and flicked a piece of the substance away with a fingernail.

'I must have accidentally hurled my dinner at the wall sometime,' he concluded. 'Anyway, good night.'

'Bilton,' I said, sitting on the foot of his bed, 'what do you actually think about Celia Stein?'

'I've formed certain judgements about her,' he said, laying aside his beans.

'She's very attractive, isn't she?'

'That is her role. Yes.'

'Does she attract you?'

'Well, she's not completely stupid, which is more than you can say for most people. She has a hunger for knowledge of the world, and maybe I can help her out there. Maybe I could help her to develop.'

With a grotesque, limbo-dancing motion, he prudishly removed his underpants while still under the bedsheets, and lofted them casually on to the top of his wardrobe.

'Good night,' I said, leaving the room.

'Right,' muttered a muffled Bilton from under his bed-clothes.

I went to bed. After a few hours, I heard scuffling in Bilton's room; his voice, and female laughter, resolving into a torrid, slowly surging mutual murmuring, accompanied by a clump, clump, clump, clump. And then the whole of my life and the whole of Bilton's suddenly became a kind of racing car that was taking corners way too fast. Celia Stein was there too, and my dream didn't disclose whether we were scared or merely having a good time. I woke and then I had to go to Bilton's room to quietly open the door and verify his alone-ness amongst the swirled sheets.

Chapter Eight

Biltonesque. That never came about. Nor did Biltonic, Biltonate and Biltonite; these words do not exist. Although there was a pop song by those smart-arsed punk revivalists Gone. 'First there was a Milton, then there was a Bilton,' they sang – an elision which the rest of the lyrics entirely failed to justify. It was a minor hit.

Bilton, though, he was a big hit. Two weeks after the incident he received a phone call from Grey Fauntleroy, editor of the stylish reactionary weekly *Hatstand*. It was a column offer. Grey Fauntleroy himself was incredibly right wing, but he appreciated unreasonableness across the political spectrum.

'It would be completely illogical of me to turn it down,' said Bilton, pacing our kitchen as I sullenly stirred coffee.

'It's a big break,' I said, 'you can't afford to be worried about selling out.'

'Look,' said Bilton, now coming to rest next to the fridge, 'I can see that you're a bit . . .'

Jealous. That was the word he was looking for. Bilton was ceasing to be an underdog. He was becoming an overdog, for heaven's sake, and I couldn't handle it. The other day he'd even palmed off on me a couple of 'My Favourite Things' which he was too busy to do. It was this display of casual magnanimity that had really got to me.

'I'm biting the hand that feeds,' said Bilton. 'It's actually more subversive to accept these offers than to turn them down.'

He looked at me, and then opened the fridge door.

'Beer?' he said, proffering a can which was clearly a peace offering.

'No thanks,' I said, and trudged up to my bedroom.

'You can talk about selling out,' said Bilton, not really very angrily, as I closed the door; '"Me and My Fucking Pen"!'

I flopped on to my bed, and lay there thinking.

Bilton had already been restored to 'Downbeat'. Harry Piper had given him a year's contract to run the slot as a freelance. It now covered an entire page, and featured a large shot of the lavishly remunerated Bilton, looking not so much depressed as suicidal.

Bilton had commissioned a couple of pieces from me concerning the short life expectancy of North Sea fishermen. Generous, I suppose, but I hadn't got around to doing them because I was having problems with 'Pen'.

'It's just not working,' Harry Piper had said, 'and you're being completely outshone by Hailey Young's new regular slot.'

'"Me and My Teeth"?' I said incredulously. 'Come off it.'

'It's good,' said Piper. 'And bringing in more toothbrush ads than we can handle. Little Willie actually read one the other day – personally, and with his own eyes. He hasn't read "Pen" of course, but I'll be honest with you, I've given him a memo, telling him it's not working.'

I nearly blubbed, and that night I had a dream. Well, not so much a dream, more a straight rerun of memory. I was standing on the platform of York station, overwhelmed by strong emotion: premature homesickness plus regular sadness. My father stood next to me reading his *Spotlight*, and I sublimated my feelings by attempting to control a wind-whipped *Globe*. The train pulled in and, as I climbed aboard, my father handed me his newspaper. 'Write!' he bellowed, as the train began to inch away, creaking along the platform.

The word echoed in my head as I blearily righted myself in

bed. It had been an injunction both to keep in touch and to find a job in journalism – by implication a worthwhile job, not 'Me and My Fucking Pen'. In the old days, my father had been a bit of a socialist. He'd had ideas; wanted to change things. He knew that that's what journalism should be about. And Bilton was doing that sort of journalism: confrontational, idealistic. And I wasn't.

I picked up a copy of the book I'd just bought, *International Relations for the Young Journalist*, and flung it out of the open window into the rustling depths of a nearby tree.

For a while it seemed as though Lazenby might resign in the wake of the incident, such was the weight of favourable coverage for Bilton (there were only a couple of token condemnations from the editors) and such was the scale of Lazenby's embarrassment. It now seems likely that he'd had some sort of nervous breakdown. He disappeared from public view for about a month and then was forced to resurface when it emerged that his working party on Russia had, unbeknownst to him, been in the Bahamas for three weeks.

'They needed a break after their very intense session at Cap Ferrat,' he was reported as half-heartedly mumbling.

Bilton had some fun with that one in the short, weekly TV programme he now did for Channel 6, *Lazenby Watch*.

When Bilton started at *Hatstand*, his first column – a condemnation of the power of the media barons – was rapturously received. Grey Fauntleroy threw a party for Bilton, to which he (Bilton, that is) invited me.

At first I couldn't bring myself to attend. I'd had several feature ideas turned down by Grey Fauntleroy, and I couldn't bear to see him disporting himself on home territory with his gilded acolytes. Even his pop columnist was called Chaucer: *Geoffrey* Chaucer, for God's sake!

But, emboldened by four pints, I drummed the famous bronze knocker against the Georgian door, and was escorted by a relay of pretty, right-wing girls through the hallowed, narrow corridors that housed *Hatstand*. I noticed the actual hatstand itself, unencumbered by hats, of course; the altarpiece, as it were, which had once belonged to Lord Salisbury. Geoffrey Chaucer, I noticed, dressed in motorcycle leathers, was diverting one of the girls into the bathroom.

In the garden, successful and (which was worse) genuinely happy-looking people were in a variety of carefree poses: laughingly shaking hands, chucking black olives about, sipping wine from ornate, priestly goblets. The background reminded me, somehow, of an idyllic stage set for a light-hearted, upper-class farce: there was a hint of violet and pink in the balmy evening sky; vines tumbled across the ancient powdery pink bricks of the garden walls. Celia Stein was there, walking towards me with a drink. Now there was something to make *me* happy, too.

'Grey's just about to speak,' she said, falling slightly against me and sending my mind into frantic ratiocination: had that been a sexual ploy?

I smiled uncontrollably as Fauntleroy – round, pink and elegant – climbed on to a chair at the far end of the garden. He was wearing jeans, which, despite his age (mid-fifties) and girth, he carried off well.

'Martyn Bilton,' he said 'is left wing, bolshie, anti-social, reckless and uncompromising. And when I first saw him, I thought fantastic!'

Titters here.

'He joins a distinguished team of columnists who have *carte blanche* to write whatever they like – against the magazine, against me and, above all, against our infinitely tiresome Prime Minister.'

Prolonged applause.

'Please raise your glasses in a welcome to Martyn.'

The ceremony was performed.

'I'm not going to say anything else,' continued Grey Fauntleroy, 'except that we have a coffee percolator, permanently on the bubble, in our editorial offices.'

Long laughter.

'I'll be turning it off when Martyn comes to see me!'

Hysteria.

Bilton now arose from the centre of the throng. Yet again, there had been a transformation. His hair had been driven roughly backwards so that he looked like a vampire after a long night. He wore a new suit; still Dickensian, but more spacious. He reminded me of old footage I'd seen of those long-gone guys The Rolling Stones. He looked like all of that lot rolled into one. He wore something around his neck that was somewhere between a tie and a cravat; a bit Disraeli-ish, I thought. He must have bought all this stuff today, and clearly his latent dandyism was emerging. He was like a flower unfolding in the sunshine.

'Would you say he was unknowable?' whispered Celia Stein.

'I'd say he was unknown,' I said, 'until now.'

Bilton spoke.

'I would like to thank Grey Fauntleroy for giving me the freedom of the pages of his magazine to attack the pages of his magazine, and everything that he stands for. My second column will concern poverty in rural areas and deals in detail with the suicides of three farm labourers in the south-west part of . . .'

'He's going to be *such* a big star,' said Celia, drowning Bilton out completely as far as I was concerned, 'and he's even starting to look the part. We had a massive response, you know, when he said my show was garbage. Just hundreds of letters.'

'People agreeing?'

'Absolutely. But that's not important. It's the response that counts. So hard to get. Media consumers are just asleep nowadays, or punch-drunk or something, and it takes someone like Martyn to wake them up. Did you see the review in *The New Seeker*?'

She fished a cutting out of her handbag, and passed it to me. I read:

'. . . Watching last night, I sensed the presence of a spirit which has not been abroad in this country for many a year: the spirit of punk rock. It was embodied in the scrawny frame of one Martyn Bilton, the young communist (of all things!), who brought a little café au lait to bear on the personage of the Prime Minister . . . '

I skipped to the end.

'. . . This fiesty young firebrand had the iconoclastic rigour of the true intellectual, and I'll look forward to seeing him on the box again.'

'Good writing,' I said bitterly.

'Come on, you,' said Celia, and gave me a playful thump.

Eventually Celia Stein drifted off to talk to Geoffrey Chaucer. He was her boyfriend, it transpired.

I walked up the narrow stairs, and the word going around was that, upstairs, Grey Fauntleroy was getting the Monopoly board out. His parties traditionally culminated in Monopoly; he had been single-handedly responsible for the revival of the game as an acceptable activity in high society.

Bilton was in a blue-and-gold drawing room, standing, restrained, with a small red wine, and talking to one of the pretty girls who was sitting on the window seat. I'd seen the girl in a gossip column.

'So tell me,' she said, 'the communists. Was that Stalin and his lot or Hitler and his lot? Sorry, but history has never been my strong point. I must seem like a frightful airhead.'

'It was Stalin,' said Bilton, 'and his lot. Hitler was a fascist.'

'Fascist?' said the girl. 'That rings a bell.'

'Right,' said Bilton, 'well, there's still a lot of it about . . . Golf clubs, and so on.'

'I could talk about political history all night,' said the girl, 'but going back to K.C. and the Sunshine Band . . .'

I listened in for a while, eating ridiculous amounts of peanuts.

'Now then,' Bilton said to me, when the girl had finally walked away.

'Who was she?'

'Some aristocrat,' said Bilton.

'Isn't she the cousin of Lord Somebody of That Ilk?'

'She's not of *that* Ilk,' said Bilton. 'She's of another Ilk altogether if you want to go into it. She's also the assistant producer of a Channel 9 thing called *Rebels*, which she wants me to go on.'

'Well, why don't you be a rebel and say no?'

Bilton sighed, and I felt a little guilty.

'Good party,' I said.

'Give me the Cock and Flower any day,' shrugged Bilton.

'Don't give me that,' I said, trying to keep my tone bantering rather than angry. 'You're loving it all. Honestly, you don't have to pretend to . . .'

'I'm moving out,' said Bilton.

'What?'

'I'm leaving the house. I'll pay my rent until you get a new tenant.'

'Where the hell are you moving to?'

'Halls of Holborn.'

'Halls of Holborn? It sounds like a bloody shoe shop.'

'Yeah,' said Bilton, 'well it's not.'

A young, chubby bloke who actually looked about fifty

and had a pipe in his mouth, came up to Bilton.

'Martyn,' he said respectfully, 'I'm just starting out in journalism and I'll be quite honest with you, I'd like some tips. I mean, I know I'm not going to be the next Martyn Bilton, but if I could just get some . . .'

As the pipe smoker kept talking I minimally signalled a goodbye to an embarrassed but pretty damn fucking pleased Bilton while the young/old person spoke words like 'honesty', 'bravura', 'grave-yet-wry'.

I decided to go straight home via about seven pubs, being unable, in my upwelling misery, to face a bleak descent into sober sleep.

The next day I read about the Halls of Holborn in the *Globe* library. They comprise – for the benefit of any readers as ignorant as I was – not flats but high-ceilinged, wood-panelled 'halls', arranged in a graceful, approximately Art Deco-style, figure-of-eight-shaped building. There are shops, restaurants, inner gardens and outer gardens and helicopter pads. The Halls also have their own tube station – on a security-screened sub-branch – and a penthouse apartment, the so-called 'High Hall', is reserved for the use of any member of the royal family who happens to be at a loose end in Holborn.

It was, and remains, a secretive place with high security. Paranoid billionaires live there, distinguished foreign fugitives, cabinet ministers' mistresses and furtively decadent Arab princes.

Bilton, of course, could not afford to live there from his own resources, comfortably off though he now was. His Hall (one of the smaller apartments) was sub-let to him by Grey Fauntleroy, in what seems to have been a simple act of generosity. Bilton was taken there in a van sent by Fauntleroy,

and tootled west with his entire possessions in a single knackered trunk. There was no goodbye from me. I was at work.

My profile of Bilton went through four irksome rewrites at
the behest of an increasingly irritable Harry Piper, further
alienating me from the subject. It went unnoticed amongst a
dozen or so similar 'exclusives' on Bilton.

A week after the *Hatstand* party, Bilton called me, and we
made an arrangement to meet. But the next day he called
back to cancel. It seemed that he had to go to a recording of
the television show called *Go Cook Yourself*, in which well-
known people were shown how to make a dish that suited
their personality.

'And what dish are they doing for you?' I enquired.

'Cheese on toast,' said Bilton.

He promised to call back and arrange another meeting,
'. . . when I get past this log jam of bloody chat shows.'

A couple of weeks later he sent me an incomplete letter,
eloquently attesting, in a peculiar sort of way, to the distract-
edness of the truly in-demand.

'We'll meet for a drink sometime,' the note prophesied. 'By
the way,' it went on, 'I left some socks at your place. Keep
them if you like, although they're a bit . . .'

And at that point, no doubt, the phone had rung and Bilton had taken another bound towards megastardom. He was
a regular on the *Pundit City* programme now; and his journalism was everywhere, always with that blandishment in ital-
ics at the end which testified to the esteem in which editors
held him: 'This article first appeared in . . .'

But then, within days of its receipt, the promise of the socks
letter was made good, and Bilton summoned me to the Halls
of Holborn.

Chapter Nine

(A month after the incident)

I climbed on to a tram in Charing Cross Road that was going towards the Halls. I wasn't comfortable with my own churlishness towards Bilton. It went against my idea of myself as a basically quite decent bloke. I would be nice to him, and in his dark, secret way he would note the fact and be pleased by it.

I was in a good mood; the whoosh of the trams sweeping past the stalled traffic always made me feel better. Every window was open; I savoured the rushing air; the flashing sunlight, the conductor's quaint shouts of 'More room on top', and 'Move along inside.' I alighted at the Holborn Interchange and approached the towering Halls feeling like someone in a movie. High above me, I could see, against the bright sky, the silhouette of a billionaire being landed on the roof by helicopter.

Bilton wasn't in.

'Mr Bilton is not in,' said the annoying man at the Halls' acre-wide, parquet-floored reception. 'He is not answering my call.'

'Could it be that he's in bed? It's only midday after all. I could go up and knock on his door.'

'Knock on his door?' said the man. 'People do not, as you put it, knock on doors at the Halls.'

'What kind of place is this anyway?' I said. 'I mean, these are flats, aren't they? Why call them halls? I've never heard of anything so whimsical and pointless.'

But the man was facing the other way, watching his little TV. Banished to the limbo of the lobby itself, I walked backwards and forwards. I'd forgotten my mobile, otherwise I'd have called Bilton. Then I heard an atonal dink from the edge of the lobby, and lift doors silently parted to reveal Celia Stein, comely in a sunbeam.

I felt cold, low, old.

'How are you?' she said, approaching me. 'You're looking for Martyn?'

'You've been to see him?'

'Absolutely.'

'But he's already been on your show . . . I mean, that's something that's gone.'

'I'm asking him back.'

'Oh.'

'And we're having a what do you call it . . . affair. Bilton and me.'

'You're seeing each other?'

'I'd put it more strongly than that. We're having an affair, as I said.'

'Oh,' I said again.

'Go on up and see him. Ask him all about it. Don't worry about the bastard on the desk.'

I ascended in the lift, spirits sinking all the time. The lift, I glumly noticed, was more like a drawing room. There was a chandelier. And a desk.

I trekked bitterly along the vast corridor. Probably Bilton and Celia had been communing all month. They were of equivalent media stature, after all. Before long they would be in the *New Globe*'s 'Made It Big' slot, or Piper would be pressurising me to put them in 'Pen', and I would have to give copy approval to their respective agents, and wait for six months for their answers to the questionnaire. The corridor was airless, and disturbingly silent. I decided to turn around and go home.

But then I noticed that the door to number thirty-six, Bilton's place, was open.

Inside, about ten metres across a mainly empty room, was Bilton. He was sitting cross-legged next to a single, quite small, can of beer. Against one wall was a fireplace, as large and austere as some altar from the ancient world. Against the other wall was an isolated pink sofa – the only furniture in the room – and Carol Crane was sitting on it.

'A threesome!' I thought, but then I noticed the casualness of their glances.

'I'm surprised they let you in,' said Bilton, in a neutral tone.

'The bastard downstairs said you weren't in,' I said.

'That's what he's told to say,' said Bilton. 'I forgot to mention that you were coming.'

'Well, thanks a lot for that,' I said.

'Hello,' said Carol nicely. 'I'm going in a minute.'

She was writing in her big book. 'So that's Stein two for the fourteenth,' she said. 'Now I do think you should think about pushing the gardening thing. A Marxist gardener – I could do so much with that, and it gives you an almost human face. I mean, look at Rupert Granger. He's got a good thing going: an absolute Rottweiler in his interviewing technique, but he's got this very nice sideline with his interest in butterflies. It gives him endless lifestyle outlets.'

'Yeah,' said Bilton, '"Me and My Fucking Affectation".'

'It makes him seem deep,' explained Carol.

'He didn't seem particularly deep to me,' said Bilton.

'Incidentally, Martyn,' said Carol, 'I do think you should do the Granger show, but you must be careful. The guy goes for the jugular every time. I think you should wait: get some more stature under your belt if you know what I mean. Adrian –' she turned to me suddenly – 'have a look at that; tell me what you think.'

Carol Crane indicated a large poster crudely tacked to one of the white walls. It contained a dense matrix of images: a 3-D painting. I stood before it and unfocused my eyes so that the hidden image reared into view. It was Bilton, of course, in a discus-throwing pose with swirling coat frozen in space, a long splash of liquid – coffee – flying from his hand.

'We're calling it "David and Goliath",' said Carol. 'Ten thousand come off the presses tomorrow. We think it's going to be the big thing with students this coming academic year.'

'God knows they're thick enough,' said Bilton.

He yawned, and rolled a can of beer towards me, which he had produced, like a magician, from underneath the light, long aviator's coat he was wearing. I collected the can, walked over to the window and looked at the garden of the Halls. Across the lawn there were large trees from which white blossoms were falling slowly down. A pampered family was picnicking on the lawn, attended by two butlers. The day dreamed, and I was happy with that. Bilton was not having an affair with Celia Stein; she had been merely behaving oddly. People sometimes did things like that. But – was he having an affair with Carol Crane? There was certainly an easiness about him with her.

'You see, it's all about positioning, and once you're positioned, you've got to be repositioned to stay ahead of the game. Do you realise that we could be heading for over-exposure? It could be time for you to take a world cruise. Just you and a TV documentary team; satirising the social pretensions of the – what do you call it? – *petit bourgeoisie*. I wouldn't mind coming on that myself, actually.'

'I haven't got a passport,' said Bilton, standing up and

concluding the conversation with his new air of authority.

Carol, who had packed her book, said her goodbyes, and kissed Bilton, but only on the cheek.

The one door in Bilton's room, I discovered, opened to reveal six other doors.

'Only kitchens and bathrooms,' said Bilton, 'nothing special.'

'Why don't you put something in this place?'

'I don't like furniture,' said Bilton, 'not in rooms.'

'Can you show me around? Outside, I mean?'

Bilton shrugged.

After another ride in the lift we were walking through the Hall of Halls, a long arcade of luxurious shops. We entered a refulgent butchers with sweeping, circular counters of white marble; low-slung fans set the cool slabs of perfect meat slightly but rapidly wobbling. The cleanest man I have ever seen, dressed, apparently, in white paper, approached Bilton.

'Morning, Mr Bilton,' he said, 'we have your order.'

Bilton nodded, and the man returned with a small white cardboard box. He opened it for the inspection of Bilton, and revealed a tin of corned beef wrapped in flouncy tissues.

'We don't have a lot of call for the actual tinned meat,' said the master butcher.

Next door to the butchers was a shop selling booze. Sun filtered through the shelved liqueurs as if through a stained-glass window. The stacked red wine had the purity of a blood bank. Two foppish employees were jemmying open an exotically branded wooden crate.

'Nice off-licence,' I said to Bilton as we inspected the bottles.

'Wine merchants,' said the browsing Bilton. 'Different thing.'

'Are you still drinking too much?'

Bilton shook his head.

'Just don't have the time,' he said regretfully.

'Hey,' I said, 'Celia told me she was having an affair with you.'

'Yeah,' said Bilton.

'Are you? I mean, is she?'

'No.'

'So why would she say it?'

'Probably because she's pissed off.'

'About what?'

'About everyone saying that me and her are having an affair.'

'Oh,' I said.

'You're going back on her show, I hear.'

'So Carol says.'

'So soon after your last appearance?'

'Every so often Stein does a show where some guests are invited back to discuss what they said on an earlier show.'

'So it becomes a chat show about a chat show?'

'Suppose so,' said Bilton. 'But chat shows are a good subject for chat shows. Might as well get the shallowness out in the open.'

Later we sat in the public house that served the Halls – a deserted wood-smelling haven. It reminded me of an old-fashioned signal box with its array of long, graceful brass beer pumps. There were no uniformed staff, no televisions, no fucking virtual-reality machines. No theme. A proper, old-fashioned pub.

'You've done very well out of Grey Fauntleroy,' I said, as we settled on to plush barstools.

'It's a perk of the job,' said Bilton, 'a traditional emolument. It's like a tied cottage, in fact, no diff . . .'

'All right, all right,' I said.

For a while Bilton looked surprisingly sheepish, and then said, 'You won't believe what they asked me to do last week.'

'What?'

'Present a lottery cheque . . . I mean, I'm an egalitarian.'

'Obviously,' I said.

'I turn down ten things a day. Madness.'

'Anyway,' said Bilton, as we lay on the rough wood benches of the Halls' sauna centre and the twin brother Turkish masseurs began thrumming on our backs, 'I've been invited to Grey Fauntleroy's place in the country next week, and he's asked me to bring someone.'

'Are you asking me?'

'If you want.'

'Why don't you take Carol Crane?'

I was pushing a boat out here, which Bilton sank.

'Do you want to fucking well come or not?'

My response was drowned out in backslapping of a suddenly heightened intensity.

Chapter Ten

Fauntleroy's place was out west, so I met Bilton at Padding-ton Station.

That day there'd been a big news story: the resignation of the distinguished Foreign Secretary, Hugh Home (which was pronounced Hulme). His motives have since become pretty clear, of course, but at the time they were entirely mysterious, and he did nothing to dispel speculation that he was simply tired of governmental drift and indecision regarding the Pro-tected Republics. Hearing the news, General Zubarov broke off from terrorising the Ukraine and put out a crowing state-ment in which he referred to Lazenby by a word which trans-lated, with surprising precision, as 'pillock'.

It was also noticed, on that Saturday morning, that in his recent public appearances Lazenby had lost a great deal of weight, and his walk – never his most impressive feature – had degenerated alarmingly.

The train was soon banking around hills, scattering sheep, dashing into and out of apparently gratuitous tunnels. It was another beautiful, freakishly hot day; a typical summer's day in England, in fact. In our carriage, people were talking hap-pily, drinking wine from little railway-customised bottles, ignoring the sprawling newspapers on the carriage tables. The conductor told us that we touched 220 miles an hour approaching Exeter; the driver seemed to be showing off.

Sitting alongside Bilton and me was a fat couple who'd been eating from the buffet all the way. The woman had already purchased two lots of drinks and food when she said to the man, 'Do you want anything from the buffet – again?'

'Couldn't eat a thing,' said the man . . . 'except a couple of pork pies and maybe a packet of crisp'd be nice.'

I looked at Bilton. He never actually laughed at anything. Not as such. But he looked up from some formidable political tract and glanced at me. A couple of minutes later the woman returned and placed a sandwich down in front of her place, and handed the two pork pies to her husband. He unwrapped the first pork pie and placed it in his mouth, eating it with a ten-second bout of remorseless chewing. He did exactly the same with the second one, and then looked sadly out of the window.

'Those pies were absolutely dreadful,' he said.

I glanced again at Bilton, and this time he was already looking in my direction, the light making mirrors of his eyes, but still no smile. Sometimes, I reflected, turning back to *The New Globe*, I liked Bilton very much indeed. I hoped our weekend would be a success.

Grey Fauntleroy's place was impressive. Well, of course. Our taxi flew along an undulating but perfectly straight drive aimed at a large door in the dead centre of a symmetrical, neo-classical mansion. Grey was waiting at the end of the drive. He watched us, amused, hands on hips. He wore white slacks belted with a beautiful orange and gold tie.

'Toad of Toad Hall,' observed Bilton as we pulled up and paid the taxi driver.

'Morning, boys,' said Grey. 'Maisie will show you up to your rooms.'

Maisie was a very pretty middle-aged woman who took us up wide stairs, and led us to two big doors.

'Mr Bilton in here; Mr Day in here,' she said delightedly, before curtsying (or did I just imagine that) and disappearing.

'Well, my room's enormous,' I said, strolling into Bilton's room having unpacked. I looked around Bilton's room. '. . . but yours is twice the size,' I added, openly dismayed.

Bilton also had flowers, which I didn't. There were two enormous bouquets of funnel-like white and violet blooms on either side of his broad, high bed.

'I've never seen such massive bouquets,' I said, 'and so exotic.'

'Yeah,' said Bilton, 'well, saving the Amazon rain forest isn't a big thing with Fauntleroy. He prefers to just buy it up and give it away to his friends.'

Bilton put on a rough-textured white suit, and we drifted down to pre-lunch drinks at the west side of the house, on the fringes of a scorched meadow. Attendance was sparse. Most of the guests hadn't arrived yet. Grey Fauntleroy, looking comically shopkeeperish behind a long table covered with jugs of tawny booze in which luminous lemons bobbed, began introducing Bilton and me to a worn-looking but attractive woman with a grey bob.

'Elicia Tate,' he said, 'meet . . .'

But the process was short-circuited when the woman simply leant over and kissed Bilton.

'Get home all right after Thursday night?' she said. 'God, it was a fantastic party, but when Sir Arnold Barnet started doing the can-can I just had to leave.'

'Yes,' said Bilton, 'I was hoping he'd fall head first into that pile of broken glass.'

'He's coming here later,' said Grey rubbing his hands. '. . . Probably the richest man in England,' he continued, turning towards me. 'Made an enormous pile in fertiliser.'

Grey moved away while Bilton and Elicia Tate – who was actually, as I later divined, Cinema Verity, doyenne of high-brow film critics – discussed the iniquities of Arnold Barnet. I was reduced to saying 'Oh really?' occasionally, and 'How shocking.'

I noticed that Bilton was not drinking. I, on the other hand, had become listless and bleary after two glasses of Fauntleroy's punch.

Grey returned and introduced us to a man with a big round head and a small amount of centre-parted hair. It looked as if there was a butterfly sitting on his head. This was Dennis Cambridge and he was a blustering sub-editor who worked on the absurdly contrived, snobbish-and-yet-striving-to-be-hip green wellie magazine *Grass*. Neither Bilton nor Cinema Verity knew him. Not only, I miserably reflected, did Bilton now know all the right people, but he also *didn't* know all the wrong people, which was equally important.

Dennis Cambridge knew Bilton, though.

'Tell me,' he asked, as Bilton and Verity drifted away. 'Is he really as cool in person as he is in print? And do you think he'd do a piece for us on coming here this weekend? I'd love to get his angle on nature.'

After an al fresco lunch, Grey was sitting on a bench in the middle of a field. Bilton was on one side of him, and Rex, Fauntleroy's surprisingly stupid deputy editor, was on the other.

'You know Martha, the rather attractive girl who does our letters page?' said Grey, turning towards Bilton. 'Well, she's wild about you. Saturnine. That's what she calls you.'

'Can't place her,' grunted Bilton.

'No,' said Grey, 'of course you can't. Too busy thinking about the proletariat. The man who came to mend the photo-copier the other day, I think he's one of those. There's a propensity for revealing the buttocks while working. I think it's a call-sign to other members of the same tribe. I liked your piece condemning the public vilification of muggers, by the way. The whole thing was from a perspective I'd never thought of . . .'

'Where are your daughters, Mr Fauntleroy?' I asked, anxious to forestall any further long-winded praise of Bilton. 'You have six, don't you?'

'Please call me Grey. I have seven, and they've all gone out into the wide world.'

'I.e. Chelsea,' snorted Bilton.

'More interesting question is where my bloody wife is,' said Grey. 'Haven't seen Chantal for two years. D'you think one of those two is going to fall in?'

We looked down the long slope towards the brown glitter of the trout stream. Just next to an elaborate bridge, two men were wrestling playfully.

'Who are those chaps?' said Rex.

'Couple of halfwits from the village,' said Grey.

'Making one fullwit in total,' said Bilton, rolling up his sleeves. 'It's no wonder socialism's so late coming to this country,' he sighed. 'We've never got beyond bloody feudalism.'

Grey stood up.

'What are you doing this afternoon, Martyn?' he asked. (Why the hell didn't he ask me what *I* was doing this afternoon?) '. . . There's golf practice on the South Hill, sunbathing on the terrace, fishing down there –' he pointed to the stream – 'Monopoly in the Monopoly Annexe, and tennis on the tennis courts.'

'I think I'll go to my room and read,' said Bilton.

'Christ!' said Grey. 'I do my best.'

Employer and employee walked off in different directions, and I was left alone with Rex.

'You the chap that does "Me and My Pen"?' he asked.

'Yes,' I said glumly.

'It's very good, you know. I've always thought that. I

especially enjoyed that one where Gavin Tyndale . . .'

'The prolific belletrist . . .?'

'. . . Where he spoke about that French eighteenth-century cut-glass pen that had been rescued from Marie Antoinette's personal bureau just before the Revolution. And how its delicacy symbolised the poignant transience of all literary endeavour.'

'Right,' I said. 'Shall I tell you the real situation there?'

'How do you mean?'

'After we'd published the piece, Tyndale confessed to me that on his desk is a shoebox, and inside it he keeps about three hundred . . .'

'Oh God, I know what you're going to say . . .'

'Three hundred E-Zee Scribble Bungaways.'

'The most disposable pens on the market,' said Rex, ruefully.

I nodded.

'Make your average biro look like a bloody family heirloom.'

I left a disillusioned Rex and, being much too hot and having a terrible headache, walked into the dark, cool house. It was impressive: walls of dusty orange, faded lilacs; great gilded mirrors; there were bathrooms with fireplaces and coal scuttles, and baths with lions' feet. I lay down on a *chaise longue* and went to sleep.

I woke up sweating. I still had a headache. I stepped outside, and saw Cinema Verity enjoying the sun in a little bikini. I waved to her and shouted, but she just looked at me with a puzzled expression.

In the distance I saw Bilton. He was enjoying the shade, lying fully clothed under a big, lonely tree and watching a small boy – where the hell had *he* come from? – keeping a football aloft with repeated kicks. Or trying to.

'I can do it better than this,' the boy was saying to Bilton as I approached, 'only this ball's a bit flat.'

'Yeah?' said Bilton.

'Do you think I can kick this ball higher than the top of this tree on the first go?' said the boy, changing tack in his attempt to impress Bilton.

'No,' said Bilton, and he was right.

I sat down next to Bilton.

'What were you talking to Cinema Verity about?'

'Cinema – funnily enough,' said Bilton. 'And she was asking me about you.'

'What did you say?'

'I said that you did "Me and My Pen" in *The New Globe*.'

'Is that how you define me, then?'

'I don't define you at all,' said Bilton. 'It's society that does that to us all.'

'Still coming out with that Marxist claptrap, then? Honestly, I have to say . . .'

'Do you have to say "I have to say"?' said Bilton. 'It's the authentic voice of the whining *petit bourgeoisie* . . .'

'Honestly,' I said, 'I have to say that I'm beginning to wonder why you asked me here in the first place. I mean, was it just to show off? To say, look at me, how well I'm doing.'

'I've got to go and return a phone call,' said Bilton, standing up.

'Another interview? I'll say two words to you, Bilton: "over exposed".'

'Yeah,' said Bilton, 'well, I'm feeling a bit over-exposed to you right now.'

Bilton was hurrying away. The little boy's ball came towards him, and he kicked it back, hard.

The little boy gamely ran after it, and I yelled 'Bilton!' but there was no response.

I was still feverishly wrenching fistfuls of grass out of the ground twenty minutes later.

Grey Fauntleroy stood before a huge wood fire which had been lit as soon as the sun went down beyond the tall windows of his drawing room. He was doing another round of introductions. Somebody bald who was something in the City. Somebody bald who was something in the City's wife. A gamine cookery writer called Cleo (evidently Grey's girlfriend), Dennis Cambridge, Cinema Verity, Rex, Bilton (wearing a rather too small dinner jacket that merely emphasised his suddenly graceful height; introduced by Grey as being 'mind-bogglingly but amusingly a Marxist') and me (referred to by an uninterested Grey as 'Aiden').

'Oh, I'm forgetting something . . .' said Grey, coming amongst us with champagne, '. . . later on we will be honoured with the company of Sir Arnold Barnet, although I believe he is under an injunction preventing him from attending social gatherings at which more than a strictly limited amount of gin is available. And John Hobday will be here too, if, that is, he can drag himself away from Croydon, the constituency which he rather embarrassingly represents.'

I looked at Bilton, who was scrutinising the ceiling. John Hobday was one of Lazenby's media ministers.

We moved towards the dinner table, and it turned out that I was placed next to Bilton – awkward, since it was clear that we would not be talking. But then Verity walked up to Bilton and started gabbling away to him, bashing me on the nose with her dangling necklace all the while.

'Look,' I said, swiping the necklace out of the way, 'why don't you sit here, and then you two can talk all night?'

I stood up, moved to the far end of the table, and gloweringly lowered myself into Verity's place, which put me

between Rex and Dennis Cambridge, both of whom I immediately started to ignore.

We were half-way through pâté de foie gras when John
Hobday appeared through the French windows, making an
entrance like a character in a farce, which, in a way, he was.
He was chubby, suspiciously tanned, his face matching his
beige suit. He was wearing a yellow tie and – ambitious creep
that he was – a pair of Lazenby loafers. His luxuriant, auburn
hair had been formed into an aerodynamic shape. Sports car,
I diagnosed.

'Sorry ahm late,' he said, 'the wife was navigating.'

And now his flushed wife stepped through the French windows after him.

As he approached, Hobday beamed at us all, and then
stopped beaming.

'Ah,' he said.

'Something wrong, John?' said Cleo.

'Now I'll be honest with you all,' said Hobday . . .

(At least that is what he almost said, but it came out sound-
ing suspiciously like 'Ah'll be honest with yerall.' Hobday, I
subsequently found out, was nicknamed 'Obday' by the
lobby correspondents on account of his imperfectly sup-
pressed Yorkshire accent).

'. . . I'm going to get into big trouble with the papers if I sit
down to dinner with a certain person 'ere.'

'Good God, man!' sighed Grey.

Bilton was staring evenly at Hobday. I admired his guts,
which in turn made me even more jealous of him.

'Ahm sorry, Grey,' said Hobday. 'I don't approve of Mr Bilton. Philip's not just my Prime Minister, 'e's a personal
friend.'

'Bollocks,' said Grey.

'Ahm adamant. Ahm going.'

'Go then,' said Grey, 'but it's a bloody shame. I got the Lebanese red – the '79 – up especially for you.'

Hobday sat down and grabbed a bread roll.

'Very pleased indeed ter meet yer,' he said, with a full mouth, to Dennis Cambridge.

But then Bilton stood up.

'I'm reading a very good book at the moment,' he said. 'I must get back to it.'

Seeking to make an emphatic gesture, Bilton chose, peculiarly I thought, to chuck his cigarette lighter into an ashtray, and set off towards the door with a wayward stalk.

'Sit down,' said Grey very quietly and quite threateningly, without looking up.

Bilton havered most uncharacteristically.

'You two have a fight,' Grey went on. 'It'll do both your reputations good, and we'd all enjoy it. But do it after the coffee . . .'

Grey hadn't realised what he was saying, which made this all the funnier to the rest of us. There were diverse good-natured pleas to the adversaries, and Bilton eventually flopped back into his seat, accepting a consolatory mineral water from the beaming Maisie. The dinner party was back on track.

At the end, of course, Hobday and Bilton were talking. I flitted past a few times . . .

'Ah still think Marxism's important philosophically,' Hobday was saying, 'but politically? No way.'

Later, Hobday was still talking.

'But surely there isn't a working class any more? I mean, 'ow would you define it?'

'Start with those people who don't worry about how to define the working class,' said Bilton. 'Then look at all the people whose interests your government and every British government feel able to ignore.'

'Mmm . . .' said Hobday.

And later.

'It's just a false religion really, intit?' Hobday was saying.

'But what's a true religion?' Bilton was saying. 'And how would anyone know?'

Then they were joined by Grey Fauntleroy, who began questioning Hobday about the unpopularity of Social Dynamics.

'Ah can't discuss the deliberations of cabinet,' said Hobday.

'Pompous prat.'

'Not 'eard of collective responsibility, Grey?' said Hobday, piqued.

'Both words are complete anathema to me.'

Hobday shook his head.

'Come on,' said Grey, jerking his head towards the Monopoly room. 'Monopoly!'

I was one of the first to follow Grey through to a long, graceful, chilly room. I took a seat in a cluster of faded arm-chairs at one end. But everyone else was convening at other end, sitting down on a slightly ragged pink rug. Fauntleroy had the board and was laying it out; he was always the banker, of course. This Fellow of All Souls derived tremendous satis-faction from facilitating house purchases or punctiliously handing out £200 for Passing Go, and sometimes, indeed, such was his efficiency that the money changed hands before 'Go' was actually passed.

The guests were reaching for their favoured tokens; all had clearly played Monopoly with Fauntleroy before.

'Dear little flat iron!' squealed Hobday's wife, and actually kissed the damn thing.

Bilton and I were the only two not playing, I not having

been invited to, and Bilton declining on grounds of conscience. Bilton was sitting near me, but his chair pointed towards the board, mine away. He was holding, not drinking, a glass of wine. I wasn't drinking either. The pâté de foie gras had been rich and cold like a slab of butter, and I felt that I hadn't seen the last of it that night. I was squirming in my seat, unable to get comfortable, unable to join in with the Monopoly repartee.

'First law of Monopoly,' Grey was booming at the City gent. '. . . The Utilities are absolutely bloody useless. Can't build on 'em, so don't buy 'em.'

The game ground on for half an hour, and then Cinema Verity, sparkly eyed but wan, approached Bilton.

'I'm the top hat, and I'm rather dizzy,' she said, in a Lewis Carrollian sort of way. 'You must take over from me while I get some air.'

Bilton sighed, puffed out his cheeks and blew.

'Monopoly,' he said, now shaking his head for good measure, to make it clear that he was entering the game under sufferance.

As Bilton approached the table, Dennis Cambridge, who'd been gawping at Cinema Verity all night, also rose from the Monopoly board.

'Air!' he said. 'That's a jolly good idea. Adrian,' he said, turning to me, 'maybe you'd like to take over the Scottish terrier.'

'Okay,' I weedily replied.

Ignoring this minor-league exchange, Grey was booming at Bilton, who was now sitting down.

'Know what it says on the top of the Monopoly box, Bilton?' he said.

'Suitable for children aged eight and upwards?' said Bilton.

'No,' said Grey. 'It says "The property speculation board

game". Even Mr Lazenby doesn't approve of property speculation, let alone your friends in the mysterious Group.'

He handed Bilton the dice, and Bilton threw.

Two sixes.

'God,' gasped Cleo, 'you're good at this!'

Bilton's top hat came to rest on Chance.

Grey picked up the card to read it, but Cleo, unable to bear the suspense, snatched it out of his hand.

'Congratulations,' she read. 'It is your birthday. Collect £15 from each player.'

There were calls of 'bravo', 'well done', 'many happy returns'.

My nausea intensified as I saw that by handing Bilton £15 I had nearly gone bankrupt. Dennis Cambridge was evidently not very good at Monopoly, for he had bequeathed me a miserable portfolio: Old Kent Road and Whitechapel with one house apiece, the Waterworks, £207 and a Get Out of Jail Free card.

It was my turn. I threw the dice, moved the dog, and landed on Community Chest.

Grey picked up the card.

'Go to jail,' he read. 'Go directly to jail. Do not pass go. Do not collect £200.'

'All right, all right,' I said bitterly, 'no need to rub it in.'

This was meant to be funny, but I had only succeeded in engendering another nasty little silence. I couldn't get the pâté de foie gras out of my mind, and the tension of my new relationship with Bilton was making matters worse.

At exactly midnight I landed on Mayfair. It was Bilton's, and he had a hotel on it.

'That'll be two thousand pounds,' he said, looking resolutely into the middle distance.

'Actually . . .' I said, standing up and staggering across the

121

board, sending houses skittering and, I think, actually demolishing one hotel, 'I've got to just . . .'

I lurched into the garden via the conservatory attached to the dining room and vomited gushingly. Afterwards, having walked unsteadily to the tree under which I'd talked to Bilton, I fondled a low leaf and, breathing deeply, savoured the cool breeze against my still-clammy temples. Across the lawn I could see a skipping, zigzagging tweed-suited figure with a man in a chauffeur's uniform trotting doggedly behind him.

So, Sir Arnold Barnet had arrived after all.

Later, I was in a cab going back to London. The ride would cost me a fortune but I didn't care. I had left a note for Grey on the hall table, apologising fulsomely but casting subtle aspersions concerning the pâté de foie gras. I felt pretty good, having made my escape, although I did wish that the taxi driver would turn his radio off. The news was coming every ten minutes as we hurtled past the dark, high, striding trees, and I half expected to hear something about Bilton and myself on it, so momentous did the end of our friendship seem to be.

Chapter Eleven

Bilton was on television regularly throughout that summer. Typically I would leave the house, being unable to face watching whatever programme it might be, but then I would sometimes relent, and watch tensely on fast forward, waves of envy and sadness at a friendship ended buffeting my brain.

Late one balmy evening I watched Bilton on the first of a new Channel 14 series, *My Sunday Morning*. The effect of *cinéma vérité* was tiresomely contrived with hand-held camera as Bilton boarded the Highgate tram and rode that dusty switchback up the hill to the village. Clutching a wonky flower, he stalked imperiously through its streets of sunshine and shadow in what appeared to be high-laced, white, pointed boots, ballooning white trousers and a sweat-stained and creased, but palpably expensive, cricketer's shirt. With his white face, he looked like a negative of himself: a ghost.

Fittingly, then, he was next seen crunching through the gravel, past the shockingly collapsed, jungle-engulfed tombs and precariously elevated angels of Highgate Cemetery. He was suddenly before Marx's grave, absurdly with head bowed. The unseen interviewer attempted a question but Bilton irritatedly signalled that he should remain silent. After a respectful interlude, Bilton moved forward and placed his flower at the base of the grey cube.

There was another flower, dead, already there.

'I wonder who put that dead one there?' said the whimsical off-camera voice.

'Me,' said Bilton. 'And it wasn't dead when I put it there. There used to be a lot of flowers on this grave. In years gone by socialists from all around the world would come and pay their respects. But now the ideas are going through a period of temporary neglect . . . I think of it like Catholicism in England: banished for a while but then coming surging back; roaring back. On the other side of the tomb, someone's written "wanker" in big letters. Indicates a lack of respect.'

'*Why* precisely do you come here?' said the off-screen voice.

'Read the inscription,' said Bilton, and the camera dutifully panned across the angular golden words. Not the 'Workers of the world unite' part (I had accompanied Bilton on one of his pilgrimages, so I knew my way around), but the other part: 'The philosophers have interpreted the world in various ways. The point, however, is to change it.'

The camera lingered on this for a while, and then moved upwards to the carved head of Marx, and remained there for a shaky minute. Distant tourist voices faded in and out; a single bird sang a staccato song.

'He had a weird hairstyle,' observed the off-screen voice.

And on that bathetic note, the short film ended.

The coffee advert – I videoed that too. It was extremely futuristic, in a *passé* way, with many flickering shots of Bilton, dressed like an archly conceptualised tramp, striking balletic, coffee-hurling poses, and accompanied by the arbitrary 'beat bursts' of the avant garde group Lion. The advert was acclaimed in dozens of media-on-media magazines as brilliant, but I can't remember the brand.

The most widely celebrated of Bilton's interviews took place with – indeed, was graciously granted to – the highly successful but in my opinion lightweight left-wing journalist Rich Hayes. Within a week of its original broadcast on Channel 19, the encounter – a one-off entitled *In Conversation with Martyn Bilton*' – became a regular fixture on the Instant Classics Channel. The overall tone was sycophantic but, early on, Hayes asked some ostensibly difficult questions.

'You've made a lot of money out of professing egalitarianism,' he said. 'Are you not at all materialistic yourself?'

'I *am* a materialist,' said Bilton, who was wearing a gypsyish neckerchief and what appeared to be a cape, 'a *dialectical* materialist.'

There was a shot of Rich Hayes laughing, ruefully hoist by his own petard.

'I bought a new pair of boots the other day,' Bilton went on, 'and they hurt my feet. That's materialism for you.'

'But you live in one of the most select blocks of flats in London,' said Hayes.

'Well, I like to think that I'm lowering its reputation with every day that I'm there,' chortled Bilton.

Of course it had all been stage-managed. Later on Bilton and Hayes took their conversation on the road, around arts centres, theatres and bookshops. It was usually a sell-out, I believe.

I didn't talk to Bilton over that summer; nor the following winter and spring. We had fallen out, and every day that fact shocked me. I was writing the occasional feature and struggling to give 'bottom' to 'Me and My Pen', while Bilton continued to soar.

I avoided his regular appearances on the Channel 16 spin-off from *Pundit City*, *At Home with the Pundits*. I was also careful to miss every episode of *Top Marx*, his pithy tea-time slot summarising Marxism, a show buttressed by fancy, award-winning graphics, or so I was told. And never once did I see his mimed political commentaries on the revoltingly whimsical, totally silent, five-minute current affairs show *No Comment*.

His . . . shall we say distinctive face appeared for weeks as the hologram inside the egg-timer on the Interlude Channel. He was incorporated, thinly disguised, into three novels, none of which have I read, and a never-before-or-since-heard-of gay, experimental dance company called The Seven Stevens worked up a piece called *Disgrace* which was based on the incident and received rave reviews.

During that freezing, frightening February when London rediscovered the recipe for the peasouper, on the very day that the new Poet Laureate turned down my request that he do a 'Pen' in terms that were far from poetic, I came back from lunch to discover that I'd been invited on to Channel 24's *My Friend the Star* to discuss Bilton. I said no.

Lazenby's descent continued of course, although by now he seemed to be denying some fundamental law of physics. I mean, what goes up is supposed to come down . . . but not Lazenby. His approval ratings in the perma polls were in single figures every month, and he couldn't keep the incident out of interviews; the more he tried to banish its memory, the more his inquisitors wanted to bring it up. For Lazenby, it was like a baleful black star, flaring and sulphurous, malevolently hoisted to be the focus of his failure. Put another way: as a media event the incident had what Harry Piper called topspin. It just kept rolling.

Much of Lazenby's time was taken up with his massively bureaucratic and expensive Second Reorganisation of local government; his confusing plans were like a prism, accepting and refracting ideological input from all angles, attracting no support and much loathing. Bilton, the tormentor-in-chief, had a great time with these in his newspaper articles.

And then there was Zubarov. He began making lumbering, sinister jokes about Lazenby, always referring to him as Dr Farrago. The situation in the Protected Republics had quietened down over winter, but then, of course, came the full-scale occupation of Estonia, after which the Poles started to get very jumpy. They appealed repeatedly to the newfangled Pan-Nationalist Defence Network for help, and Lazenby kept formulating ever more rarefied and irrelevant, almost narcis-sistically complex resolutions, which were always voted down. He just didn't have a clue what to do, as Bilton – now a regu-lar sidekick to Damon Potter, the smart-alec presenter of the hip foreign affairs satire/jazz and dance music show *Diplo-matic Bag* – regularly affirmed in his sarcastic, quarrelsome tones . . .

One other event that occurred around the time of that sum-mer following the incident . . . I received, and opened, a letter that was meant for Bilton.

'Dear Mr Bilton,' I read. 'You shouldn't kick a chap when he's down. Didn't anyone ever tell you it's not English?'

It was unsigned.

Chapter Twelve

(One year after the incident)

At the precise moment, on that momentous 21 July on which Britain declared war on Russia, I was sitting in the bath, tentatively lathering my hair with a shampoo which I had only just realised was suitable for dry, wind-damaged hair. Why can't they just make shampoo for dirty hair, I reflected, at about the time that General Stepan Zubarov attempted to fire the first of three nuclear weapons at the heart of London. I had got out of the bath and was abstractedly urinating when my mobile phone rang. It was Harry Piper.

'Please come into work immediately,' he said.

'Hang on,' I said, 'it's my day off.'

'I think the seriousness of the situation warrants a suspension of holidays,' he replied.

I asked into an electronic void what he was talking about. Piper had hung up.

I drove through the blustery rain-flecked dusk to the offices of *The New Globe*. I could only assume that Piper wanted to discuss something to do with the fact that this was the first anniversary of the incident. Maybe he wanted yet another profile of Bilton. Well, I would quit rather than do it myself.

He was sitting on my desk in an irritatingly proprietorial way. Everybody around him was talking to everybody else; the atmosphere was upbeat. Everything seemed somehow different; I was suddenly nervous of Piper once again.

'Hello,' I said.

'Yes,' he said, coldly. He looked over my head for a while

and then lowered his gaze. 'I was not impressed, to be honest, by your response to my phone call. But I shall say what I intended to say in any case.'

He coughed.

'For the past few months, me and the top brass in ads have been kicking around an idea for a new Sunday supplement, and now is the perfect time to launch it. It's going to be a leisure and lifestyle type of thing . . .'

'Another one?' I gasped, appalled.

'. . . and we've decided to call it "Easy Like a Sunday Morning", after the Lionel Richie song. Before I go any further, what do you think of the name?'

'Well,' I said, 'it's . . .'

'The beauty of this whole idea,' Piper ploughed on, ' is that "Easy Like a Sunday Morning" will never, and I mean *never* –' he banged the table ferociously – 'mention the war. It'll be consumer-oriented, lively, funny, irreverent and, above all, irrelevant, and we think you're just the man to edit it.'

He held out his hand.

'Congratulations.'

'Excuse me,' I said. 'Did you say war?'

And that's really how it was.

When I got home, I poured myself a whisky. It was funny how life could put on a spurt like this. 21 July. I had been braced for an evening of what Carol Crane might have called Biltonia. But now this. I went into the sitting room and turned on the television. A small man with the sort of long, bald head that you didn't often see on television was pointing with a stick at a large map of what used to be called the Commonwealth of Independent States. Dotted around this map were small, jagged symbols of flame, and these, it transpired, were the 'potential flashpoints'.

I had not seen this man before. Underneath him was a little message to the effect that all scheduled programmes had been cancelled until further notice. This man was not a regular TV presenter or pundit. He'd been dredged up, by the etiolated looks of him, from deep academe. He spoke of the situations within the various republics; the degrees of chaos and economic disarray obtaining in each.

The 'potential flashpoints', it turned out, were the civil and military nuclear installations, and these, the expert repeatedly and dourly insisted, would also be the 'nodal points' of the conflict. The academic was boring, which was interesting: he'd been given a licence to go into detail, to lecture, betokening, of course, the seriousness of the situation.

Thin red lines extended from the General Zubarov symbol – rather absurdly, a small, braided military cap – to the capitals of the republics within the former Russian empire. Moving his high-tech stick between the two points on each line, the academic explained Zubarov's relationship with the republics one by one. 'The picture,' concluded the academic, as his face filled the screen, 'is one of complete chaos, and I would like to stress that I have absolutely no idea what is going on.' His image was promptly superseded by that of the usual presenter.

'Thank you for your analysis, Dr Dwyer,' he said. 'We'll be returning to you shortly.'

But why? I thought to myself.

Suddenly there was a bang from the direction of the door. I walked into the hall, into which a piece of paper had swooped. I picked it up. 'Watch television at nine o'clock,' it said. 'Lazenby is on.' It was signed 'Oswald'.

Oswald was the next-door neighbour that I had inherited when I moved in with Bilton. It was a role he played to the hilt, by which I mean that he was a sort of paradigm of domesticity. You could always rely on Oswald to be sunbathing in his garden when it was sunny, to refrain from watering his garden when there was a hosepipe ban, and to do so when there was not. One fifth of November, Bilton had told me, he'd actually seen Oswald light the blue touch paper and stand well back. He was a nice bloke.

The phone went. It was Oswald.

'Did you get my note? I've just delivered it to you, so it should be somewhere on the floor near your letter box.' (Oswald was inclined to pedantry). 'I knocked but you didn't hear me. Or maybe you were ignoring me. That happens a lot, I find. The government have been putting out news bulletins all day saying that everybody should watch Lazenby tonight at nine o'clock. He's making a statement from Number Ten – all channels. We – that is the people who were in – were told by news bulletins to leave notes for the people who were out. But I suppose they told you at work.'

I looked at my watch: seven minutes to nine. Oswald would stop talking in a moment.

'Honestly, it's a bad business this,' he continued. 'Of course, I could see it coming. All that talk about Holy Mother Russia. And that mad declaration: the Seven Sins of the West . . . I knew there'd be trouble.'

'I never saw it coming,' I said. 'I feel like Rip Van Winkle – you know, been asleep for forty thousand years or something. Just proves: you should keep an eye on the news.'

'But you're a journalist,' said Oswald, appalled.

'Ah, but a different type,' I said. 'The stuff I do is primarily concerned with the writing implements of celebrities. At least it was until today.'

'I just don't understand it,' said Oswald, heart-rendingly. 'I mean, how can we have a war with Russia? They can't attack us. We're too far away.'

'Well, they do have nuclear missiles.'

'Oh,' said Oswald. 'Weren't they supposed to have got rid of all those long ago?'

'They said they had, but in fact, of course, they hadn't, and in any case they have all the plutonium they need to make new missiles.'

'I see,' said Oswald. 'That's bad.'

'Also, Zubarov could conceivably send a flotilla of gun boats around from the Baltic. I mean, it sounds absurd but he could. We've cut back our navy quite a lot in recent years, and we'd be no match for them. And Zubarov's always made out that he's got, you know, agents operating in this country, so there could be a fair bit of terrorism, I suppose.'

'But surely,' Oswald plaintively enquired, 'our allies in the new Pan-Nationalist Defence Network will come in on our side?'

'Not necessarily. You see, if Russia had declared war on us, then they would have all immediately piled in – albeit incredibly reluctantly – on our side. But *we* declared war on *Russia* in response to provocation which was, arguably, not that serious, hence the other powers' policy of so-called 'pro-active hyper-vigilence', which comes down to doing absolutely nothing for as long as possible. Of course, we have their sympathy. We have their good wishes, if you like.'

'Well, that's something, isn't it?' said Oswald.

'No,' I said, 'not really.'

Oswald sighed. 'The thing is,' he said, 'I've got two young kids.'

He had as well.

'Don't worry, Oswald,' I said. 'It's probably all talk, and if there is any fighting, it'll almost certainly be confined to the Protected Republics of the former Commonwealth of Independent States.'

'Eh?'

'The places we're supposed to be guarding against Russian intervention,' I reminded him.

'Right,' said Oswald, his voice brightening slightly. 'All those places whose names I can never remember.'

'Exactly,' I said.

'I'll tell you what, though,' said Oswald, 'I'm with him all the way. Mr Lazenby, I mean. He's just had as much as he could stand. He'd had a bellyful. He's only human, after all.'

'It's an interesting theory,' I said, 'but I've got to go now.'

'Yes,' said Oswald, 'Lazenby's coming on in a minute.'

I turned on the TV, and there was Philip Lazenby, who looked different. It took me a minute to work out what it was. He was wearing glasses: heavy black ones that made him look like a handsome man deliberately downplaying his looks out of magnanimity or sheer gloominess. It was an impressive effect. His hair was looking strange too: no longer bouncy but crinkly and grizzled. His suit was black, and the shirt was white; Lazenby was looking like a vicar, or an old-fashioned banker.

The tie was a superb red silk thing but the knot was no longer fulsome and tubular. It had been snatched, drawn into a too-tight, perfunctory triangle as though under pressure of more important business than the correct putting on of a tie.

'Good evening,' said Lazenby, with unfamiliar decisiveness in a voice which suddenly had something of the compelling quality of a tenpin bowling ball rumbling towards the target. 'This evening, our country finds itself at war. It's not the first time it has happened. Our opponent is a dangerous and sinister man who threatens every value that we hold dear. It's not the first time that we have faced such a man. We've won our wars in the past and we will win this one. For months, we have tolerated absurd, verbal provocations from the illegitimate Russian leader, General Stepan Zubarov, and he has singled out our troops for attack at every stage of the international peace-keeping operation. So be it. If Zubarov wants a fight, he shall have one.

'We have information that, at this moment, Russian forces are massing for another incursion into the territory of the Protected Republic of Estonia. We are going to take charge of the international effort to repel this and General Zubarov's other incursions. Our military strongholds on the border of Russia may now be singled out for attack; they will be strongly defended. We are at the moment the only country formally at war with Russia, but we have received a pledge of support from our American allies, and from our friends in the Various Nations. My negotiations within the Pan-Nationalist Defence Network are continuing.'

The camera moved in closer to Lazenby, and he frowned in a new, beguiling, wry way.

'Talk of war is always alarming,' he said, softly, 'but please do not be over-anxious. The capacity of General Zubarov to do direct harm to this country would appear to be limited.'

That's right, I thought, limited to a nuclear attack.

'As events unfold, I will be making regular broadcasts, and revealing as much information as is compatible with the need for tactical surprise. We must all simply go about our normal lives, and see what happens. But let me state briefly a few of the things I know about General Zubarov.'

He paused, and spread his hands on the desk. I looked at the desk. *Only* the hands were there. No papers; no cue cards.

'Firstly,' said Lazenby with a confident snort, 'I know that he is not actually a general at all. He simply adopted the title upon assuming power four years ago, which, by the way, is typical of the man. I know that he was expelled from the Moscow Military Academy for cheating in examinations. I know that he has usurped the legitimately elected government of Russia without any regard whatsoever for the constitution; I know that General Zubarov is prepared to put his people through great suffering in order to divert attention from his dictatorial, brutal regime. I also know that he is a bloodthirsty coward.'

Lazenby paused. (What he had become, I decided, was a man that women rather than girls would find attractive – a distinction I had frequently seen employed in women's magazines. He no longer looked like the little one in The Monkees. He now looked, through half-closed eyes, like the long-dead, humorous but grave Italian actor and sex symbol Marcello Mastroianni. He still looked small, of course. He *was* small. But he no longer looked trivial.)

'. . . and I know one final thing,' he was saying. '. . . In threatening the free people of this country, General Zubarov has made the biggest mistake of his life.'

And he nodded slowly. (Good grief, he was going grey; but it didn't matter.)

'Good night.'

It was a brief but pleasingly straightforward speech. Lazenby had not gibbered or stuttered, and I felt slightly disappointed that it had ended. I realised that, having switched Lazenby off, I felt alone and unprotected.

I entered my bedroom, and looked at my personal effects: my diary, my latest unfinished novel, my list of goals tacked above my desk. All revealed, in the light of events, as grubbily crumpled bin candidates. All now sidelined. I shakily put my diminished wispy artefacts away. I would have to go into abeyance, put my life on the back burner. But I had an uneasy sense that not everybody would be putting their lives on the backburner.

At half past ten, I decided to go to the pub. Trudging through the dark, big summer raindrops in my face, I cheered up immensely. I would make a go of 'Easy Like a Sunday Morning'; it was a big step up the ladder. Then I thought, but what if the whole bloody ladder is knocked away by the war? A cat ran past me very fast. An orange streetlight suddenly fizzed and flickered, sending a shadow of a gatepost jumping. I looked around me, at the compressed, angular, suburban villas, with their glowing, tightly curtained windows, and felt a wave of sympathy for ordinary humanity in danger. But it didn't last long, because two seconds later I stepped over the threshold of the pub.

The cavernous interior of the Cock and Flower was decorated ill-advisedly in mustardy flock wallpaper. Behind the bar, above the drunkards' laboratory of optics, were rows of shelves cluttered with sentimental knick-knacks donated by generations of regulars: decaying teddy bears, a couple of shrivelled footballs, personalised tankards – the prized possessions of somebody that everyone had forgotten existed. On the top shelf, a gormless, orange fish hung in a murky aquarium.

The pool alcove was haunted by the usual desperadoes, circulating between ritualistic poses: at the table; sitting; standing; smoking. The darts players were playing darts; the man who played the fruit machine was lunging away in the corner. It would take more than the Third World War, I reflected, to stop the customers of the Cock enjoying their pub pursuits.

The barman sauntered down his enclosure towards me. His name was Clive. He had a limp, always wore a lumberjack shirt and had a bald, yellow head and no eyelashes. He was also extremely old. And he was a cockney.

'What do you make of all this, then?' he said. 'I'll tell you what I make of it: if this war's anything like the last one, it won't be half bad.'

'Were you around in the last war, Clive?' I said.

'I did my bit,' he said.

'What service were you in?'

'RAF.'

'Oh yes. What part?'

'Spitfires. I cooked the food for the blokes that flew them. God, I went through it. You've heard of dawn raids, right? Pilots flying bombing missions just before daybreak?'

'Yes,' I said.

'Well, what no one ever thinks about is the poor bugger who makes breakfast for the blokes who did the dawn raids. I was preparing fifty breakfasts at midnight. Cooked breakfasts, mind you. They called them "the few", but, bloody hell, they put away a lot of bacon and eggs. I was working flat out. It was inhuman, I tell you.'

'You never saw action, though?'

'You mean outside the kitchen? No. And I'll tell you what, I had the time of my life in that war.'

'How come?'

'The blackouts, mate,' he said, leaning conspiratorially across the bar. 'The bleedin' blackouts. Everybody was at it. I shagged my way round east London twice over, I did.'

'And you honestly think you'll be able to do the same thing again?'

'Cheeky little sod.'

He gave me my beer.

'Where's your mate, then,' said Clive, 'that Bilton bloke? Haven't seen him for ages.'

'Dunno,' I said, 'on telly somewhere.'

Clive walked away to serve somebody else, then returned.

'I'll tell you what, though,' he said, 'this war's going to put him out a bit.'

I nodded.

'Do you know what I mean, though?'

Chapter Thirteen

Just after midnight, shortly after I'd returned from the Cock and Flower, the doorbell rang. It was a policeman, with one hand on a bleary Bilton's shoulder.

'Does this belong to you, sir?' said the policeman cheerfully. 'Found him reeling around in Mile End, and he gave this address. He has been cautioned, and no further action should be necessary, provided he goes inside and gets his head down.'

Bilton was squinting into an empty cigarette pack and swaying in the blustery gusts.

'He'll be all right now,' I said, but the policeman remained on the doorstep. I felt the need to say something.

'Pity about this war.'

'Yes,' replied the policeman, screwing his hat back on to his head. 'Make a lot of extra work for us – one way or another. Good night, sir.'

I looked at Bilton on the doorstep. 'Where've you been?'

'Remember Rupert Granger?'

'That wanker we met with Celia Stein last summer?'

Bilton nodded.

'Just recorded an interview with him. Goes out tonight – in half an hour.'

'Which channel? No, wait. It'll be cancelled. Replaced by rolling news.'

'It's going out,' said Bilton.

'And I thought you'd cut down on boozing?' I said.

'Yeah,' said Bilton, 'I had.'

But it came as an enormous relief to me to see Bilton drunk again.

'Been in the Blacksmith's Arms, Mile End Road,' he said as, with a tell-tale totter, he broached the portals of what I still thought of as our house; 'quite a decent pint of Old Rusty Nuthouse.'

'Bilton,' I said, 'I take it you've heard the news?'

'Been talking long-term military strategy all night,' he confirmed, 'with a very astute dustman, who was of the view that the Middle East would be the big front in the long term; that Zubarov's going to have a go at the bloody Arabs – after the oil, and quell the bleeding fundamentalists. That's how it'll end up, according to the dustman. Can't see it myself,' he said, crashing into the hall bicycle, 'but that'll be the thing about this conflict; no one will be able to predict anything. That's my prediction.'

We entered the kitchen, and Bilton swung his head into the fridge.

'Bilton,' I said. 'I think I should apologise. About the way I behaved at Fauntleroy's place. It's just that I . . .'

'Anything left in the way of beer?' he asked, recoiling with a backwards stagger for no readily discernible reason. 'Quite fancy a couple of nightcaps.' He fumbled about in the cupboard next to the fridge, then surged towards me with a bulbous bottle in his hand.

'Transcaucasian States . . . Zubarov'll probably leave 'em alone. Complete mess. Too much bloody bother . . . Central Asia, though, different story . . .'

He grabbed two cups, neither of them clean, from the draining board.

'. . . Kazakhstan might actually want the bugger to take over. They've been very close since the old days.'

Bilton sat down at the table opposite me. The bottle he was fiddling with contained Unicum Zwac.

'This,' he said, swigging from the neck, 'is one of the very best of the Hungarian liqueurs. It's made out of herbs and . . . er, soil. Tastes like falling down in a bloody forest. The dustman,' he went on, 'as well as being concerned about the situation in the Middle East, was very worried that Zubarov might go for Afghanistan again, for old times' sake really, which is not a bad little theory, you've got to admit.'

I got myself a glass of water.

'I'll tell you what the future holds for me,' he said, 'seeing as you haven't asked . . . Margin . . . aliginal . . . isation . . . sation. I believe I'm right in saying there is such a word. Not,' he rambled on, 'that that matters in the slightest. No individual counts for anything in history; and I suppose that I have now struggled to the status of a footnote. I can't belie – that is to say deny – a certain decadent thrill in the doing of this. But . . .'

The remainder of the sentence dissolved in his brain as, with a great gulping snore, he plunged instantaneously into unconsciousness.

Bilton, I noticed, had collapsed at 12.30, the precise moment that his interview with Granger was scheduled to be broadcast. I walked into the living room and channel-hopped in search of the arrogant features of Granger. I came across Bilton's first – Channel 15.

Bilton was saying, 'If you want to go all the way back to ancient Greece, it was actually Aristotle himself who wrote that social conflicts arise from the inequality of social conditions, and I think I'm right in saying that . . .'

There was a cut to the face of Granger, who was yawning hugely. It was a common tactic of his, but the effect was nevertheless shocking.

'You're a communist,' he butted in; 'I suppose you think that's clever. Or at least iconoclastic. I mean, correct me if I'm wrong, but no one actually believes in that stuff any more, do they?'

'If you're suggesting that my political opinions are unfashionable . . .' Bilton shrugged. 'You're probably right. You'd know much more about what's in fashion and what isn't than me.'

'When you threw the coffee cup – was it a spontaneous or a premeditated act?'

'It was a mixture of both,' replied Bilton, unconvincingly.

'But I suspect that spontaneity had the upper hand. When you threw that cup of coffee at Mr Lazenby, you were completely out of it, weren't you?'

'What are you suggesting?'

'You say what you did was a political act, but you were completely blotto, zonked, gone, pie-eyed, and didn't know what you were doing.'

'Are you implying that I was drunk?'

'It was simply a rather ridiculous, adolescent prank, fuelled by booze.'

'This is character assassination; I'm not surprised; you've probably been put up to it by someone more significant than yourself, which gives us a lot of suspects to choose from. I'm not going to argue with a [a bleep here] like yourself. But I want to say that I do not, never have, and never will drink alcohol to a capacity which interferes to the slightest degree with my ability to make reasoned judgements.'

Just then a terrible crash sent me charging into the kitchen. Bilton was on the floor. At first I thought he was dead. But he'd simply rolled off his chair in a stupor.

I was about to walk back to the television when I heard Bilton begin to moan. 'Cut my head,' he muttered rapidly, 'cut it bad.' I checked; he hadn't. '. . . Get me to Chester; where's Chester?' Then he became totally incomprehensible; or at least said something which sounded very much like the following. 'Who sounded that. Took a few effusive people. Stay now.' I had no idea what he was talking about. Alarmed, I nervously prodded him awake, and he went to bed in his old room.

I was woken up the following morning by a call from Harry Piper.

'Something I forgot to mention yesterday. I don't want your mate Bilton in the new section. I know lifestyle's not his thing but I'm just giving you this warning. This is not the time to give house room to opponents of Lazenby.'

'But if Bilton was a good writer yesterday, surely he's a good writer today?'

'That's not how it works,' said Piper, 'and you know it. Haven't you seen the papers? Universal approval for Lazenby's actions. Britain stands alone. Again. And whether you're in favour of war or not . . . at last the guy's *done* something, and that's what people like. Little Willie said it was the most brilliant *coup de théâtre* in world history, except for a couple of his own things, of course.'

'What about "Downbeat"?'

'Stopping it of course. It's a pity. He was a nice guy. Well, he wasn't, but he was a decent hack. See you next week, and I want you to have a fistful of ideas for "Easy Like a Sunday Morning", because we've got a big meeting with the advertisers, okay?'

I turned on the radio next to my bed – any number of rolling news services to choose from. The latest no-confidence motion against Lazenby had been withdrawn, and replaced with an opposition pledge of loyalty for the duration of the conflict. Lazenby had met the Chiefs of Staff, and there was to be no conscription (now *that* was what I was waiting for).

Zubarov had threatened Paris with nuclear destruction following some remarks by the French President which had irritated him. England had lost a football match against Spain, a test match against the West Indies, and a game of rugby in New Zealand. 'Yesterday,' said the sports reporter, 'was a bad day for British sport.' No one, of course, knew quite how bad a day it had nearly been. I'm talking about the malfunctioning nukes. A minor comedian had died of a major heart attack. The day would be cloudy with scattered showers.

I sauntered downstairs to find that Bilton's coat, which had been left the night before on the back of a kitchen chair, was gone.

Chapter Fourteen

Five days later, Bilton called me early in the morning.

'Hello. It's Bilton.'

'I know. Where are you?'

'Scarborough.'

'What the fucking hell are you doing there?'

'An "In Conversation". It's happening tomorrow. At least it's supposed to be, but Hayes has buggered off. Night before last in Redcar, I just went on and said, "Any questions?" It was a disaster. A mass walk-out. All six people left. I thought they'd cancel the one tonight but the fuckers won't.'

'I'm not at work this week,' I said. 'Not much on. I could get the train up and ask the questions. Do the Hayes role.'

'You could,' said Bilton, 'be quite useful actually.'

So I took the 250-mph or whatever train up to York, where it is possible to change for Scarborough. I watched a goods train carrying tanks trundle deafeningly past for ten minutes; two small boys on the platform next to me jumped up and down with excitement throughout. There was a Portakabin on the platform marked 'Of Military Significance' with a sentry outside, the first time I'd seen the boxy red OMS sign, which was to become so familiar. Clearly my native town was of some strategic importance, thanks to its rail links. I boarded the little train for the branchline that went up the coast. This line, which had been closed for years, had recently been reopened by Lazenby as part of his environmentally aware, mainly privately funded 'Bringing England to the People' campaign – which was his one really big pre-war success, of course. *The New Globe*, which had doubled in size with speculative war coverage, was by my side unread.

I had arranged to meet Bilton in a pub on the front called the Bucket and Spade. I wound down the narrow salty streets towards the front. The day was hot but grey with a soft, enpurpled quality to the air, presaging thunder or some more generalised calamity; there was a great gold gash of light on the horizon over the sea. A few desperate trippers, getting a holiday in before God knows what might happen, sucked on giant prawns and lunged at elusive masses of candy floss. A sparse crowd of insectoid mods conducted a feeble reunion on the quay; it was so long since their heyday that it was probably a reunion of a reunion.

A gang of lads in Zubarov masks were doing a ramshackle can-can outside a pub called the Old Shrimp and Lemon. Many people wore the Zubarov T-shirts sold from makeshift stalls along the front. They featured an upside-down image of the General's head with his eyeballs retouched to be nearer the bridge of his nose. Very funny. Other people wore the complementary Lazenby T-shirt, on which he looked simply handsome, modest and charming. There was another, rarer T-shirt, on which Lazenby's face appeared along with the somewhat premature judgement 'He's seen off Zubarov'.

In the gift shops in the phoney-gabled houses along the front, tat had been adapted to take account of the war. You could buy Philip Lazenby mugs, model nuke-proof tanks, sticks of rock shaped like missiles.

Outside the Bucket and Spade was a sign: 'Fine old English ales', it said, 'and topless mud wrestling'. Inside, it was low, dark and crowded. There was a festive atmosphere, which is to say that there was a cigarette fug, many rapidly coalescing puddles of beer, and a sea of crumpled, discarded chip punnets. Two pimply soldiers lounged next to the bar, surrounded by blondes with bubble cuts. There was an enormous screen showing that awful, droning soap opera *Ordinary World*.

Bilton was sitting in the corner, sweating in his bloody coat, and shouting into his mobile phone.

'Look, I've been on hold for fifteen minutes now. Do you know how much this is costing me? Yes, you *can* take a message. You can tell him to take his fucking little magazine and shove it right up his fucking . . .'

Bilton looked up at me and put his phone down.

'Hung up,' he said. 'No bloody manners.'

'How's everything going?' I said.

Bilton pointed towards the bar.

'It's your round,' he said.

'We'll just take all that "How are you?" and "Glad you could make it" stuff as read then, shall we?'

'If you don't mind,' said Bilton, unfurling his farcical, bent address book and running his spatulate finger up the number columns.

I bought the drinks and returned.

Bilton was talking quite softly into his phone, without agitation.

'Yes. Maybe tomorrow then. Yes. Bye.'

'Who was that?'

'Carol. Now look, let's get these down quickly. The sooner we do that the sooner we'll be able to get some others down quickly and then . . .'

'Carol Crane? You were just on the phone to Carol Crane?'

'She's my agent. I was calling my agent on the phone. It's not an unknown phenomenon.'

'Okay,' I said, 'fine.'

Bilton sighed a big sigh.

'You like Carol Crane, don't you?' I said.

Somebody had put a record by the new beat act Duct on the juke box. Bilton was watching a man doing a running-on-the-spot dance and playing air guitar on a pool cue.

'Carol?' Bilton said. '. . . Well, of course there's a lot of bullshit there.'

He took a reflective sip of his pint.

'. . . A *lot* of bullshit. Perhaps more bullshit than I've ever known in one human being. But when you get past that, then, yeah.'

'Yeah, what?'

'What do you mean "Yeah, what?"' said Bilton, irritatedly.

He pulled out of his pocket a scrunched piece of paper and let it fall on to the table.

'More good news,' he said.

It was a letter, from the Executive Producer of *Rebels*, cancelling Bilton's appearance on the show.

'You will understand,' I read, 'that some programmes must be sacrificed in the coming months to make way for extra demands which the international situation will undoubtedly place upon our schedule . . .'

I put the letter down.

'When people want you,' Bilton said, slowly, picking up and then thoughtfully replacing his full glass, 'they ring you up. And when they don't want you, they write to you.'

'Or they simply don't contact you at all,' I said.

'That,' said Bilton, nodding thoughtfully, 'is the other possibility.

'Hello,' said a mean, small, hoarse Yorkshire voice. If a crow could talk it would sound like this. It belonged to a sinewy old man who was wearing what looked like quite a nice suit on top of a vest. He was drinking stout, but was very, very thin. 'Are you Martyn Bilton?'

147

'In what sense?' said Bilton, warily.

'Fucking are,' said the man. 'What are you doing in my town?'

'Fuck off,' said Bilton.

'You'd better tell me.'

'I'm in your town to work,' said Bilton. 'I'm "In Conversation" tomorrow evening at the New Victoria Theatre. Know where that is?'

'No,' said the man.

'Good,' said Bilton.

'That some kind of show?' said the man.

'It's a conversation,' said Bilton, 'as the name implies. Between me and my friend here.'

Thanks a lot, I thought.

'I don't have to pay to go and see a conversation,' said the sinewy man. 'I can have one any time I like for free.'

'Yes,' said Bilton, 'but this would be an *intelligent* conversation.'

'You shouldn't be here,' said the man. 'This is a patriotic pub. We're getting the War Price in tomorrow.'

'War Price?' I said.

'War Price bitter. Price includes war tax.'

It was the first I'd heard of it.

'Voluntary,' said the man, 'but anyone who doesn't buy it . . .'

He shook his head, walking away.

'You're going to have to watch out from now on,' I said. 'What's Carol telling you to do?'

'Public apology to Lazenby. Declaration of solidarity with the war effort. Major on the gardening.'

'Good advice,' I said.

'Sure,' said Bilton, doing his sarcastic nod.

We stared across towards the pool table. The man who had

been playing air guitar was now trying to limbo underneath the pool cue, which was being held out by two of his friends. Two thoughts were contending in my mind. One, a sharp sadness at Bilton's plight. And two, a sharp, guilty gladness at Bilton's plight, stemming from the fact that his rise to stardom had been decisively halted. I was ashamed of this feeling.

Suddenly the grinding angst of *Ordinary World* disappeared from the television screen, and the already familiar war logo – a map of Russia which subtly incorporated the profiles of Zubarov and Lazenby – bounced on to the screen.

'Good afternoon,' said Lazenby. He was lounging against a desk in a plush, countrified drawing room. The context was clearly informal, but Lazenby hadn't gone for that golf-club look of most prime ministers in downtime. He was wearing a slightly crumpled, yet beautiful white shirt and tight black cords. He looked young and virile. In his hand was his rarely seen pipe; no cue cards. He was smiling. 'I have received news from General Wilton-Forbes in Estonia,' he began. 'He told me that, at midday our time, he formally accepted the surrender of the Commander of Russian Forces in Estonia, Major Anatole Vinkovski. Thanks to the skill and bravery of the British Army, the independent state of Estonia is once again free from Russian tyranny. This war is not yet over, but an important victory has been won.'

He paused, smiled again, and turned to look through the window of his study; the camera smoothly closed on this window, and then we were through it to the wet, bright green lawn beyond: here, Lazenby's two children, a cherubic, Victorian-looking pair, shortly to become familiar from many a Warcast, were tottering in cute rainhats, and engaged in stage-managed play with two brightly painted tricycles. We watched them for a while, and then the scene closed with a soft fade. We were back with Mr Lazenby.

'I won't keep you from your celebrations,' he said simply. 'Good afternoon, everybody.'

I suppose everybody remembers these early, masterly Warcasts as well as me.

There was cheering, and then *Ordinary World* crashed back on to the screen, to be immediately replaced by ice hockey (i.e. fighting). The barman rang his time bell long and hard in celebration, going red in the face as he flailed. There were cheers; a massed move to the bar. I made a drinking gesture at Bilton, but he shook his head.

'I don't like this pub,' he said.

'Fine,' I said. 'Let's get some air.'

We trudged along the front. The day had gone; night was falling, and rainy gusts flying in from the black sea kept battering us into the sides of buildings. I'd told Bilton we needed air but this was ridiculous. Here was too much air. A few people crouched in the lurid foyers of amusement arcades watching the weather with dreamily sad eyes – that war look.

Eventually we came upon a small, bright caff. Rivulets of rain raced shakily along the front window. We sat down, and asked for a menu, and a man in a waist-length maroon jacket picked up a piece of paper from an adjacent table, and presented it to me: 'Fish and Chips' it said.

'I think I'll try the fish and chips,' I said.

I looked questioningly at Bilton.

'Not hungry,' he said, and put his arms on the table and his head on his arms.

Chapter Fifteen

The end of a long, tired, sunless summer's day.

We took a swaying tram up a dark, mysterious hill of tightly packed, shuttered shops. A few Union Jacks, straightening in the breeze, flew from the upper storeys. You only notice how many flagpoles there are around the place when there's a war on. The pavements were almost totally deserted. People stayed in during the early days of the war. To put it bluntly, they were watching television. Half-way up the hill, the storm began, illuminating the sea in the gaps between the shops – like a jolted black and white photograph. The flat flashes of pure daylight in the evening gloom made me feel sick.

The New Victoria Theatre was a grimy neoclassical building that loomed balefully over a small park. The advertising panels outside displayed fluttering flyers advertising 'Martyn Bilton – In Conversation', skewered on to adverts for a local amateur company's production of *The Mikado*.

I pushed through heavy double doors with round submarine windows into the sudden quiet of a purple-carpeted foyer. A tiny man wearing a dinner suit, and with bluish-grey hair walked across the deep-pile carpet to greet us. The atmosphere was warm and sleepy.

'Martyn Bilton? Terry Clarke, front of house,' said the man.

He had an elegant head: wavy hair, interesting retroussé nose, nice skin. But there was dandruff on his collar and the backs of his trouser bottoms were trampled into his shoes.

'What?' said Bilton.

'I'm the front of house manager, supervising foyer, box office and bar.'

'Bar?' said Bilton, with sudden brightness.

Clarke indicated an alcove off the hall.

'The Flora May Memorial Bar.'

He pointed to a framed, soft-focus black and white photograph.

'That,' he said, 'is our patron, Dame Flora May'.

'Dead, is she?' said Bilton, squinting at the picture; and then he remembered me.

'Adrian Day,' he said, gesturing quite derisively towards me.

I shook hands with Terry Clarke.

'Welcome to our little theatre,' he said. 'Not much to look at but there's a great feel to the place, I'm sure you'll agree.'

I did not agree; but I smiled. Bilton, on the other hand, was frowning.

'Look. I don't think we're going to get too many people tonight. Are you sure its worth going ahead?'

'Of course, of course,' said Clarke. 'I've been in this business for thirty years now and I think I'm able to gauge pretty accurately the appeal of a show.'

'How many tickets have you sold?' I asked.

'None,' said Clarke. 'But I'm sure we'll have a late surge.'

'You do appreciate,' I said, 'that Bilt . . . I mean Martyn has been placed in a slightly awkward position by recent world events.'

Clarke gave me a look which I – alarmed – interpreted as incomprehension.

'You do realise,' I said, tensely, 'that we are now at war with Russia?'

'I'm sorry,' said the little man, cocking his head. 'We are at war with whom?'

'Russia,' I said.

'Oh absolutely. I thought you said something different there. No, no, I appreciate that Mr Bilton's anti-establishment stance may be slightly more fraught than it was, but it all adds to the fun. Should be a good, lively evening.'

A thought occurred to me.

'Is there anybody here who's in charge of security?'

'Security?' said Clarke complacently. 'That's a front of house matter.'

'So you have experience in dealing with trouble?'

'Mr Day,' he said, 'this theatre is the home of the North of England Light Operetta Society.'

'Violent bunch, are they?' said Bilton, who was doing strange things with his shoulders inside his coat.

'The point is – and I yield to no man in my affection for the Society – they're not very good at Light Operetta. Requests for refunds, often heated, are a constant of my working life, so please have no worries on that score. Now . . .'

And the little man clapped his hands, once.

Bilton prepared for the show by drinking Guinness, alone and next to an electric fan provided for his personal benefit in the Flora May Memorial Bar. Meanwhile, I lay on the floor of the hot dressing room – which was filled with sprays of dying flowers, papier mâché weaponry and spangled, velvety dresses that made me sneeze – and read the informal script for the 'In Conversation' that Rich Hayes had prepared.

Bilton walked into the dressing room five minutes before we were due to go on. Terry Clarke – the only member of theatre staff that I had seen so far – was with him. Bilton sagged into a cross-legged position on the floor and began rolling a cigarette.

'This is your five-minute call,' said Clarke.

'Talk English, man,' said Bilton, licking his paper.

'Sorry,' said the manager, 'it's five minutes until curtain-up.'

'We don't want a curtain,' said Bilton, 'none of that theatre crap.'

'But this *is* a theatre,' said Terry Clarke, hurt.

'Proscenium arch,' said Bilton; 'pure bourgeois symbolism. Us and them.'

Bilton was standing up now. He began to whistle.

'Don't do that,' said Clarke.

'Why not?' I said.

'Bad luck to whistle in the dressing room. And you mustn't say the name of the Scottish play.'

'*Macbeth*?' I said. 'Oh, sorry.'

Shaking his head, Clarke walked out of the dressing room. Two minutes later he came back in.

'This is your three-minute call,' he said.

Bilton rolled his eyes at me.

Clarke was looking at Bilton.

'You look a little pale,' he said. 'Are you sure you don't want some pancake?'

Bilton shook his head.

'Don't like to eat before I go on.'

Clarke frowned. But his enthusiasm was unbounded.

'Do you want me to go on and do a quick intro? You know, please welcome that dazzling iconoclast Martyn Bilton, fresh from his great success at . . . Where was your last success?'

'I can't remember,' said Bilton.

'Thank you,' I said to Clarke. 'Something like that would be very nice.'

Bilton and I waited in the wings as Clarke did his thing. 'Ladies and gentlemen . . .' he began, and from this I deduced there must be, at the very least, four people in the audience: two ladies and two gentlemen.

Walking into the sudden, dazzling stage light, I couldn't tell at first whether there was anyone in the audience at all. There was certainly no applause as Bilton and I clomped across to the two chairs which had been placed either side of a low microphone. But as I sat down, I was able to survey the stalls, the only part of the auditorium opened for our performance.

There were indeed four people in the audience: two ladies and two gentlemen.

I just plunged in.

'Martyn Bilton,' I said, 'you are at the centre of a media storm. Everyone wants a piece of you. You are, in effect, a star. Yet you claim to be a celebrity of a different sort. You claim to have a message for a society that has lost its . . .'

A woman in the front row – *the* woman in the front row – was rising to her feet.

'Is this *The Mikado*?' she quavered.

I turned towards her, shielding my eyes, and leant towards the microphone.

'No,' I said. 'It is not *The Mikado*.'

'I must have the wrong night,' shouted the woman, quite casually, and walked out.

I glanced across at Bilton, whose eyes were closed. He seemed to be asleep, which was a bit worrying.

'Martyn Bilton,' I said, loud enough to wake him.

His startling eyes opened.

'Let's just go straight to the questions,' he said, quietly.

Four minus one is three. We were down to three audience members. There was a couple, who looked quite conventional, and, in the dead centre of the auditorium, a long, nasty-looking man who was looking nastily at Bilton and drinking from a bottle of beer. He had a face like a switchblade razor.

I spoke – surprisingly fluently in the circumstances.

'I think it would be best if I simply asked whether anyone in

155

the audience has a question. We'll get the ball rolling in that way, and then play it by ear.'

I sat back.

With nightmare inevitability, the razor-faced man stood up – he was wearing some sort of belted combat jacket – and smashed his lager bottle on the seat in front of him. Staring at Bilton, he said, 'How would you like this in your face?'

'I must insist that all questions go through the chair,' said Bilton, gesturing towards me.

'How would *he* like this in his face?' said the man, who now, with a horrible, rolling ease, was climbing over the lines of seats towards the stage. When he got close to the edge of the stage he momentarily disappeared, the stage being so high. But then his broken bottle appeared and he hauled himself up after it. His long, colourless hair was so matted with sweat and rain that he looked like a horrible swimmer emerging from a horrible pool.

'Excuse me,' I said, but my words were drowned out by the wobbling cowboy boots of the advancing man. A spotlight was following him. High up above the balcony I could see a wiry silhouette, manipulating the ancient lights. What the hell was going on? I stood up and walked to the side of the stage.

'Mr Clarke!' I called out.

Razor-face sat down in the chair that I had vacated, and leant into the microphone. In a relaxed, urbane tone – he seemed to be a natural on stage – he asked Bilton, 'Are you behind Mr Lazenby and behind Britain in this war?'

Bilton folded his arms and looked at the man. He, too, spoke calmly. Maybe this wouldn't be too bad.

'I think that my position *vis-à-vis* Mr Lazenby is pretty similar to yours, namely neither behind nor in front of. But below.'

'You are talking bollocks,' said the razor-faced man, with renewed menace.

'You've heard of the ruling class?' said Bilton.

'Are you saying that I'm part of the ruling class?'

'My point is precisely this,' said Bilton, 'that far from being in the ruling class, you are in the drooling class.'

The razor-faced man and Bilton simultaneously stood up. The man spat, hard, aiming at the middle of Bilton's white shirt front.

'Mr Clarke!' I shouted again from the edge of the stage.

None of the two people remaining in the audience moved. Perhaps they thought this was all part of the show. I glanced back at Bilton to see him spinning, his coat swirling about him. Clearly, he had tried to hit razor-face, and clearly he had missed. The man spat again, this time on to the back of Bilton's head. I was walking towards the two of them, picking up the chair that I had been sitting in, ready to engage. But now razor-face was resting his arms on Bilton's shoulders and shuffling his feet. Pointed fronds of his greased and sweat-soaked hair were lashed across his face like scars.

'In this war,' he said, his face very close to Bilton's, '. . . in this coming conflict we've got to stand . . .'

The two were like boxers in a clinch.

'. . . shoulder to shoulder; we've got to fight . . .'

. . . Or two sagging smoochers at chucking-out time.

'. . . tooth and nail . . .'

The razor-faced man sniffed mightily.

'. . . and do you know what else we've got to do?'

Bilton was silent, looking at his assailant, almost humble. With acrobatic finesse, the man tipped the upper half of his body backwards and spoke for the last time.

'We've got to put our heads together!' he roared.

And then blackness.

Later, next to the electric fan in the Flora May Memorial Bar,

Bilton's large white eyelids rolled up and his large violet eye-balls rolled down.

Thank God, I thought, he's going to be okay.

'Who are you?' he said.

Or maybe he wasn't.

'Wait a minute,' said Bilton, slowly screwing up his eyes in concentration, 'is it your round or mine?'

Bilton sat up on the crimson banquette seat, being fussed over by the couple who were our last-surviving audience.

'Tip his head back,' said the wife, who was actually quite pretty. 'That'll stop the bleeding.'

For ten minutes, the blood had been bubbling from Bilton's nose like a faltering fountain. The woman arranged the compliant Bilton in a position to her liking.

'I'll have a Guinness,' said Bilton to the ceiling.

'Front of house matter,' said Terry Clarke, starting to busy himself behind the bar.

Guinnesses came for everyone, and gradually Bilton started to talk to the couple, who were called John and Heather Turner. He was in carpets.

'I'm left-leaning myself,' said John. 'Going back in my family – they were all miners and their lives were just gradually disman-tled. In the place where they lived everyone's still unemployed.'

'Of course,' said Bilton, inadvertently putting a thin white moustache on his top lip with the pint of Guinness.

'But, you know,' John went on, 'they all did their bit in the war. No questions asked. And I was just thinking, maybe Philip Lazenby is our Winsome Churchill.'

That's what he said: Winsome Churchill. The guy was being nice to Bilton so I hoped Bilton would let it go.

'Winsome Churchill?' said Bilton. 'W-I-N-S-O-M-E? Do you mean, *Winston* Churchill?'

I couldn't bear to look at the crestfallen carpet salesman.

'Seems to be back to his old self, doesn't he?' said Terry Clarke, who was polishing glasses next to me. 'I'll tell you what, this has been a night to remember.'

'It was clever of you to think of a blackout,' I said.

'But I thought of it just that little bit too late, didn't I?'

'Well, you know, it's the thought that counts.'

'And I gave the attacker the chance to get away.'

'Yes,' I said. 'He escaped under cover of darkness.'

'Sure,' Bilton was saying, 'we need more jobs. But people have got to stop being paid less than their due for work.'

'How do you know they are?' asked the carpet seller.

'It's true by definition,' said Bilton, 'this is textbook stuff.'

'Eh?'

There were many signed pictures of soft-focus performers around the bar. Terry Clarke was pleased I was taking an interest in them.

'Who's that?' I said, pointing to one.

'Trevor Levity,' said Terry Clarke. 'Used to be a regular here. Comedian. Surely you've heard of him?'

'Nope.'

'His catchphrase is "Lovely lady, lovely lady".'

'Why?'

'I don't know. He's very big in the Highlands of Scotland. In the Highlands *and* the Islands, actually. He got a lot of coverage last year.'

'Oh yes?'

'Drove his car into a bus stop, killing four. He was completely pissed.'

An hour later, everyone was drunk in the hot little bar. The two small chandeliers were swaying quite violently with the updraught from the fan. The Turners were having their 'In Conversation' with Martyn Bilton after all, and they were certainly getting their money's worth.

159

'So you're saying that every employer is an exploiter?' Heather Turner, now rather red in the face, was saying.

'Every one,' said Bilton; by now there was quite a pile of bloodied tissues next to his Guinness.

'But hang on,' said the man. 'The employer's putting up the money, taking the risk.'

'Yes,' said Bilton exasperatedly, 'but where the fuck did *he* get that money except by exploiting some other mug? This is basics. Look, let's go back to 1917 . . .'

I said that I personally was going back to the hotel, and Bilton eventually came with me. We walked into the balmy, geenish night, leaving with John and Heather Turner as Terry Clarke locked up the theatre. Above the floating, scary moan of the distant sea, he shouted something.

'What's that?' I shouted back.

'Whistling in the dressing room!' shouted Clarke. 'Maybe he'll remember next time!'

At the hotel there were two faxes for Bilton.

The first was from Grey Fauntelroy:

'Dear Martyn . . . You write an excellent column but a magazine such as ours has only one loyalty during time of war, and that is to the leader of our country. Philip Lazenby has finally proved himself capable of decisive action, and we are now willing to provide him with our full support. I must therefore tell you that we require no more writing from you. Do keep the flat ("Hall" is not your style, I think) for as long as you like.'

I turned to Bilton in the empty lobby.

'Well,' I said, 'at least you've still got a wonderful place to live.'

The next message was from Sir Henry Pike, Chairman of the Management Committee of the Halls of Holborn.

'The Committee requires that you vacate your hall immediately. Your continuing presence would be unsuitable in the present circumstances.'

That was the nub of it.

I sat in bed with the evening paper. In the wake of his defeat in Estonia, Zubarov had of course claimed a great victory and declared a national holiday for tomorrow. He had also restored what the paper called a 'command economy'; there seemed to be some debate about whether this amounted to the restoration of communism, but a lot of people thought it did. The dead horse that Bilton had been flogging for years had got up and bitten him.

Chapter Sixteen

(One year and one month after the incident)

It turned out that Bilton's nose was broken, after all. But I remember that day in Scarborough as a good time. There's a glow about it in my mind. The sunset, in a way, of a friendship.

I didn't see Bilton for a month. It was Bilton's last day in his Hall. He sat on the floor in his big room, next to four cardboard boxes. He was putting down his mobile as I walked in.

'That was Piper,' he said.

'Good news?'

'He wants me to do a piece.'

'Excellent,' I said.

'It's a jokey piece about long-term unemployment. He said I was the only person he could think of who might do it. But he doesn't want my name in the paper and if I accepted the commission I'd have to do it under a pseudonym.'

'I hope you told him to fuck off?'

'I told him to *piss* off.'

'Excellent,' I said, again.

'Which leaves me without any income.'

'Bilton, you know, if you're really running low, I can always . . .'

The phone rang.

'Don't patronise me, you little bastard,' said Bilton, picking it up.

It was a drab, airless day. I opened one of Bilton's windows, feeling bad.

Bilton put the phone down.

'That was Cal D'Arcy,' he said.

'Christ,' I observed.

D'Arcy, of course, was one of the biggest media men in Britain. He'd made his name many years before with a magazine masterstroke which was still the subject of regular seminars at *The New Globe*. He'd combined the dominant lifestyle areas in the market, gardening and antiques, and come up with a magazine devoted entirely to antique gardening implements. Sales were phenomenal. D'Arcy (as if any of this needs pointing out) had then become launch editor of the celebrity glossy *Flavour of the Month*.

'Didn't you say you were going to be in *Flavour of the Month*?' I said to Bilton.

'Cover story,' said Bilton. 'They interviewed me for the September edition weeks ago. I mean, it must've gone to press by now, but D'Arcy wants to see me for lunch.'

'I am full of foreboding,' I said.

'Funny you should say that,' said Bilton. 'He doesn't mind if you come, by the way.'

Good, I thought. Our little spat seems to have been healed.

The arrangement was for one o'clock in The Maze in Mayfair.

Bilton and I threaded between the absurd, high-backed chairs – twice we went up a blind alley – looking at the multimillionaires drinking dandelion and burdock and eating their chic Austerity War Price lunches (cheese on toast, etc.) and watching the news on their tiny TVs. Severe classical music played, as it seemed to in every public place during those first war months.

D'Arcy reclined at the prestigious Centre Table. Like the Minotaur, I suppose, except that he was quite small. The shirt was white; the hair, of course, was as white as snow too, and crew cut. His blue suit stunningly echoed his blue eyes. He spoke in an urgent whisper.

'Sit down, Mr Bilton; sit down, Mr Day. Can I order you a drink. Gin and tonic? Margarita? Vimto?'

(The nostalgic, much-chronicled return of the so-called Old Cordials was already in full swing.)

Bilton and I had beers.

'Martyn Bilton,' he began, 'I congratulate you. Not for many a year has a young man so impinged on the consciousness of this country. You were our "Flavour of the Month", not for one month but for many.'

He sipped some water, absurdly, from a tin mug. He breathed deeply.

'If you don't mind, I would like to say a little bit about the ethos of *Flavour* . . .'

He brushed some crumbs off his knee, which I doubted very much had ever been there.

'. . . If I may?'

I nodded, blushing. Bilton was stone-like.

'By comparison with us, other magazines are unpredictable, flighty and fickle, by which I mean that they stick to their guns. They will occasionally go their own way, cover subjects which are out of step with current opinion, and damn the consequences. We do not. With absolute fixity of purpose, *Flavour* bends with the wind, goes with the flow, sells out anew every month, and thereby hangs our unique, iron integrity and consistency. Hence the name of the magazine: *Flavour of the Month*. Flavour of *this* month. We choke upon, are made sick by, the flavour of last month.'

Looking into the middle distance, Bilton spoke.

'Do you have about you any copies of the forthcoming edition of the magazine in which I appear?'

Cal D'Arcy nodded once.

'We have pulped the entire production run, scrapped the edition. There will be no *Flavour of the Month* in September . . . Waiter!'

A waiter came running.

'A whisky please. A double.'

I was witnessing the incredible: Cal D'Arcy was blowing his cool. He took out his handkerchief and dragged it across his forehead.

'I thought I should tell you in person, Martyn. Or rather, my analyst thought I should tell you in person. This is my own mistake and I must take complete responsibility, and come to terms with my own actions. I have, of course, offered my resignation.'

'I'm sorry to hear that,' I said.

'My resignation has not been accepted,' said Cal D'Arcy, receiving and downing his whisky.

'Oh,' I said. 'I'm sorry. Or rather, I'm glad. Or. No.'

I had decided to shut up. Bilton was giving me a look.

'I am going to grit my teeth and look to the future. As I said, I am entirely to blame, and therefore I will be firing only a relatively small number of junior staff who happened to be in the office on the day that I made the original mistake of commissioning the piece. All I can hope is that we come back really strongly in October.'

'I'm sure you will,' I said. 'Can I ask who'll be "Flavour of the Month" in that issue?'

'Mr Day,' said Cal D'Arcy, smiling. 'I'm surprised at you. There really is only one candidate.'

During the course of those three sentences, Cal D'Arcy's cool had returned. That's all it took. The issue would be devoted to Lazenby, of course.

'I'm sure you'll come back very strongly,' I repeated, syco-phantically, as Bilton rose to his feet and left the table.

Cal nodded gravely, watching Bilton go.

'I expected that. Or rather, my analyst told me to expect that.'

Bilton had stalked out – not an easy thing to do in The Maze. I waited at the exit for fifteen minutes before he arrived. He was very, very angry, not talking.

'I'm very sorry, Bilton,' I said, trotting down the street behind him.

'Fuck off,' he said, looking straight ahead. He was heading towards St James's Park, as though he meant to blow it up.

I found him sulking in a deck chair in a mess of fallen pink blossom. A squirrel was flitting around near his desert-booted feet. Immediately to the west were the War Offices, and presumably Mr Lazenby was in there. Intense policemen were circling, circling, the park: just to look at them made you sweat. Martial music came out of the little café by the water.

'*Flavour of the Month*,' I said to Bilton. 'It's just a bloody joke. You didn't want to be in that rag, did you?'

Bilton scratched his hair and shook his head.

'Want to go into the café?'

In the café – Union Jacks everywhere, of course – the waitress asked us what sort of tea we wanted.

'A pint of Guinness,' said Bilton.

I asked for two cups of English Breakfast.

'It's a great story for a diary, you know. A whole issue pulped. You should sell it to Kev Smith. You know, "The Boulevardier"; he's always desperate for stuff.'

'It's a great story for a diary,' echoed Bilton in a silly voice. 'That's really going to change a lot of people's lives for the better, isn't it?'

I wanted to go home but, being in a mood of gloomy lassitude, I went to a pub with Bilton and drank uneasily for three hours. In the pub, everyone was hot and bothered. On the

166

TV we watched hundreds of soldiers climbing on to monstrous aeroplanes. Their jokey goodbye messages to family and friends rolled across the bottom of the screen. (One soldier – evidently no historian – had written as his parting missive: 'Don't worry, pet, it'll all be over by Christmas.')

I turned to Bilton.

'Don't you have to move out of the Hall today?'

Bilton shrugged.

'But I thought . . .'

'Yeah, yeah, yeah. A bloke's coming at seven to help me with my luggage. Whether I like it or not.'

A thought occurred to me: 'Where are you actually going to go, Bilton?'

And then the beefy landlord approached us. He addressed Bilton.

'When you bought that last round I knew I'd seen you before. I just had an uneasy feeling, like when you're going to be sick, you know. But now it's clicked, so you can get out of my pub, and here's your fucking dirty money back.'

He threw a pile of change at Bilton.

'I don't want it getting mixed up in the till with all the good money from decent people.'

Bilton just stared back.

After a few seconds, the landlord looked at his watch.

'Now I'm not a violent man . . . No, wait. Correction. I misspoke. I *am* a violent man, and if you're still here in three minutes' time I'll bloody well prove it.'

We walked out of the door and Bilton, who was very drunk, picked up a metal dustbin and threw it through the pub's glass door, which showed a lot of maturity I thought. As I ran, I had time to see him hail a cab and get in.

Bilton had certainly, in his obtuse way, sensed my jealousy of his success and, no doubt, also my relief that it had ended.

167

Now, as editor of 'Easy Like a Sunday Morning', my trajectory was gently but undeniably upwards, whereas Bilton, well, he was in free fall. I would shortly be moving out of our shambolic shared house to a small but expensive flat I'd bought just off the King's Road in Chelsea. I hadn't had the heart to tell Bilton about this, and now I didn't know where to contact him *in order to* tell him.

Chapter Seventeen

I moved out of the house in Leytonstone in early October.

Bilton had not returned to London. Once, I thought I glimpsed him through a momentarily parted bead curtain in a cloud of steam, amongst dozens of dangling copper pans in the kitchen of a Chinese restaurant. I dashed towards him, only to be ejected by a stressed-out chef; the person I'd seen wasn't Bilton. In the same month, I saw a wolf-like man next to the bike sheds in the underground car park at *The New Globe*. As he stared up the ramp with the intrepid look of the imminently departing cyclist, I was sure it was Bilton and shouted his name before I realised my mistake.

In October I saw Bilton's byline in a magazine I happened to find on the back seat of a cab. It was called *Golden Years*, and was billed on its front cover as 'a magazine for cost-conscious elderly gentlefolk'. Bilton had contributed a small piece about an economy garden shed that provided access for bathchairs. It was well written. I could find no publisher's address in the magazine; no trace of the title in any of the media gazettes.

Carol Crane called a couple of times. Had I seen Bilton? She'd talked to him briefly, and he'd said he'd purchased some sort of old van, and was 'on a fact-finding mission'. Carol told me that she thought this was a joke, and I hoped that she was right. All of Carol's messages – by all media – had been ignored by Bilton. The line had gone dead.

Time passed. I was pleased with my new life, the threat of annihilation aside, of course.

My new flat was located opposite Lots Road power station, which was a comforting presence. With nothing more than a gentle hum, and occasional puffs of fluffy white steam, it kept half of London Underground running. It had, of course, been brought back into service to help supply the increased power needed on the Tube since Lazenby had ordered – in the interests of maintaining high morale – that no gap longer than three minutes occur between trains. Naturally, it was designated OMS and was guarded by a high security, gangly lad of eighteen or nineteen who picked his nose inside a per-spex box.

The old, Bilton-oriented pattern of my life was replaced with another pattern, equally engrossing, erasing the memory of what had gone before.

As this strange, elusive war dreamed on – initially, of course, there were no conventional battles, and later on, there were still no conventional battles – the economy boomed. Arms manufacture played a part, of course, but the chief cause – as recent research has triumphantly exposed – was that every-body assumed they'd be alive for a significantly shorter time than they'd originally been banking on, so they spent in the anticipation of their being, quite literally, no tomorrow.

There were the skirmishes, of course. Short, intense, involving professional soldiers and with limited aims. I mean, I wouldn't like to have been there, but they were nothing epic. I can't remember in what order they occurred: the Skir-mish at Minsk; the Skirmish at Mirmish. They've all merged into one for me.

The Nuclear Races gave me tension headaches, of course. These feverish struggles for control of former Soviet nuclear installations – military and civilian – fought on our side, according to the newspapers, by heroic professors carrying small arms.

And then there was War Sadness.

I had some contact with that in the shape of an uncle named Duncan who was disoriented in the familiar way: he wanted a tangible war.

He wanted, almost, to see bombs in the street, toppled double-deckers amidst the smoky rubble, Martian-like figures blundering about in exotic, elephantine gas masks. He wanted martial law, and would have been soothed had his car been commandeered on his way to buy the morning paper.

That Lazenby should've been able to run the country almost exactly as before except for very minor Reserve Powers, the implementation of which were, in any case, overseen by his new, ultra-democratic Second Chamber, and which had extremely wide public support . . . that the only opposition to the war should come from that self-conscious band The Questioners, a nebulous, ineffectual talking shop of middle-class people who lived mainly in Belsize Park, and included some Mild Greens, and marginal liberals, feminists, and irrelevant MPs on the left fringes of Start Again . . . this sent my uncle's brain boggling. He was hospitalised for a week: 'Incomprehension of the war', they wrote on his records, and there was a lot of it about.

I think that Bilton's and my former neighbour Oswald, who'd striven so hard to get his ordinary life and his two point two kids, came close to being War Sad. I happened to know that he was one of the hundreds of thousands prescribed tranquillisers.

I liked Oswald, and, after leaving Leytonestone, revived my acquaintanceship with him by requesting that he contribute a column to the *Globe*'s 'View from an Ordinary Person' slot, about which he'd been flattered to a touching degree.

Oswald was a devotee, of course, of the revived all-channel

Sunday Night at the London Palladium shows. The mixture of anti-Russian stand-up routines, mainstream songs and semi-naked women with feathers on their heads went down very well with him. He was particularly keen on Lazenby's talks, and had a habit of calling me after the shows to enthuse about them. He was in raptures after Lazenby had appeared on stage with his favourite pigeon, around which he constructed his famously eloquent, pseudo-Christian 'All Creatures Great and Small' homily.

Lazenby had, of course, not only sorted out for himself a perfectly decent walk, he had even learnt to saunter. Yet any hint of insolent self-possession was missing as, dinner-jacketed, he approached the centre of the stage for those live Warcasts. They've been compared, in their wit, their effortless breadth and casual lyricism, to television lectures given by the long-dead historian A.J.P. Taylor. I've seen those films and, in my opinion, Lazenby's talks were even better. It was confidence, I believe, that enabled him to do this. It's confidence that enables anybody to do anything. (Of course, he had the finest wits in the country desperate to write for him; we shouldn't forget that.)

I liked those Sunday nights just as much as Oswald did. I liked the uniting of middle- and highbrow as Lazenby spoke about the revival of nationalism in Europe, say. Patiently, sadly, and with those deliquescing moments of, yes, humour, he'd explain again why he'd had to take a stand against Zubarov. 'I couldn't talk any more,' he'd say, a lump in his throat. And then there'd be the footage from the War Zones: suave English guys with surgical masks around their necks, explaining about the latest Russian atrocities.

I liked the fact that everybody was watching, just like in the old days: mild, attentive families with children kneeling in their bedtime clothes. Lazenby, scrupulously tasteful, avoided sentimental mention of this new national harmony. But you felt it, especially on Sundays.

Many youngsters, of course, voluntarily joined the so-called Young Armies, to acquire fitness training, a small amount of military lore and to participate in socially useful projects. Others joined more traditional groups.

Close to my house was a circular church hall which some sea cadets – poignant, dry-land sailors – rechristened HMS something-or-other and used as a ship. One of these bell-bottomed fantasists cadged a fag from me at a tram stop once, and we got talking. 'Us lads in the fukkin' navy . . . we fukkin' 'ate those Russkies, we do. Sometimes I can't go to sleep for finkin' abaht it.'

Always in search of lifestyle angles on the war for slots outside 'Easy Like a Sunday Morning', I thought about writing up these nautical naughty boys, but it never came to anything.

I never really got anywhere with war stories.

I tried to interview a member of the so-called Dizzy Farmers, who created such a furore in those early months with their claims to have been subjected already to small- scale nuclear attack. General Zubarov, they thought, had ordered that a nuclear device be detonated in the Norfolk village of Hole. I phoned a resident to ask him about this.

'What are the symptoms felt by the people of Hole who have been victims of this attack?'

'A few aches and pains, and they get occasional moments of dizziness . . .'

'Doesn't sound too bad.'

'. . . which is followed by death. A dozen people have died in the Hole area recently, and it's definitely the nuclear. No question about that.'

'Could I come down and talk to you about this?'

'First,' he said, 'you've got to ring this number.'

I was quite surprised to find that the number was that of Carol Crane, who was representing the Dizzy Farmers, and had already fixed them up with dozens of interviews and appearances.

'One of them might agree to do a "Pen",' said Carol, 'but that's all I can offer you.'

I did manage to interview Lionel Furbilow, survivalist, however.

Furbilow, an ex-soldier, was one of the first people to build a nuclear fall-out shelter in his garden, ignoring the soothing words of government spokesmen, who, of course, said almost every day that such precautions were unnecessary.

He was a thin, wiry old guy with a prisoner's haircut and a face that was a mass of twisted scar tissue. He was tough, but mad. He lived in Sydenham.

'There it is,' he said, kicking the corrugated-iron shack that was at the bottom of his sodden and chaotic garden. It resembled a half-submerged workman's hut.

'Have you got . . . you know, supplies in there?' I asked. 'You know, to live on?'

Furbilow nodded.

'Tea, biscuits, etc.'

'Can I go inside and have a look?'

'Well, it's a bit damp in there at the moment, old boy, with that rainstorm we had last night.'

'Hang on a minute,' I said, 'how's it going to keep out the radiation from a nuclear bomb if it lets rainwater in?'

Furbilow looked at me, his head pulsing.

'I hope this isn't going to be a hostile article,' he said. 'Obviously the final laminates have yet to be applied.'

'Laminates?' I said.

Later, inside Furbilow's house, we slurped tea from billy-cans, and Furbilow lit his pipe, which took forty-five minutes. (Of course, and for psychological reasons which are all too obvious, pipes became immensely popular during the war, but I suspect that Furbilow had smoked one all along.)

'It's quite interesting that you're a journalist,' said Furbilow, finally settling back to draw on his pipe and realising that it had gone out. 'I'm one myself in a small way, although for a long time I had writer's block. Ever had that?'

'I . . .'

'Quite curious. Manifests itself in an inability to put words on paper. Over it now, though.'

'What's your subject? Civil defence?'

'Survivalism in general,' said Furbilow. 'All aspects of staying alive in hostile terrain. I've been a survivalist for ten years, and so the prospect of a nuclear war ties in quite nicely with my hobby. It's a big thing amongst ex-servicemen.'

'How long were you in the army?'

'Thirty years,' said Furbilow dreamily. 'But I don't use my rank; don't believe in standing on ceremony.'

'What was your rank?'

'Private.'

Furbilow slurped from his cup.

'I used to edit the travel page of a jolly nice little magazine called *Outland*,' he went on. 'Nice, cosy offices in Soho. Lovely bunch of chaps. Ex-army in the main.'

'You visited and wrote up places that survivalists would enjoy going to?'

'Enjoy?' said Furbilow. 'There's only one object in this game: avoidance of death. If you can fit in a couple of rounds of golf, so much the better.'

'You've spent a lot of time in deserts, then?'

'Deserts we officially categorise as very hospitable. If you've got enough water, you can live pretty easily in a desert. You know the key to not dying in the Sahara, say: *remember to take water*. Once you've drummed that into a chap's head, he's away. But that's your hot desert. Your cold desert – very different. I've knocked around the polar ice-caps quite a bit, and I can honestly say I enjoyed myself more there than anywhere else. Or should I say less?'

I was standing up, trying to leave.

'Know anything about emergency bivouac construction?' Furbilow said, reaching ominously for a copy of a magazine that was on the floor at the side of his chair. 'Here's a little piece by me on the subject.'

He opened the magazine and passed it across to me. I saw a picture of a hut made of twigs.

'Now the beauty of this little number,' said Furbilow, 'is that the design principles can be adapted for whatever survival medium is at hand. In a desert we're talking about sand, whereas in the polar ice-caps we're talking about s . . .'

'I've got to go,' I said. 'I'm late for something.'

'Oh,' said Furbilow, 'don't suppose you've got a card, have you?'

I gave him my card, which, I realised fractionally too late, included my home number.

Chapter Eighteen

(Two years after the incident)

That torrid July the war was a year old, and there seemed to be a constant thrum and drone in the air as the heat beat down. Sometimes this was the sound of the heavy transport planes which scraped across the skies on their way to the Northern Bases in Friendly Poland, but usually it was just collective psychological tension of a very high order.

There was a universal expectation that the war would come to Britain. In a sense, of course, it had already done so, in the form of the quite regular but small explosions caused by Russian agents. The baleful black-edged posters warning of bombs were everywhere.

I constantly expected Bilton to get in touch.

Early in July, while on a day out in Brighton, I came across a torn-out page from a gardening magazine above the stalls in a gents' toilet. As I urinated, I looked at pictures of suspiciously brightly hued flowers. I read some of the captions: 'Botanical tulips mixed: a beautiful combination of various types of botanical tulips which will give a splendid show for up to six weeks in the spring.' Then I happened to glance at the bottom of the page. 'Picture captions by Martyn Bilton,' I read. Unfortunately I could not trace the magazine from the page I held in my hand.

Also in July, early one weekday evening, they repeated a short TV programme he'd made the previous year. It was called *I'm a Believer*. In it, Bilton, apparently frock-coated, speechified on the necessity of believing in things and conducted interviews with a French fellow Marxist, a Catholic priest, a Green, and a man who believed in fairies. At least, they repeated the first half of the show, but after the first commercial break it was replaced by the celebrity hiking/cooking show *Cake Walk*, in which well-known personalities took a walk through some of their favourite scenery, waxing lyrical about the features of the landscape that most impressed them. And then baked a cake.

Just then the phone rang.

'Hi,' said a creepy, slow voice, 'my name is Ed Billion, and I produce and present a TV show called *Blown Away*.'

'*Blown Away*? I think I've seen that. Goes out on Channel 6 at 4.15 a.m.?'

'We're renegotiating transmission time for the new series.'

'Right.'

'*Blown Away* is about people whose media careers have, as we like to put it, gone down the toilet.'

I was immediately on the defensive.

'Oh yeah . . .?'

'I'm not talking about you. I'm talking about your friend Martyn Bilton. I called his agent but she just kept talking about some guy called Josh something and what a tragedy his illness had been for tiddly-winks . . .'

'How strange,' I said, and replaced the receiver.

It rang again immediately; it was Furbilow.

'No point talking on the bally phone,' he said; 'where do you actually live?'

He came around the next day.

'This thing you edit,' said Furbilow, sipping white wine on my patio. 'What's it called again?'

'"Easy Like a Sunday Morning".'

'Comes out on a Sunday, does it?'

'That's right.'

178

'And it's pretty sort of easy in terms of literary style?'

'Correct,' I said.

'Well, how does this grab you for "Easy Like a Sunday Morning"?'

He leant forward, seizing my wrist and fixing me with his slowly swivelling bloodshot eyes: '"Staring into the Void", a series of articles on different life-endangering situations. Accounts of being trapped on mountains with frostbite, and no food and a broken leg and wild wolves on the loose; lost in subterranean caves or suffocating in malfunctioning submarines; running out of provisions while lost on Dartmoor in fog, etc.'

'Well,' I said, 'those ideas may be more appropriate to our men's pullout; it's called "Boy's Own", and it's edited by a guy called Tom McNair. I could introduce you to him if you like.'

'Would you?' said Furbilow excitedly. 'I'd be awfully grateful. My writing's come on no end recently.'

A few days later, I provided for Tom McNair a quick account of Furbilow's abilities as a journalist (thus ensuring he would never be commissioned for *The New Globe*), yet Furbilow was eternally optimistic of making it into print in a national newspaper, and he visited me frequently in the following weeks. I didn't mind seeing him. Most of my contemporaries, while not exactly War Bores, talked competitively about the war so that I felt the need to have a new theory or a new perspective every day. My conversations with Furbilow were conducted on an altogether different level – a lower level, you could say.

Furbilow, like everyone, was a great fan of Philip Lazenby. 'He's a young man, never been tested *in extremis*,' he said, one too-hot day in the dazzling, concrete 'garden' of a Fulham pub, 'but he's keeping his nerve; completely on top of the situation; playing a blinder I'd say . . . And did you know that he once played cricket for England?'

'No he didn't,' I said.

'Okay, not *for* England. He played *in* England. At school, I believe it was. What are you working on at the moment?'

'When I go back to the office tomorrow I'll be editing a long article in our "We're All in This Together" series.'

'Sounds good,' said Furbilow. 'Accounts of ordinary individuals standing foursquare against the menace of Zubarov?'

'This one's about three actresses who all go to the same hairdresser's,' I said. 'Last week's was about four game-show hosts who had the same chiropodist.'

'Same chiropodist, eh?' said Furbilow. 'I'd love to read that. Do you think you could modem it over to me?'

He started wittering on about the excellence of *The New Globe,* especially 'Easy Like a Sunday Morning'. Of course, his motives were not entirely unselfish. In fact, they were entirely selfish, but I felt sad that here was a person who, for all his undoubted eccentricity, was a man of action; a person who had actually done things rather than just interviewing people who had done things. And yet what did he aspire to be? A bloody hack.

Gradually, I stopped listening to him. I was watching a barrage balloon in the sky. Its dangling mooring rope put me in mind of the string on a child's balloon; its bobbing motion seemed, also, to suggest an inappropriate frivolity. Yet, for all their low tech, they were apparently the best thing for protecting the capital's skies.

'Have you ever heard of Martyn Bilton?' I said to Furbilow.

Furbilow put his pipe in his mouth and sat back.

'Isn't he that piece of filth that did the terrible attack on Lazenby?'

'With the lukewarm half-cup of coffee, yes.'

'I've read about that troublesome little toad. Isn't he in a revolutionary and subversive organisation called The Organisation?'

'He is not part of an organisation called The Organisation,' I said. 'He is a member of a group called The Group. Or was. They've disbanded now.'

'You seem to know a lot about the fellow,' said Furbilow, suspiciously.

'Well, he's a friend of mine.'

Furbilow tapped a little heap of tobacco on to the table top. His pipe seemed to combine never lighting with frequently going out.

'Frankly I'm amazed,' he said.

'Why?'

'I'm amazed that a top-flight journalist like you should know a chap like that.'

'Don't be ridiculous,' I said.

'Is it or is it not true,' said Furbilow, who, to my secret delight, had become quite angry, 'that this man is actively undermining the war effort?'

'He is not undermining the war effort,' I said. 'On the contrary, he is writing gardening articles for a small-circulation magazine aimed at elderly gentlefolk of limited means.'

'Subversion can take many forms,' frowned Furbilow.

I was irritated by Furbilow. I was irritated by this absurdly nebulous war; I was irritated by lifestyle journalism. I was too bloody hot.

I went home and turned the television on. I wanted soothing jazz but accidentally strayed into the rarefied realms of Channel 19, and got current affairs chat by mistake. The conversation was by way of a preview for a programme coming up that same evening which would celebrate the apotheosis of Philp

Lazenby. (It was called *Guiding Light*, of course, and featured a long section with a rugged-looking Lazenby masterfully in charge of his boat in the Thames basin. It won many awards.)

'Oh absolutely,' some languid brainbox was saying. 'One's never seen the like. I mean right through the roof. We're actually seeing ninety-five per cent approval ratings, which of course is absolutely unprecedented for a prime minster. I mean, it's strange; but his prosecution of the war tactically, in so far as one can understand these things from the sidelines, seems to be little short of brilliant. And his propagandising, if one might use that word – which has critical overtones although one doesn't necessarily intend them – likewise has been quite impeccable thus far. Have you noticed, he's even looking different? Leaner, hungrier.'

The man reached for a lit cigarette that had been sending a thin line of smoke up the side of his face, and smoked it strangely.

'But why?' drawled an equally, if not even more, languid voice from off-camera (lateral puffs of smoke came from this direction; this was about the time when general nervous tension excused smoking on television). '. . . Why did we have this breathtaking, er, this . . . declaration, as it were, of war. I mean, quite stunning. Of course we know that Lazenby regards Zubarov as a serious threat to the whole of Europe; and we know the history of antagonism between the two men. But one never thought that Lazenby would respond. What I suppose I'm asking is what was the psychological trigger for Lazenby?'

The smoker put down his cigarette; then he picked it up again and smoked some more.

'Interesting,' he said. 'And funnily enough one seems to be able to pinpoint this quite precisely. If the accounts from those close to the Prime Minister are to be believed, we must look to the incident involving that young man. His name escapes me, although he's become quite notorious . . .'

'Martyn Bilton?'

'Bilton, that's it. With the cup of coffee. The Prime Minister was terribly unsettled, not only by the incident itself but also by the approval that it seemed to garner. And it was at that point that he resolved to go to war. Erm, of course, it took a while to get things in place strategically, so there was a hiatus.'

The horizontal smoke appeared.

'I see.'

The vertical-smoke man resumed.

'The declaration of war did actually come on the anniversary of this incident with the coffee, and that, from what one can gather, was absolutely no accident. It was as though, by acting on that date, Lazenby was attempting to somehow banish the memory of his humiliation. There was, I believe, something of a media jamboree planned to coincide with the anniversary – it was all cancelled of course – and undoubtedly Lazenby wanted to forestall that as well.'

The lateral smoke came again.

'And so from a tiny little event, insignificant in itself, a whole . . .'

I turned the TV off, feeling sick. Why couldn't these pundits just fuck off: sooner or later they always said something that you hated, so why let them ramble? The incident had caused the war and I, as the catalyst of the coming together of Bilton and Lazenby, had caused the incident. It was a thought I had formulated to myself, only to dismiss it as impossibly whimsical – a crabbed, self-centred conceit, the function of a self-obsessed and neurotic personality. To hear it echoed and given what passed for intellectual legitimacy on television was nightmarish. I went immediately to bed, and pulled the sheets over my head.

Chapter Nineteen

That summer, we all tried to alleviate the stress with music, and the revival of jazz was one of the stranger cultural ramifications of the war. In August, I began to frequent a small basement club off the King's Road called The Bunker. Often I entered its smoky interior with that familiar tension across the scalp: some nuclear issues unresolved. The Bunker, as was the fashion of the time, had an area set aside (a 'Wartalk Zone' as it was known here and in other places) for people who wanted to talk about the war, and another for those who didn't. For myself, I talked about the war if I was feeling good; didn't want to know if I was depressed. For the last hour of the evening, until 3 a.m. or so, there'd be smoochy, slow blues tunes. Very often, the endless, weary circling of the couples sent me to sleep. The war brought a lot of people together.

At home I'd listen to complex, melodic, wailing music – Charles Mingus, Ornette Coleman – sometimes while sitting at my desk cross-referring between newspaper articles and atlases, picking out hotspots from the Black Sea to Siberia, floating gradually out of panic on a sea of Bloody Marys, above my pin-stuck charts.

I didn't go on holiday. Russian agents, of course, were believed to be tracking the British abroad. Probably a myth. I spent most of my time off in Battersea Park, reading, and half-listening to the test matches while sitting under the shade of a beautiful ash tree. I remember the way the shadow of its branches swooped across the pages of my book in the playful summer gusts.

Lazenby attended a couple of the tests. He was interviewed by the BBC's new cricket correspondent, Charlie Golightly, during the tea interval one blistering August day at Lord's. At first there was a lot of arch stuff about the game and then, inevitably, Lazenby got serious.

'Do you know,' he said, 'this war is all about a lot of high-flying principles: we're fighting for freedom, toleration, democracy and the British Way of Life, but it's hard to talk in abstractions.'

There was a humble pause.

'I suppose what I'm really trying to say is that if you're looking for something to symbolise, to encapsulate, the things we're fighting for, you might do worse than just look out there . . .'

'At the cricket pitch?' said Golightly.

'Look at the bright, golden green; the spiralling wood pigeons; the shadow of a clock tower; twenty-two white-clad lads . . .' The next two words were uttered with a brilliantly restrained intensity: '*Batsmen, bowlers.*'

Sitting on the grass, I gasped.

'. . . I've got to go now, Charlie. There's a war to win.'

His last sentence was drowned out by applause, at first sparse, the individual claps identifiable, and then so loud that it distorted – a spontaneous expression of warmth from the hardened professionals around Lazenby: soundman, producer, interviewer, and Lazenby's own bodyguards and assistants, I supposed.

Millions of people must have heard that broadcast. I don't know why I remember it particularly.

Over the next few months I became, I suppose you could say,

a small-scale socialite; commissioning articles from my peers across dinner tables. I was frequently at parties with Celia Stein, but our peculiar encounter in the Halls of Holborn had made me wary of her.

My attention had now been diverted towards a small red-headed girl called Eleanor Hopkins, who was beautiful in a worried-looking sort of way. When I met her she was working all the hours God sends on 'Lazy Days', *The New Globe*'s massively successful canal-cruising supplement. She was five years younger than me, and I must have looked like a big shot.

'Easy Like a Sunday Morning' was certainly deemed a success, and I was flourishing at the *Globe*, to the extent, indeed, that I was summoned to a congratulatory meeting with Little Willie Meltchitt himself.

I waited in the ante-room to the high, gilded conference chamber, where Little Willie was conducting a features conference. As the ornate clock that was incorporated into the golden globe on the wall above my head began to chime ten, they walked out: the Heads of Lifestyle. I counted seventeen of them. There were in fact twenty on the books but at any one time about three of them would be away having nervous breakdowns. Harry Piper was bringing up the rear, lighting a fag as he left The Presence.

'Good luck,' he said.

'I don't think I need any luck,' I said. 'From what I gather it's just a pat on the back about "Easy Like a Sunday Morning".'

'Ever heard of Christopher Brittain?'

'No.'

'Very promising young journalist four years ago. He was called in just like you; Willie started by saying well done, called him a genius, the lot. Two minutes later he sacked him.'

'Why?'

Piper shrugged.

'Little Willie just suddenly decided he was a wanker.'

'God. What's he doing now?'

'Edits *Bide a Wee.*'

'Is that the magazine that's only available in . . . '

'In public lavatories, yes.'

'You've got me worried now.'

'The thing you've got to remember,' said Piper, 'is that, like most people, Willie has his good days and his bad days. It's just that, unlike most people, he only has about one good day a year, and that's usually Christmas Day, when he's not actually at work.'

'But surely,' I protested, 'he's not going to decide that *I'm* a wanker?'

Piper put his hand on my arm.

'As I said, son . . . good luck.'

The bastard. I do believe he was jealous.

I walked into the conference chamber. The art on the red walls – shadowy, medieval stuff depicting sour-faced priests and doomed, ill-looking princes – I knew to be priceless. But the actual conference table and chairs were modern and looked quite cheap. Meltchitt lolled enormously at the top of the table. He wore no tie, and his collar was spread-eagled right across his chest. Austere, beautiful, efficient-looking females sat on either side of him. One of them motioned me to a chair.

'Now,' he said. 'Heard good things about you, young man. This section you edit . . . Er, can't recall the actual name, er . . .'

One of the women hastily scrawled something on a piece of paper and shoved it under Little Willie's huge nose.

'. . . but I'm told it's easily likeable on a Sunday morning and that's good enough for me.'

'Thank you,' I said.

187

'Good,' said Little Willie.

This was going pretty well.

'Now,' he went on, 'what about the future, eh?'

My brain went into overdrive; I panicked.

'The future of what?' I said.

It had come out all wrong; sounded positively rude. As Little Willie's hobgoblin face mutated slowly but inexorably into a scowl, I nearly resigned on the spot.

'Your future,' he said, with hatred in his colourless eyes.

Maybe, I thought, Christopher Brittain has a vacancy for a deputy on *Bide a Wee*.

'Obviously,' I said, sweating crazily and feeling sick, 'I'm enjoying myself tremendously at the moment, and I'd love to stay here at the *Globe* for as long as possible.'

'Why?' said Little Willie sourly.

'It pays the most money,' I said.

But – sod it – that was wrong too.

'. . . Which is completely irrelevant, of course,' I went on. 'I think, very simply, that this is the best features department in the world, and therefore I'd be quite mad to want to move to . . .'

But Little Willie was now talking to one of the severe women and glancing at his watch. He turned back to face me.

'It's been very nice talking to you,' he said, 'and keep up the good work with . . . er . . .'

He glanced at the scrap of paper again.

'. . . your "Early Look at Sunday Morning".'

I had to go to the Ink Spotte immediately afterwards, and I could see why Piper needed his rugby ball.

One broiling Sunday shortly afterwards, I was walking in Battersea Park with Furbilow, who was carrying a complicated stick arrangement.

'This,' he said as we strolled past the glittering pagoda, 'is a snake catcher. For catching snakes. You simply hook the loop around the blighter's head, and then pull tight with the drawstring. Effective against most breeds.'

I looked at him, perplexed.

'Ever been attacked by a venomous snake?' he asked casually.

'No,' I said.

'You're pretty safe against anything with this stick, except the puff adder, of course, which is positively *seething* with poison, and so fat that it can't get out of the way even if it hears you coming. I've never been attacked by a snake either,' he said, regretfully folding up his stick and gazing at the slow, mustardy river. 'Been at close quarters with a mountain lion, though, while doing a spot of death climbing at Yosemite National Park, California. Death climbing, by the way, is climbing that's technically impossible. You ought not to survive; you're gambling on pure luck. By the way,' he droned on, 'one of my military contacts has news of your man Bilton.'

'What?' I said, astounded.

Furbilow carried on walking, swishing his bloody stick.

'Fellow's in hiding. Government safe house. Best place for him.'

'Is it possible to get in touch with him?'

'I jolly well don't want to get in touch with him,' said Furbilow. 'I can assure you that I would not be seen dead . . .'

'Not you,' I said, 'me. Do you think I might be able to get in touch with him?'

'It might be possible,' said Furbilow. 'I don't know.'

He stopped and took out a pen, scrawled something on a page of his diary, ripped it out and handed it to me.

'You might start by giving this fellow a call. Say that old Bodger Furbilow sends his regards.'

I could have kissed him.

'This is wonderful,' I said. 'I'm incredibly grateful.'

'Think nothing of it,' said Furbilow.

'Now,' he said, replacing his diary and pulling an ominous - looking manuscript from the back pocket of his indestructible canvas trousers, 'do you think your pal McNair might be interested in a little something I've cooked up? It's a travel piece really, and contains what I believe to be an element of humour: "Swimming in the South Seas with sharks: why it needn't cost you an arm and a leg".'

I promised to make enquiries.

On the Monday, I phoned the number which Furbilow had given me. A brutal-sounding man said 'War Security', and I asked for the name that Furbilow had scribbled: George Warden.

'Warden,' said a drawling, upper-class voice.

'Hello,' I said, 'you don't know me. My name is Adrian Day. I'm a friend of Martyn Bilton's.'

No response.

'I gather that he's under your protection, and I was wondering whether I might visit him.'

'Mr Day,' said Warden, 'I don't know what you're talking about. If I can *find out* what you're talking about I will phone you back.'

Two days later, amazingly enough, he did phone me back.

'Martyn Bilton,' he said. 'Now, what about him?'

'You've found out who he is, then?'

'I knew all along, Mr Day. But it doesn't do to be too forthcoming about these matters without checking the enquirer's bona fides.'

'Which you've now done?'

'I'm calling you back. You can read into that what you will . . . What can I do for you?'

'First of all, why is he in a safe house?'

'He has been assessed as being at some risk of what we call "effective nullification in terms of basic validation".'

'You mean he might be killed?'

'Yes.'

'Who by?'

'Hotheads. This young man has made himself very unpopular.'

'Does the Prime Minister know that he's being protected?'

'It was done at Mr Lazenby's personal suggestion, as a matter of fact.'

'Very magnanimous.'

'Mmm.'

'Obviously you can't give me a specific address, but could you tell me what part of the country this safe house is in?'

'No.'

'Could you give me a clue. You know, are there a lot of sheep there, or is the place famous for . . .'

'Mr Day, I am a busy man. Are you formally requesting to see Mr Bilton?'

'Yes.'

'Then you can expect to hear from me again.'

Chapter Twenty

My evenings, late that summer, would usually start at the Public War Room in Sloane Square – so much more comfortable, with its chintzy ambience and excellent coffee, than the makeshift Bulletin Booths of the West End. I would read papers and try to comprehend the charmingly primitive magnetised maps with their many metal symbols – Us and Them – as they were repositioned at the end of every day by the War Room manager.

The manager of the Sloane Square War Room was a big, jovial guy with jet-black hair, blue eyes, and a slightly blue-grey nose. He was called John Pennistone. He'd been a Cambridge don before the war, had excellent contacts within the Ministry of Defence and often received information early. I got talking to him in the week of America's first limited and temporary intervention on Britain's side.

I had two subsequent conversations with him: the first took place when the São Paulo agreement was signed, by which, of course, both parties agreed to conduct the war without resort to nuclear weapons; the second took place when General Zubarov tore this up.

Despite our age difference, we got on well. He had a sort of morbid fascination with my trivial journalism; it was light relief compared to his business of chronicling the war.

Late that September, he walked across to me carrying two coffees.

'Next few weeks are going to be a bit hairy,' he said, sitting in the armchair next to mine. 'Could even be touch and go.'

'How come?' I said, my coffee cup wobbling on its saucer.

'There's a battle going on for control of a nuclear missile station outside Kiev.'

'God. I suppose that's one we've got to win.'

'We're not involved.'

'Eh?'

'Remember Colonel Shalovchikha?'

'The Rebel Colonel. Leader of a breakaway force. Thinks Zubarov's a wimp.'

'A wanker is what he actually called him, but you don't speak Russian, do you?'

'I thought Shalovchikha was dead. Killed in a car bomb.'

'So did we all.'

'What if he gets to this missile station first?'

'There could well be a strike.'

'You mean the people who work there will go on strike?'

'I mean the missiles could well be fired at London.'

'Oh. I suppose it would be a way of Shalovchikha showing that he's in the driving seat.'

'It would be a way of killing hundreds of thousands of the enemies of Mother Russia, which is even closer to his heart.'

'Will this be coming out on the news?'

'I think the danger will be played down,' said John.

'Well,' I said, 'thanks for telling me.'

For the rest of that week, I felt the constant welling of tears behind my eyes. Self-pity, pure and simple. That's what the onset of war produced: millions of people asking, 'Why me?' I found that I didn't want to be with people. The strain of keeping upper lip stiff was too great. I couldn't concentrate on reading; I had to take time off work. All I *could* do, funnily enough, was watch football on television, and there was no shortage of that.

One night that week, my wardrobe rattled at 3 a.m., and I nearly had heart failure. A rattling wardrobe seemed – by the all-dominating law of bathos – to be an appropriate domestic prelude to global nuclear war.

But it was just the wardrobe rattling; I opened the door and found an overcoat slumped.

I walked the streets aimlessly, not stepping on the cracks; constantly stopping and arching my back in an attempt to unclench my whole body. It was a dirty, blustery, post-summer time; in the sky, marbled miles of grey.

I called my doctor to make an appointment. 'It's my ears,' I told his receptionist.

'Is it a genuinely physical ailment or war stress?' she snapped back and, even as she spoke, I knew the answer. I had a touch of the War Sads. I put the phone down. On the Thursday of that week, I telephoned John.

'Is the nuclear danger at Kiev over?'

'It will be after tonight,' he said, 'one way or another. Lazenby's moved to his bunker under Whitehall.'

'Bastard,' I said. 'John, do you ever think, why does this have to happen?'

'Ah,' said John, 'that's the writer in you.'

But I was beyond flattery in those dark days. I think we all were. The bullshit between people just faded away. The news of the danger had come out, and a lot of people left work early. At the *Globe* there were no huddles at the newsdesks. The reporters just sat there, smoking even more than usual, and waiting. I was taking hours over proofreading a caption for the latest in our 'Sunday Girl' series. 'Melissa hopes to be a model,' I read. I wished very much that there would be a world around for Melissa to be a model in.

Afterwards, I wandered along to World's End, Chelsea. Half the *Globe* features staff were there, Harry Piper having decided that it would be really neat to profile this area in lifestyle terms ('best eats', etc.) during the night on which the world might end. Obviously this was a gamble, in that, if the world *did* end, there might not be another edition of *The New Globe* to carry the articles. ('This,' Piper was said to have intoned, 'could be the end of lifestyle on earth as we know it.')

Some television crews had had the same idea, and I walked past a crush of link men towards a little Italian caff, where I drank a coffee and started a bun which I couldn't finish. The proprietor had placed a large Madonna in the window. He shook my hand when I paid him. At about nine I walked towards the river and into a pub I'd never seen before. Opening the door, a cacophony hit me. People were dancing to a jazz band whose wild-haired players were like puppets operated by a drunken puppeteer.

I struggled to the bar and asked for a whisky, which I then amended to a double.

'Why not?' said the barmaid with a grin. 'It's a special occasion after all.'

The cheerfulness in this place was disturbing and, it seemed to me, heretical. At ten o'clock the music was stopped and the TVs were turned up. It was the all clear, of course. The all-channels logo; classical music, followed by Lazenby in fine, sombre yet lyrical form at the microphones outside Number Ten. This time Shalovchikha really was dead. Lazenby added that the month's War Price takings had reached a new record, as they had done, indeed, every month since being introduced.

The sign-off was as usual: 'Congratulations, I am proud of you all.'

How the jazz boomed from the doorways of the King's Road that evening. How the bugs jittered.

Chapter Twenty-One

(Two years and three months after the incident)

'Adrian Day?' said the man on the phone. 'George Warden.'

On the Tuesday of the previous week, the day on which Zubarov had scorned the Second Chinese Peace Initiative by going back into Belarus and killing 650 British soldiers in one night, I had married Eleanor. The day after that we had moved into a salubrious, rather embarrassingly large villa on the edge of Hampstead Heath. Two days later our child was born: a boy, Barnaby.

'Hello, Mr Warden,' I said.

'Got a pen on you? Take this down.'

It was Bilton's address. It was in Cornwall.

'He'll be expecting you at tea-time on 29 October.'

Tea-time. It didn't sound much like Bilton.

'His name is Pete Stitt.'

'What?'

'Pseudonym.'

'Right. Thanks very much,' I said.

'Oh, by the way,' said George Warden, 'keep the address under your hat. If you're feeling peckish you might eat it.'

He was very droll.

That evening, I sat in my study with a cup of War Price cocoa and a glass of sherry, thinking about Bilton. I gazed over the night-time gardens at the charmingly variegated, electric-lit colours of the curtained rooms of the houses beyond. Children's rooms, dads' messing-about rooms. It was shortly after my baby's bath time. The family smell of talcum powder hung in the warm, soft air. He was in bed now and alongside my desk, plugged into a wall socket, was the electronic receiver which enabled me to hear his snuffles, trumpetings and small, quavering wails as he slept in the nursery – the first room that Eleanor had earmarked for decoration. On some evenings, I seemed to hear the ghostly windswept cries of a hundred babies through this gadget; a coalescing lamentation from the new generation against what the world is doing to itself.

Downstairs my wife was watching the all-channels News Extension, which this week featured Mr Lazenby being solicitous towards some child refugees from somewhere, and then consoling relatives of the victims of recent Russian terror strikes. A nail bomb in Wolverhampton had killed three.

I was a family man now, and I was aware that I should be wholly concerned with the safety of my family in these troubled times. But, dammit, I was vastly excited at the thought of seeing Bilton. With the breakdown of the European powers' official line of conditional neutrality, and the entry of France and Italy into the war on Britain's side, Lazenby had reached a level of public regard approaching deification. I wondered whether the old equation continued to apply: could Bilton fall any lower? I doubted it. After all, when your end of the see-saw is touching the ground you can't go any lower.

The front half of the train to Cornwall was marked OMS, and therefore was no-go. Annoyingly this part included the buffet. I packed a book for the journey: *Modern Islam*, or something. I was becoming a swot, I'm afraid, and that morning I had found out that my small war analysis, 'Which Way Will Khirgizia Jump?', had been accepted by one of the smaller war journals. At last, I was taking steps towards a more serious, engaged form of journalism.

The latter part of the ride was beautiful. Past rolling winter fields in many of which stood the Zubarov scarecrow: a mass-produced moustachioed mannequin designed for the purposes of patriotic symbolism rather than scaring crows.

We wound along the coast, and I stared at the indigo sea. I saw a small warship, hung with bunting, proceeding south. We stopped at a station where a man with a tinkling bicycle rode up alongside the guard's van and hoisted the machine inside. 'Morning!' he positively shouted at me, as he entered my carriage. A flock of sheep crested the brow of a hill and drifted diversely down. I formulated my attitude to Bilton. I would be cool, solicitous, unboastful about my son, modest about my career, impressed by whatever he had achieved. I would not talk about Eleanor.

It was only two-thirty as I stood on the deserted platform of the village station with the locomotive raucously discharging steam from a grille on its flank. In five minutes the loco at the other end would pull the train out for the return journey. I could just climb on board again. The friendship between Bilton and me had, surely, gone beyond its elastic limit.

I wandered over the road, into a small, grey square with a stone cross and flowers underneath to commemorate a local boy killed in action.

It was a dingy, grey village. It suited the slow, sleeting rain which had now begun to fall. I approached a post office with two or three scrawled postcards in the window – 'Pane ting and decorating. All so garden work under taken' and 'Would you like to swap houses with us? We will swap our house here for a house anywhere else in the UK.'

Next to the post office was a dusty toyshop. Immobile mobiles dangled in the window and a faded toy train circled on an inch-wide line.

I walked out of the square, around the corner into a pub

with scarred seats and a steady grey light. There was a notice behind the bar: 'Banned from this pub,' I read. Then the names: David Mibbs; Richard Mallinson; Vince Briggs; Joe Slater; and, yes, Pete Stitt.

I soaked up a filthy stout. Alongside me at the bar, a fat man was eating an knackered old egg sandwich. His jaw clicked repeatedly. The click tocked repeatedly – I mean the clock ticked repeatedly. I read my paper.

Georgia had surrendered to Zubarov, or so it seemed. But there was a commentary next to the piece saying that the two sides had not fought so much as a skirmish, and that the surrender was a put-up job, literally paid for by Zubarov, and designed to make him look good. I ordered another stout.

'You're the first person to have ordered two pints of that in succession,' observed the barman.

'Yes, well,' I said, 'it's not very good, is it?'

The barman gave me a bright-eyed smile and said nothing. I asked him whether he had a number for a taxi.

'I'll phone you one now,' he said, reaching for his mobile.

The taxi driver was a man called Graham Mann. He was a lean, shrewd-looking guy with a crew cut. After our phone conversation, George Warden had asked me to take a taxi only as far as the head of the little valley in which Bilton lived. I was to ask for Badger's Meadow. Warden had sent me a map to show me the way from there.

'Badger's Meadow, please,' I said.

'You going to see Pete Stitt?'

Surely, I thought, this was something he ought not to know. But there was something in the confidence of Graham Mann's tone which told me that no deception would work.

'As a matter of fact I am, yes.'

He nodded, and looked at me in his mirror.

'Or should I say Martyn Bilton?'

'Good God,' I said. 'That's supposed to be secret.'

'Absolutely,' said Graham Mann, as the car took off slightly, on a humpbacked bridge that was in the middle of a copse.

'*Top* secret,' I said.

'That's right,' said Graham Mann.

'How do you know?' I said.

'How do I know what?' asked Graham Mann.

'That Pete Stitt is Martyn Bilton.'

He looked at me in the mirror again. He was frowning.

'I don't know,' he said. 'It's like saying, how do you know that the world is round? I can't remember who first told me.'

'Does everyone around here know?'

'Yup.'

'I'm appalled.'

'I think what happened is that he was in a pub – I mean, he likes a drink, this guy – and he was getting a bit stroppy, which he apparently has a tendency to do when he's had a few. When the landlord refused to serve him he said, "Do you realise who I am?"'

'I see.'

It sounded a fairly plausible scenario, I had to admit.

'So I might as well take you all the way, don't you think?'

I trudged towards Bilton's house along a narrow track bounded by towering, black hedges which shuddered in the wind. Around a corner, a large, bull-faced tom-cat skulked across my path, looking like he'd been up to no good. Was this Bilton's cat?

Bilton was pacing backwards and forwards in front of a grey, blank-faced, pebble-dash house hung with dead pot plants which swayed hither and thither in the wind. It was built in a sort of hole at the confluence of two ditches, which was surely illogical. Bilton turned to face me. His hair. Well, the whole front of it wasn't there any more. For a millisecond

I considered this a rectifiable fault; that he'd somehow over-looked the necessity of attaching it that morning. Then the horrible, time-locked irreversibility of everything tumbled down upon me: the declaration of war; the terror strikes; the nightmarish missile race at Kiev; our lives burning up like sweet wrappers put to a flame. Nothing had scared me so much.

Bilton had lost weight, too, which I would have thought impossible; he looked like a madman on hunger strike. He had acquired a new old coat, if you see what I mean; and when I say that parts of it trailed on the ground you'll get some idea of the state it was in. But not only had Bilton's appearance changed for the worse, so had he, as I realised as soon as he spoke.

'Nice to see you,' he said, shockingly, and then attempted awkwardly to embrace me, which made me freeze. I noticed the beer on his breath.

'Good journey?' he asked, walking into the kitchen. The room was big and cold with an isolated fifties cooker, a little rickety table with a plastic cloth and an old stone sink from the bottom of which hung what looked alarmingly like stalac-tites. There were three large, arched windows. Inside the room, dusk was falling early.

'Nice place. Do you get the sun in the morning?' I asked, accepting a cup of tea and trying to strike an optimistic note.

'No,' he said. 'We get the wind. This place gets no sun in the morning, but it also gets no sun in the afternoon as well. We're in a deep depression. I have biscuits,' he went on, indi-cating a plate of moody Nice, 'and a little something to help you get over the journey.'

He indicated two cans of lager set daintily on opposite sides of the table.

'You look well,' I said. An obvious untruth.

Bilton made no answer, but just gave me a poignant, dubious look. 'Well, obviously the hair . . .' he said, touching the edges of his remaining locks. I had never noticed the fault line, the vulnerability in Bilton's hair.

'We can go to the pub later,' he said, hastily changing the subject. 'Although I may as well tell you, I went along to a few meetings of Alcoholics Anonymous. I started doing a piece about it. I referred to the organisation throughout as Alcoholics Anomalous.'

'Pretty funny,' I said. 'And what did the piece say?'

'Not much. I didn't really get beyond that initial play on words.'

'You're not an alcoholic, Bilton,' I said. 'You're just a heavy socialist drinker.'

'How did you like the village?' said Bilton, with phoney perkiness.

'I found it a bit depressing actually.'

'I know what you mean,' said Bilton. 'It's not one of those chocolate-box hamlets, is it? But they're good people. Farm labourers mainly.'

'Ruthlessly exploited by the big landowners,' I blurted out.

Bilton gave me a puzzled look.

'I'm sorry?' he said.

'These country folk,' I elaborated. 'They're forced to work for minimal wages, and endure a pitifully low standard of living . . . presumably.'

Bilton was still staring at me strangely.

'I'm just looking at things from your point of view – from the communist angle.'

'Didn't you know?' said Bilton. 'I've dropped all that.'

'You're not a communist any more?'

'Nope.'

'Well, what are you?' I said, rather rudely.

'An aspiring bourgeois like yourself . . . Someone who just wants to get by the best he can.'

'You're having me on,' I said.

Bilton ignored this accusation.

'For a long time,' he said, 'I felt a terrible void at the centre of my life, and I don't mind admitting that I turned to religion for a while – shortly after I sold the van.'

'Which church?'

'I joined a prayer community in Shropshire. It was a completely communal way of living, with at least ten hours every day devoted to spiritual contemplation. The idea was to raise oneself up to a higher level of spiritual existence, and be at one with the Godhead.'

'What happened?'

'Couldn't stand the food,' said Bilton. 'Sloppy vegetarian muck all the time.'

'So what are you doing now?'

'A little gardening,' said Bilton. 'Yes, I've actually started to put into practice what I wrote about for all those years. Oh, and I'm learning to play the banjo.'

Sure enough, he pointed to a banjo in the corner of the room.

'That was in this house when I arrived; the last person to live here was persecuted for his art, you see. He was an experimental folk singer, and after his latest record came out his life was threatened.'

'Wow,' I said, 'it must've been really terrible.'

'It was,' said Bilton, 'but it was the political content that got him into trouble. Anti-Lazenby sentiments.'

'What happened to him?'

'Topped himself. Not such a bad idea,' Bilton went on, chillingly. 'I've often thought of doing the same myself.'

'Bilton,' I said, appalled, 'what are you talking about?'

'I'm just saying that there may come a time when I will

have to go. You might wake up one morning, and you will see that I've had to say, "Well, yes, that's that then."'

'Well, you'd better not.'

'Why not? What have I got to live for?'

'Look, I don't want to hear this. You're a very talented writer and . . .'

But I couldn't think of anything to add.

I suddenly felt very sorry for Bilton. He'd had a terrible childhood; been written off in his prime as a writer, and now forced to live in this hell-hole. To distract him from the tears welling in my eyes, I picked up his banjo, and thrummed the strings discordantly.

'Nice instrument,' I said.

'I bought a book,' said Bilton, 'called *Play in a Week*. That was six months ago, and I've nearly learned how to hold it correctly.'

'What about work?'

'I receive a small allowance from my protectors at the Home Office. They recognise the difficulty of earning money in a place like this. But I've applied for a part-time job over the way at some stables. Saw the ad in the paper: "Are you interested in shovelling large amounts of manure on a daily basis?" it said. "Please write, stating your relevant qualifications." I haven't heard back . . . How's the war going?'

'Oh, you know. Complicated.'

'And how's the kid? I read about that somewhere. You did a "Me and My Baby".'

Oh dear. I was hoping that he wouldn't have heard of that egregious piece of self-promotion. Eleanor and I also had a 'Two at the Top' and a 'Lucky in Love' – both in *Be Like Us* magazine – to be taken into consideration.

'Barnaby?' I said. 'He's good.'

'Funny time to have a kid, isn't it? What with the end of the world coming up. Still, each to his own.'

Bilton gave me a quick, amused look as he slurped his tea – a flash of the old sardonic spark.

'It's stopped raining,' he said, 'and that doesn't often happen around here. I think I'll hang my washing out.'

'Oh really?' I asked, thinking I'd better feign interest.

Bilton stood up and collected a big sports bag from next to the sink. I followed him through the shuttered living room towards an open door and into the garden.

'The thing about having children . . .' I said to Bilton, sitting down on a damp, fraying deck chair, falling through it on to the wet grass, getting a splinter in my finger as I extricated myself and wiping some mud off the back of my trousers, '. . . it's a matter of showing that you have . . . hope.'

Bilton nodded silently to himself. He'd come to the end of the line – literally, and with half a bag of damp laundry left.

The garden was surrounded by grassy banks, and one of the banks formed the foothill to a large . . . well, it was almost a mountain. Four static sheep were visible just above the garden wall. Bilton's small lawn was slightly overgrown but tolerably neat. Alongside it were several rows of vegetables.

'Are you doing any writing these days?'

This was the first on my agenda of difficult questions.

'I'm doing my memoirs,' he said, ferreting around amongst some underpants. 'I might call them "Recollections of a Dead Man". I think the world will be interested in what I have to say.' He draped a large pair of purple nylon Y-fronts across the line, and stabbed them with a peg. 'I could certainly give the inside story on one or two matters.'

This was his first reference to the incident and, immediately afterwards, he turned away and looked up to the top of the mountain.

'Some analysts are putting forward the theory that the incident was actually the thing responsible for the war,' I said.

'Yes,' he said, 'I know.'

'The basic argument is that . . .'

'I know the basic argument,' said Bilton with sudden ferocity. Then he immediately calmed down again. 'But thank you,' he added.

I followed Bilton back into the kitchen, where he made some more tea, dispiritedly dragging the tea bags over the rims of the cups with a spoon, and letting them slump down into the saucer, instead of flinging them about with his old, unhygienic *joie de vivre*.

'Have a biscuit,' he said, indicating the (I now noticed) slightly fungoid Nice. He blithely lit a cigarette, not offering me one. Another flash of the old Bilton.

'I still interpret history through Marxist eyes, I must admit,' he said, 'and sometimes the dialectic is very hard to read. I mean, in this war, is Zubarov a communist or a fascist?'

It was almost the only question he'd ever asked me. And what an elemental question it was.

'Well,' I said, 'he's currently presiding over a People's Revolution. But on the other hand, he's doing it all himself. So, I suppose he's sort of both.'

'No. You can't be both,' said Bilton, 'that's one of the rules.'

'Well, he's anti-Western,' I said, 'but also anti-Semitic and racist. But then you could say the same for Stalin.'

'Leave Stalin out of it,' said Bilton with, again, some of the old spark. It was a relief to me that his old loyalties still, residually, survived.

That evening, we traipsed down dank, winding streets into

the centre of the village, past battered, gloomy shops. We came upon a bleak little pub in the middle of a sort of gravelled rubbish dump, adjacent to a burnt-out garage.

'Just one thing,' said Bilton, 'before we go in. I'm known around these parts as Pete.'

'War Security told me you were using a pseudonym,' I said, 'but just out of interest, why Pete Stitt?'

'Some guys, when they die, they leave their names to the state, just like some people leave their livers to medical science. A patriotic gesture, you know. They leave the birth certificate, passport, etc. Of course, you've got to look a bit like the guy, and be the same age.'

'So who was the original Pete Stitt?'

'A lumberjack. Lived in Northumberland.'

'How did he die?'

'It's a long story but, basically, a tree fell on him.'

The red regulars at the bar merely regarded the shambling Bilton with disgust. Clearly they knew nothing of his past. We sat down next to the fire. Every so often, a draught banged into the grate causing a brief, tense surge of orange. Outside, the branch of a tree clattered and rattled against the high window. We drank more or less in silence, but then I plunged in.

'Are you happy these days?'

'Happy?' he said, in his irritating, elusive way. 'I'm not happy, and I'm not sad. Above all, I'm not happy. I can't find publishers for my work, you see. Even "Questioners" don't want to know.'

There was a silence.

'You were drunk, weren't you?' I said.

'Of course I was drunk,' said Bilton, 'that's the heart of the matter. Granger knew that. Bright guy.'

This was a thrilling admission, and I sought to capitalise on his expansive frame of mind.

'Have you ever been banned for life from any pubs in this area?' I asked casually.

'Actually,' said Bilton, 'I was having quite a decent discussion with a local bloke about politics. There was just a brief moment of violence when he broached the idea that I was a wanker. We shook hands on it outside. I may have been banned from the place; I'm not sure.'

I could not breathe the heady air of such frankness for long. We talked amicably enough and then, four pints into the session, when Bilton had just zigzagged back from the gents', he said, 'The incident, okay, it's over.'

'Fine,' I said.

'Closed,' said Bilton, 'the incident is closed. Now I want to tell you something. Little tip, really. If you ever get a lot of money, which maybe you already have . . .'

'Not at all,' I said.

'If you ever do, and you go into a restaurant, get the red wine not the white.'

'Well,' I said, 'sure, but it depends what you're eating.'

'No,' said Bilton, 'get the red, because then they leave it at your table. The white they take away.'

'That's true,' I said, 'to put it in a fucking ice bucket.'

'Exactly,' said Bilton, 'you've got it.'

It was eight-thirty by the clanking clock on the wall. We didn't say anything for ten minutes and then, slowly, Bilton seemed to relax; he didn't become his old self though. Or at least not quite. There was a kind of creepy niceness about him which was rather disturbing, betokening a resigned, defeated outlook. After one more pint, we changed pubs. The new one was cosier; quite full, and giving off a reassuring orange glow. There was jazz on the juke box.

Bilton asked me about 'Easy Like a Sunday Morning'. 'I don't buy newspapers myself,' he said, 'but I often see it around the place. In bins and so on. I'd say half the villagers here must take it.'

I told him about *The New Globe*'s new two-hundred-page weekly supplement, devoted entirely to golf. (Eleanor was going to be in charge of the art direction, but I didn't say that.)

'Sounds good,' said Bilton, 'if you like golf.'

I also cautiously mentioned that *London Sunday* had lifted his 'Downbeat' idea with their new regular feature: 'Lowpoint'. Bilton just shrugged.

I told him that I was becoming bored with lifestyle journalism and wanted to address the war in my work.

'I always thought you had a brain,' he said, with a touch of the old patronising tone, 'underneath all the crap, that is. I still think about the old days. Have you noticed how, at *The New Globe*, all the guys *looked* like the fucking newspaper?'

'No,' I said, 'how do you mean?'

'Short, squarish, neat, and with a little flash of colour somewhere near the top.'

'You mean the tie . . . the little flash of colour somewhere near the top? Yes, you're absolutely right. I must admit that I wear a tie to work now.'

'Well, you would do,' said Bilton. 'You're on the fast track from what I hear.'

I squirmed.

That night, I slept on a camp bed in Bilton's one bedroom.

'Shouldn't we shut the window?' I asked.

'A bit of a crosswind helps me sleep,' replied Bilton complacently.

Later on, as I lay beneath my billowing duvet, I asked Bilton whether it wasn't true that a safe house normally came equipped with some sort of bodyguard.

He thought about this. 'Yes,' he said, 'I suppose it normally does. I have a telephone,' he added at length; 'it's in the kitchen next to the bread bin. It's a special telephone of an old-fashioned sort, and if you dial nine you get straight through to the emergency person at the Home Office. In the event of any trouble they'd have a local man on the spot within minutes. Or so they say.'

'And do you believe them?'

'I couldn't give a toss, quite frankly.'

The next morning, I awoke early and walked into the kitchen to find a sullen Bilton stoking a feeble fire. His singing-in-the-kitchen days were clearly long since over. I wandered over to his yellowing fridge and picked up a carton of fruit juice. I handed Bilton a small piece of paper on which I'd scribbled a telephone number.

'This is my deputy Jim French's direct line. I've told him all about you. Give me a ring any time you fancy contributing to "Easy Like a Sunday Morning".'

I poured a little of the fruit juice into a glass, tasted it and read the label: it was called 'Breakfast Juice', which seemed to me an absurdly generic title. I should have left it at that, but instead, of course, I said, 'This is peculiar stuff, you know. Neither orange juice nor grapefruit juice. The two flavours seem to fold over each other. Incredibly frustrating.'

Bilton looked at me. I smiled. Then I noticed that the piece of paper with Jim French's telephone number on it was crumpled into a tight ball on the table next to him.

'Look,' he said, 'would you mind just going? I'm rather tired.'

I phoned for Graham Mann, and went upstairs to pack my bag. 'I'll wait outside,' I said when I came back down.

Bilton held the door stiffly open as I picked up my bag.

'Bilton,' I said.

But Bilton was looking at his watch.

'There's a train at nine; you should catch it easily.'

I walked down the track to the point where the taxi would wait. Graham Mann arrived and took me to the station. I sat on the platform. There were no trains, no people. My friendship with Bilton was over. Ironically, this was going to be a sunny day. I even felt quite hot, and I took my coat off.

At one minute to nine I started to be concerned about the train. And then somebody sat down next to me.

'Bilton!' I exclaimed.

'You know I said there was a train at nine?' he said.

'Yes.'

'Well, there isn't.'

'Why did you say there was, then?'

'Just to get rid of you.'

'Thanks,' I said.

'Well, you were being so fucking annoying.'

I didn't say anything. Petulant.

'There's quite a decent café in the square, actually,' said Bilton.

After breakfast I called Eleanor to say that I'd be staying for another day.

And it was a wonderful day. We turned a corner, and saw the sea, shockingly serene, with a few scattered offcuts of cloud floating slowly above in a high blue sky.

Bilton wonkily led the way along the dry white sand of the beach. We sat on a barnacled hulk of a sea barrier of some sort and read newspapers. At twelve o'clock exactly two fighter planes appeared and did some aerobatics for our personal amusement. We watched a bizarre, amphibious tractor drag two fishing boats on to the sand, and Bilton got talking to one of the fishermen, asking him detailed, unpatronising questions about the decline of the fleet – there used to be twenty boats – and the absence of anything for the young people in the village to do.

As evening fell we went to the fishermen's pub, which was warm and crowded and smelt of oranges and burning wood. All day, Bilton had been a little quiet, perhaps; but the self-pity of the day before had gone, and he was back to his admirable old habit of not talking about himself.

Nobody around us seemed to pay Bilton any undue attention.

'Maybe they don't know who I am, after all,' he said. 'Why should they? I doubt if they read newspapers. They're too busy trying to make a living.'

'But I bet they're on the Net,' I said.

There was no response from Bilton.

'That was a joke.'

'I thought it was,' he said.

At closing time Graham Mann came to collect us. Lolling on the back seat, Bilton turned to me.

'You know I said they're wasn't a train at nine o'clock in the morning?' he said.

'Yes.'

'Well, there was.'

And that was the one that I caught the next morning.

In London I called Carol Crane, and she did me the honour – as it seemed to me – of inviting me around to her house for the debriefing.

It was in Camden, of course. Like her office, it was entirely white: a traditional mews which had been substantially gutted to give two big bare rooms. We sat in the upstairs space, which had a big bookshelf that somehow went in a figure of eight. There was a metal table which was about two feet wide and yet about twenty feet long, and yet was only about a foot high. As in her office, there were no chairs as such, but things resembling scaffolding poles jutting out of the walls.

'Nice place,' I said, accepting a cup of coffee.

'Thanks,' said Carol Crane. 'All the stuff in here is Deke Swayne, of course. His stuff is inspired by the interior of a Vietnamese high-security prison.'

'Wow,' I said, 'he's seen the inside of a Vietnamese high-security prison, has he?'

'Absolutely,' said Carol, 'in a colour supplement. Changed his life. But what about Martyn?'

And I gave her a full account of his circumstances. Half-way through she began fiddling with her eyes in an alarming way.

'Sorry,' she sniffed, and I saw that she was removing her contact lenses – to release tears. She went away and came back wearing a pair of ordinary spectacles. She looked fine in them, but I was touched that she'd bothered to put in her contacts for me.

'Well,' she said, more composed now, 'how can I get in touch with him?'

I told her about George Warden.

Later, she stood on her doorstep, saying goodbye, shivering in her simple black robe.

'This war is so terrible,' she said. 'Just so terrible.'

She kissed me on the cheek, closed the door, and I heard her putting the locks on. A sad sound.

Chapter Twenty-Two

(Two years and six months after the incident)

Late in that second January of the war, I was standing in Battersea Park under a high tree with two brown leaves still attached to the very top, and wondering what to do next. It was a very bright and windy day, and a sudden gust seemed to make the shadow of a branch judder slightly to the left like the pointer of a big old clock. I looked up and saw a man sitting on a bench with his dog alongside him, and such was the intensity of the moment that he seemed to be the archetypal Man on a Park Bench with Dog.

The man on the bench was reading a tabloid newspaper and the headline said 'PEACE'.

Of course, it wasn't quite as simple as that.

The details of the peace would be arranged by the very boringly named Compromise Boards, which Lazenby and Zubarov had set up with the assistance of the Europeans. Their task – bureaucratic and pernickety in the extreme – of settling the nature of Russia's relationship with the Protected Republics was only just beginning.

That afternoon, I watched Lazenby's broadcast announcing that the war was won, and detected a slight slippage in his features; a certain crumpling loucheness creeping in; the product, no doubt, of too many secret nocturnal peace negotiations. His tie knot was back to its pre-war fulsomeness. At the end of the announcement, he shuffled papers in an old familiar way.

The next day, there was an uncommonly studious air at *The*

New Globe. For hour after hour news people and the top brains of 'Comment and Analysis' scrolled through the thousands of words in the peace communiqués. They were trying to work out whether this really was a victory. The answer, of course, would determine the line the paper took on Lazenby, which would determine, in turn, whether he survived in power. One exhausted C and A man summed up the issues for me at the water fountain.

'Firstly, we've gained a consultative role in the future foreign policy of Russia.'

'Excellent,' I said.

'But what does the word "consultative" mean, and will it be honoured?'

'Oh,' I said, 'I don't know.'

'Secondly, we get to chair the international sub-committee of the Internal Reconstruction Commission.'

'Very prestigious, surely.'

'Or is it just a pain in the arse? The stationery bill alone is expected to run into multi-millions, and we've agreed to buy all the rubbers and pencils . . . Thirdly, the Boards are trying to sort out the Republics and until then Zubarov is suspending all military operations, so the world is a safer place in the short term and may well be in the longer term too.'

'A major achievement, then?'

'But that's discounting the possibility of a new rebel commander emerging and saying, "Sod all that, I'm going to carry on doing what I want in the Protected Republics."'

'All right,' I said, 'but Zubarov has admitted he's lost the war, so the victory is ours, at least symbolically.'

'Remember, there was no surrender. The agreed formula was that, and I quote, "Bearing in mind the wishes of the British Government, and in the interests of humanity, we agree to a conditional suspension of military activity."'

'It's a tricky one, isn't it?'

The C and A man looked at his watch.

'I've been looking at the documents for ten hours, and I expect to be here for another six. It's going to take a hell of a lot of sweat to get an angle on this.'

In the end, of course, *The New Globe* acclaimed the settlement as a triumph for Lazenby because Little Willie Meltchitt – who'd been given a ten-word summary of the peace communiqués – tossed a coin and it came up heads.

But the whispering against Lazenby had begun, and it grew, of course, as the bodies began to be flown home.

It must have been about a fortnight later that I was walking with Eleanor and Barnaby along the towpath at Camden Lock. The barges, heaped with cargo, puffed peacefully along the dark green waters. Joggers were passing us on the inside and on the outside, and my little son seemed to find them amusing, positively laughing in his pushchair as they wobbled into view and disappeared.

Single file only was possible for joggers on the towpath, which is why, when I saw Carol Crane approaching us in lycra, I couldn't immediately tell who was jogging immediately behind her.

'Good grief!' I said, when I made out the figure.

'Oh,' said Carol, running on the spot. 'Hi.'

Bilton, also jogging on the spot, steam tumbling upwards from his mouth, possibly nodded. It was hard to tell as his head was bobbing about so. His hair was shorter. That was the first thing I noticed. He looked like a guy who was going a bit bald (the recession didn't seem so drastic as it had in Cornwall), and was doing the decent thing: keeping it short and neat. Despite the jogging he seemed to have put on a bit of weight around the face; it seemed to be squarer, taking away some of the wildness. He now had the face, I thought, of an intrepid young army officer.

His running kit, though, was pure Bilton: black slip-on plim-solls with flesh-coloured bottoms; inappropriate slumped, black socks, billowing shorts and some sort of weird singlet. He looked like one of those guys from your schooldays who, in the hope of getting out of PE, 'forgets' his gym togs, but whose ruse fails because he is immediately supplied with a lucky-dip outfit of mildewed clobber from the changing room lost-property basket.

Rudely ignoring Carol Crane, I said to Bilton, 'How long have you been jogging?'

'About fifteen minutes,' he said, panting. He'd stopped running on the spot now. He was looking warily at Barnaby.

'That yours?' he said, pointing rudely.

Eleanor said yes on my behalf.

'Thought so,' he said. 'Got the same expression as you.'

'Bilton . . .' I said.

'Cynical,' said Bilton.

'. . . this is absolutely incredible,' I said. 'What the hell's been happening? We must all meet up for a drink.'

'I know a good place,' said Carol. 'Ever heard of The Watering Hole?'

The Watering Hole was in Camden, funnily enough. All the furniture was glass or some other transparent material, and the only drink you could buy there was water. Bilton and Carol were already there when I walked in, talking happily as the little bubbles rose and popped in their elegant glasses. Bilton, no doubt under Carol's tutelage, wore a tweed jacket and a crisp, white open-necked shirt. He looked good; like a young professor.

'What do you think of this place?' said Carol.

'It's funny,' I said wistfully, 'but when one thinks of a watering hole, one thinks of a pub.'

'There is a problem with the name,' said Carol. 'I must agree with you there.'

Bilton leant forward and took a sip of his water. He grimaced slightly.

'They should call it "Water Water Everywhere",' he said, and Carol fluttered her hand up towards his ear.

'Such a genius,' she said.

A stranger would have interpreted Bilton's expression as impassive, but I detected a hint of a pleased look.

Then Carol told me how she'd been appalled at Bilton's circumstances in Cornwall; how she'd persuaded him to come and live in her house; how she'd installed a retired security guard in the basement; how she was determined to revive his career.

'The buzz words for Martyn are going to be "inegrity"; "noble suffering"; "wronged but not bitter". Here is someone who's been burned by life. He's haunted by the past, but that incredible spark, that incredible smoulder, is still there. That undaunted, almost noble savage quality.'

'I'm just off to the bog,' said Bilton, embarrassedly, and stalked off.

He was wearing, I noticed, some beautiful grey, baggy turn-ups and a pair of nice, simple black shoes.

'Do you think Bilton will be safe in Camden?' I said.

'Why do you call him "Bilton"?' said Carol.

'Well,' I ventured trepidatiously, 'it's his name.'

Carol shrugged.

'Of course he'll be safe in Camden, at least until it becomes trendy to kill people. We tried to keep a low profile initially, which is why we didn't contact you, and I'm sorry about that. But Martyn will soon be back in full circulation. With the end of the war the whole climate's changed. You can just see it in people's faces. The tension's gone.'

'That's true,' I said.

'Do you want to hear about the projects we've got lined up for Martyn?' said Carol, smiling coyly.

I did.

She whisked a bangle from her wrist to her elbow and back again.

'Firstly,' she said 'and this is totally Martyn's concept, we're going to get a gardening magazine up and running, in which readers' questions will be answered by other readers. Of course, it's going to be on the Net too. It's going to be incredibly functional, incredibly chic, and just incredibly beautifully presented – in words, no pictures.

She paused, and pulled both sides of her hair right back from her forehead.

'It's going to be called *Daisy Chain*,' she added breathlessly.

'Great title,' I said.

'Also, Martyn's memoirs – I mean the book of the decade, yeah? – are now in the pipeline. He's started writing, and we've got three publishers interested for big money.'

My old jealousy of Bilton was beginning to resurface. I had not expected this.

'TV interviews?' Celia went on. 'The diary is full. Channel 11 is dedicating a whole programme to Martyn in their *Me and My War* series. Oh, and he's writing up that thing by Casey and the Sublime Band or whatever they're called for "The Song That Changed My Life" in your paper.'

Bilton, back from the gents', sat down again, sipped his water and returned it hastily to the table.

'I don't think I like water,' he said. 'It's too . . . watery.'

'Have you stopped drinking?' I asked, suspiciously.

'Cut down a bit,' said Bilton.

'Dramatically,' corrected Carol. 'I'm so proud of him.'

'Your relationship . . .' I said. 'Something tells me it's more than purely professional.'

Bilton shrugged, noncommittal.

'I'm pregnant,' said Carol.

And now Bilton did actually smile.

I kissed her; shook Bilton's hand.

'If only we had something to drink except this bloody water! Well, well,' I went on, fatuously, 'Barnaby will have a little friend to play with.'

'No child of mine is playing with anybody called Barnaby,' said Bilton. 'My child is going to have a good, solid proletarian name.'

'We'll see about that,' said Carol.

'Stan,' said Bilton.

'Never!' squealed Carol.

'Maybe it'll be a girl . . .' I said, continuing in my fatuous vein.

'Ron,' mused Bilton. 'Ron Bilton. That's got a nice, lyrical quality to it.'

Carol was laughing, her hands intertwined with Bilton's, and they both looked at me, smiling.

'I'm flabbergasted,' I said. 'I just do not know what to say.'

I met Bilton three more times over the next month. Twice in pubs and once, radically, in a tea shop. He never drank more than two pints of beer; he was amusing, dry – still, perhaps, slightly subdued.

His left-of-centre viewpoint remained. But he was no longer out on a limb. His intolerance of mainstream terminology, of a mainstream frame of reference – that sneer, in a word – had gone. He was taking a particular interest in the discomfiture of Lazenby. The peace, it seemed, had been more or less forced on Lazenby by leftist factions within his party: a process which had started the day after that terrifying night during which everybody waited to be incinerated by a missile from Kiev.

A sarcastic speech by the new political *enfant terrible* Rufus Mallory ('Well, that was a jolly nice little war, but what was it for?') had severely embarrassed Lazenby. And Roz Newbold's 'Royal Body Language' correspondent had departed from her usual brief to proclaim the Lazenby marriage in tatters, having observed a series of photographs showing the way that Mrs Lazenby's left foot pointed at a reception in the American Embassy.

Lazenby's hold on national-hero status was ever more tenuous, and it was in an obvious attempt to shore it up that he proclaimed 29 February (it was a leap year, of course) a day of thanksgiving and celebration: Peace Day.

Chapter Twenty-Three

At 6 p.m. on Peace Day, I met Bilton in a small, buckled pub in one of those little Georgian streets that you might glimpse through a chink in the wall as your train pulls out of Charing Cross station.

The pub was dusty and dark, and smelt of black treacle. It was only just beginning to fill up. There were a few streamers about the place; some Union Jacks. Bilton was sitting at the bar in a lovely blue suit.

'Nice suit,' I said, taking my place next to him.

'Carol chose it for me,' he said.

'You surprise me,' I said.

He bought me a pint.

'Hey!' I said when it arrived. 'Congratulations. I think that was the first time you've bought the first one . . .'

Bilton grunted.

'How's the kid?' he said, not, admittedly, with much enthusiasm, but such conventional solicitousness was also new.

'Good,' I said. 'Very good as a matter of fact.'

'What's his name again? Willoughby?'

'Barnaby,' I said.

'Right,' said Bilton.

'Do you think it's a nice name?'

'I think it's a nice name . . . for a rabbit.'

The old Bilton resurfacing.

'Fuck off,' I said, quite happily. 'I tell you, when you see that weird little thing come wriggling into the world with all the determination, all the complication and hope there, right from the word go, it'll turn your head, man. It's the most momentous thing you'll ever see and you've just got to sit down and think, where on earth did this person come from, and then you've just got to close your eyes and try to come to terms with . . . What are you doing?'

Bilton was squinting at his pint.

'Do you think this is a short measure?' he said.

Later, we walked towards Trafalgar Square. The shops were closing (some had never opened), computer screens flickering like candles as the last calculations were done. It was cold; a mist was beginning to swirl; the red buses, warm phosphorescent light inside, swarmed and jostled.

A young man in a fashionable long coat strode up to Bilton. He had a microphone in his hand. Behind him was a team of technicians clad in bulky jackets.

'Oh no,' I muttered to Bilton. 'It's *Spotted in the Street*.'

'Martyn Bilton, yeah?' said the young man to Bilton.

'I guess so,' said Bilton, but I sensed that, deep down, he was quite pleased.

Someone behind the young man made a note. Somebody else, with a big technical box strapped to his back, spoke to the young man, who looked at his massive, glowing watch.

'Mind if we just, like, right in?' said the young man to Bilton. 'We're live in two.'

'Two what?' said Bilton. 'I'm not standing around here for two hours.'

But already the young man had started talking to one of his team – the one with the camera.

'Welcome back to *Spotted in the Street*, and now we have Martyn Bilton with us . . .'

The young man turned towards Bilton.

'Martyn, in the early time phase of the conflict you suffered a very major downfall, shall we say, on your personal quote unquote Richter Scale of public approval and I was just wondering what, that is to say, how you . . .'

'You're a good talker,' said Bilton. 'Keep going.'

'What projects, I mean, have you been working on since you effectively slipped below the limelight?'

'I've been living in a safe house in Cornwall,' said Bilton, 'drinking a lot of tea and eating a lot of so-called Nice biscuits.'

'A safe house? So that could be interpolated as a house that's, like, safe?'

Bilton nodded.

'A lot of people wanted me dead. I expect you have the same problem.'

But fortunately, at that very moment, one of the young man's team had spotted someone else in the street, and was tugging at his sleeve.

'Thank you very much, Martyn Bilton,' said the young man distractedly, and the whole lot of them moved off.

Bilton and I walked on. We came to Trafalgar Square, which was thronging with people – people meeting other people, embracing and moving off to their place of celebration. There were intermittent cheers, and hats thrown in the air. Fireworks blasted giant dissolving jellyfish into the sky – becoming falling willow trees of light. Happy policemen patrolled, breathing steam, dressed in capes, lumbering like old carthorses.

The buildings, bearing their forests of rippling flags, seemed to converge on the Square like ocean liners on a harbour. TV vans, tiny under their great rotating discs, were everywhere, throbbing and fairy-lit. Celebratory arc lights pierced the smoky clouds. Bilton said something to me, but I couldn't hear what.

We entered Pall Mall. Long cars drew up outside the clubs, some with the hieroglyphics of foreign number plates. They disgorged one important man each, and then some other less important ones. These lesser ones stood, taking notes, talking into phones and watching staged handshakes taking place within enclosures bounded with dark blue ropes. We walked past the doors of the clubs: honey glow, red carpets; usually a gilded, altar-like clock; dinner-jacketed ambassadors smoking pipes in the warm distance.

We moved on, towards The Place near Green Park. It was packed, of course, beautiful people swarming under the mighty, rotating televisions. Carol and Eleanor were there, waiting for us. As the niceties were spoken, and cocktails summoned, I watched the screens. Lazenby was on one of them, waving with his wife from an open-topped car. On the television nearest to me, a big Russian guy was talking, most respectfully, in his underwater voice of 'Myeester Byird . . . steeyatesman of the highest calibure . . . gale-orious neeyew era for our two neeyations'.

I looked about me. Just to my right was the enigmatic, monocled pop star 'Mr E. Guest'. Over to the left the billion-aire DJ Nick Dunn, who apparently owned half of Scotland, was drinking from the neck of his bottle, and periodically returning to the neck of his girlfriend. Here, alongside me, were some of the beautiful boys from the experimental the-atre troupe Flail.

Now Mr E. Guest was walking towards us, two body-guards following in his wake. He was tiny, looked more like a jockey than a singer, except that he was wearing a dress. He removed his monocle.

'Mr Martyn Bilton?' he said.

He called everybody 'Mr'; that was part of his gimmick.

'Yup,' said Bilton.

'I am most honoured to make your acquaintance, and I would be graciously obliged if at some stage you might trouble yourself to communicate further with me.'

He spoke like that; it was another part of his gimmick.

Bilton pocketed the card.

'Yeah,' he said, 'we could have a pint and a pie one day.'

Mr E. Guest replaced his monocle and walked away.

'Do you know what his real name is?' said Bilton. 'Wally Bottoms. And if you print that, he will sue you and then have you murdered, very, very slowly.'

'Right,' I said. 'I'll bear that in mind.'

On we went, to have dinner in the prestigious front part of The Back Room in Shaftesbury Avenue. Harry Piper was there, holding on to June Brown. He had fallen off the waggon. He walked (after a fashion) across to our table.

'Well, well, well,' he said.

He was looking at Bilton.

'Well, well, well,' he said again. 'Hey, how come you're not writing for us any more?'

'You sacked me,' said Bilton.

'Oh,' said Piper. 'I wonder why? Well, it's all water under the bridge now, eh. Forgive and forget. New spirit abroad. By the way, did you get those death threats we forwarded on to you? . . . Tell, you what,' he said, falling over and getting up again, '. . . I'll have a little word with Little Willie. See if we can't get a chap like you back on board.'

Bilton was shaking his head; a melancholy smile.

'No chance,' said Carol Crane. 'But if you want to bid for serial rights on his memoirs, here's my card. I warn you, they'll cost a bomb.'

I looked at Piper and thought it politic to try an I'm-sorry-but-what-can-I-do-about-it shrug. I'm not sure it worked.

After dinner we went to the Radio Café. Here, of course,

you could ask the DJ to play you any record ever made and, as we stood amongst the crowd on the balcony over the dance floor, Bilton said to Carol, 'Come to think of it, you know, there is one record I'd like. It's . . .'

'You don't have to say it, you idiot,' said Carol, making off in the direction of the DJ.

When she returned, 'Queen of Clubs' was already blaring, and we all started dancing. Yes, even Bilton, whose style was oddly reminiscent of somebody kneading dough while walking across hot coals and balancing a precious vase on top of his head.

'Bloody good song, that,' he said, when the song finished, to ironic cheers from the smart brats around us.

After that, we just went to an ordinary pub off Haymarket, and settled down at a cosy corner table. At about midnight I stood with Bilton in the gents'. He was singing one of his strange little songs, just like the old days. As we washed our hands, we exchanged smiles in the mirror: proper, unselfconscious ones on both sides, just before steam from the hot taps made the reflections cloud.

Five minutes later the landlord announced that he'd run out of beer.

'Sorry, folks, it's been one of those nights.'

And we all spilled out on to the street.

We couldn't decide what to do. It was cold. Carol and Eleanor wanted to call it a night. The fireworks were still going on, but without booze, in the late-night cold, their resonance had changed, and the bangs put me in mind of big hoardings falling into empty streets. We drifted towards The Mall. A man under a statue was playing a guitar for a small crowd; there were a few gatherings around the braziers of St James's Park. And then there was a heart-stopping bang: a particularly big hoarding falling a particularly long way.

'I'm off,' said Eleanor, simply.

Everyone sort of nodded, and we started to cross The Mall, but now somebody was flagging Bilton down. It was nobody really, just a boy – sixteen or so – with an autograph book.

'I know you're famous,' said the kid, 'but I don't know exactly who you are.'

'Ha!' said Bilton.

As he signed the book, a church bell tolled four, and when it had finished, the rain started. Looking back at St James's Park, I saw a line of running people. At the head was a naked man doing a silly, prancing dance, and he was being followed by line of fully clothed runners, all moving with an amazing stylistic consistency: knees high, arms akimbo, heads looking down and then up; pointing. It was some sort of Keystone Cops or music-hall-policeman routine and, as I watched, the chase resolved itself into a fluid, continuing figure of eight between the trees.

Down The Mall from my left came a slow street-sweeping vehicle of the sort that has displaced the rising sun as the symbol of dawn in a city. Its several spinning lights gave it a festive look that sat oddly with its humdrum function.

Then a police car came down The Mall and overtook the sweeper with a contemptuous surge of speed. Handing the autograph book back to the kid, Bilton stepped out on to The Mall, and the long, black car that was following like a solid shadow behind the police car crumpled him with a soft, sinister sound that seemed to say 'that's your fucking lot'. Then the black car stopped.

On the dull pink tar of The Mall, the blood was gushing from Bilton's mouth, as though it had never wanted to be inside him in the first place. I saw his chest subside and, outrageously, not rise again. Or not yet. I would give him time.

Looking at the naked runner, I saw that the line was breaking up behind him. Some of the followers were falling down and laughing but some had seen what had happened and were running towards me and the dying Bilton, whose face, which I was mostly keeping below my line of vision, was violet. With a monstrous, rising roar, the street sweeper was coming alongside.

Carol was screaming; Eleanor was screaming; and a man in a suit was walking towards me with considerable momentum. He was making a sort of ushering gesture with his hands, as though urging me back, away from Bilton. Behind him, an elegant, dainty man had emerged from the car with a fawn coat over his shoulder. At first the man simply looked rich: a generic. And then I saw who it was.

There were a dozen or so people alongside me now, and the little crowds were peeling away from the braziers of Green Park and coming towards the sound of the screams, along with the young people who had been chasing the naked man. My view of Philip Lazenby was blocked by the man in the suit, but I had had time to notice that a woman was standing next to him. Not his wife.

The man in the suit was now talking on his mobile phone.

'Yeah, sorry. What was that? Yeah, now.'

Behind him the big black car was racing away. Lazenby and the woman had gone. Ambulances stressfully converged.

Chapter Twenty-Four

Why had Lazenby climbed out of the car? That, of course, was his big mistake. Too many people had seen him, and one of them, of course, had photographed him standing in The Mall with the woman. It took a week for that shot to appear in the newspapers, but I'm rather ashamed to say that, five minutes after the car hit Bilton, I had enough composure to phone the newsdesk of *The New Globe*.

They couldn't run a splash just on my say-so – I was pretty obviously pissed for one thing – and the story appeared as a downpage item on page three, couched in terms of being a mere report of a rumour. But it was enough to trigger the famous Official Version.

For a long time I just couldn't think about that scene in The Mall.

My son's crying began to cause me unnecessarily profound anguish; I took cold winds personally; the sight of an empty chair seemed unsustainably poignant. There was a not-so-mature mature student who lived alone near us. In the past I had observed his lifestyle through his bedsit window with amusement: half-eaten cans of beans; cheap clothes thrown over chair backs; crumpled fag packets. Now I couldn't bear to look. He reminded me of Bilton.

One rainy day, I accidentally stood on a snail on my garden path, and burst into tears at the terrible, complicated crackling and then grinding sound. My wife ran out to console me.

'What's the point of them having shells,' I wailed, 'if that's all the fucking . . .'

'Leave it,' said Eleanor.

I was hysterical.

I found therapy in work. My tip-off to the newsdesk meant that anything was possible for me. Little Willie himself said that there was a place for me in 'Comment and Analysis' any time I liked. But I wanted to stick with the soft stuff; I needed the balm of my harmless journalism.

I even came up with a new lifestyle regular.

'Shoot,' said Harry Piper, when I walked into his tenth-floor den and sat down.

'How about this . . . "Me and My Car"?'

'We've already done it,' said Piper.

'We haven't.'

'It's there in one of the motoring supplements – I can't remember exactly where. Now I've got to get on.'

He pointed at his door.

'Look in your file.'

'I tell you, we've done it,' he said, but he was scrolling down his screen and looking for it. 'I mean, it's such a basic concept. When it comes to lifestyle regulars, it's idea number one.'

After a couple of minutes, he looked up at me.

'Can't find it. Must be looking in the wrong place.'

'We haven't done it,' I repeated, 'and nor has anyone else.'

'It's *vieux chapeau*, I tell you,' said Piper, resuming his computer search.

After about five minutes, he suddenly stood up, walked across the office floor and kissed me on the mouth.

'You are a fucking genius,' he said, sitting back down. 'Of course, you know what Little Willie's going to say?'

'The true brilliance,' I said, 'of all brilliant ideas?'

'Something like that,' beamed Harry Piper. 'Oh, and by the way, piece of news. This is Hailey Young's last day. She's leaving. She's been sacked, if you want to put it that way.'

I was pleased.

'That's a shame,' I said.

'Okay, she made a go of "Me and My Teeth", but "What I Did Yesterday" has been all over the place recently. The basic trouble being, of course, that she's not put enough effort in. Called her into the office yesterday, and said, "Hailey, what the hell did *you* do yesterday?" That put her on the spot, I can tell you. Now I must get on. We've bought serialisation rights on that actress Harriet Courtneay's new book.'

'*How to Bake an Orgasm*?'

'You bet. One of the most momentous things ever written about cakes.'

'We're publishing extracts, are we?'

'Publishing extracts?' said Piper. 'Do you realise the popularity of this stuff? We're publishing the whole bloody thing. We're publishing extracts of the *newspaper* on the days that we're running this.'

That was the day of Rupert Granger's all-channels interview with Lazenby about the events in The Mall.

A summary of the background is surely unnecessary, but here it is.

The Official Version was that Lazenby was not driving the car. It would certainly have been irregular if he *had* been driving the car, but I – as I was eventually prevailed upon to observe in print – thought I had seen him emerge from the driver's seat, and so, it transpired, had others.

Had he deliberately, vengefully killed Bilton? Or ordered his driver to step on the gas, having seen and identified him? Of course not. The whole thing, like everything in life, was just a ghastly coincidence.

For about five minutes after her photograph was published, the woman in the car was known as 'The Mystery Woman'. Then, of course, it emerged that her name was Pandora Barclay. Her profession? The oldest.

The Official Version – it's pretty mind-boggling even after all this time – went as follows. Philip Lazenby had seen Pandora Barclay walking down Whitehall, and he had ordered his driver to stop and offer her a lift. She was scantily clad; she looked cold. He had never seen her before. He was unaware that she was a prostitute.

Pandora Barclay, of course, sold her story to *The New Globe* after a lunch with Little Willie, and then gave the money to a children's charity. According to her account, Lazenby (who was always at a loss to say where he'd been heading that night as his car entered The Mall) was taking her to a hotel in Victoria. It would have been their fifth assignation. They'd never had sex. They just lay on the bed and talked about Social Dynamics, or at least Lazenby did. But there had been 'a funny kind of love' between them.

Initially, on the questions concerning Bilton's death, Lazenby was quite cool.

'He was a political enemy of yours,' Granger said. 'You had what is called a history.'

'Oh, come on,' said Lazenby, who was at his most sumptuously dandyish (he looked like an orchid), 'don't be absurd.'

'You were driving the car, weren't you? Several people have attested to that.'

'My driver hasn't attested to it,' said Lazenby with a really quite effective sigh, 'possibly because he was the one who actually *was* driving the car. That's what drivers do, you know.'

'What a lot of people think,' Granger went on, 'is that this man, who is now facing possible prosecution, has fallen on his sword for you.'

'The man comes from Bethnal Green,' said Lazenby. 'He hasn't got a sword.'

'Let's turn to Pandora Barclay,' said Rupert Granger, 'which I believe is something that you did quite regularly.'

'Preposterous,' said Lazenby, shaking his head, and tossing away the one cue card that he had brought along with him.

'You think her story is all lies?'

'*All* lies. Here is a woman, a perfect stranger. She was standing in the street in a short skirt and I decided to pick her up – let me rephrase that; I decided to offer her a lift. After all, I had a big car. Just me in it and some detectives, why shouldn't I do that?'

'Did you not even suspect that she was a prostitute?'

'She told me that she was in corporate hospitality.'

'And so she was, in a sense,' said Granger. 'Is it true,' he went on, 'that on your first visit to Ms Barclay, you pretended to be a Philip Lazenby lookalike, and that she disbelieved you because she thought you didn't look sufficiently like yourself?'

'This is absolute balderdash,' yelled Lazenby with sudden fury. 'I will not be toyed with in this manner. You are simply trying to take the lid off a Pandora's B . . .'

It was the end of his political career. For poor Mr Lazenby, indeed, it was the end of everything.

Bilton's funeral took place in a rapidly encroaching sea fret on the east coast of Kent. The crematorium was Victorian Gothic, almost falling off the edge of a bloody cliff. Carol had arranged it all; generations of her family had finished up here. There had been strenuous attempts to keep the location from the press, and Harry Piper had been surprisingly good in not forcing me to write it up.

I arrived early. The place was deserted except for a small, ancient gardener toiling at a smoking pile of twigs.

'Excuse me,' I said, 'I'm here for the funeral of a friend, and I can't see anyone around.'

'What's the name?' he said in a soft, unpleasant voice.

'Do you mean my name?'

'No.'

'Bilton. Martyn Bilton.'

'Isn't he the nutcase that attacked Lazenby?'

'Oh, come on,' I said, 'there's no need for that. You're supposed to respect the dead.'

'I respect the dead,' he said, snapping a branch across his chest and dropping it on to the fire. 'I do their garden.'

The gardener of death, I thought; it would've made a lovely piece for 'Downbeat'.

'It's a beautiful place,' I said.

'I do my best,' said the gardener, but I was gazing at the broiling, purple and green sea and the crooked, black rock towers and arches juxtaposed at demonic angles about the cove rather than the man's insipid rows of hardy perennials. High above us, a screaming seagull was being bundled backwards in turbulence.

'Your friend is very lucky to get into this crematorium,' said the man, absurdly.

Clearly, his pride in his own work required some further comment.

'Bilton – my friend – he liked gardening.'

The man prodded at the fire with his boot; there was a lot of swirling smoke but no flame.

'Well, he didn't exactly like it,' I continued, 'he *wrote* about it.'

'He wrote about it, did he?' said the man with contempt. 'I'll tell you something, if I was writing about this fire I'd put down that it was alight by now. I'd put down that it was roaring like a . . .'

The man had suddenly stopped speaking.

'Like a what?' I barked.

A sudden, sustained blast of wind sent the man's ragged clothes fluttering and rippling about his scrawny frame and pieces of rural debris flew directly from him to me; his eyes slowly widened as the blast increased and the flesh underneath his prominent left cheekbone began to twitch. Then it stopped. The wind had died down, and the man pointed behind me.

'There's the vicar,' he whispered. 'That's his car.'

I scurried gratefully towards the pale vicar emerging from one of the new Japanese three-wheelers. He had been supplied, I think, by the local council.

'Mr Day,' he said, 'thank you so much for coming.'

Carol had done Bilton proud. She'd rounded up Timm the cartoonist, who arrived with one of his blondes in one of his sportscars ('I say!' blurted the vicar), and Allan, from Bilton's Group, came. Lifting off his motorbike helmet, he revealed himself as a surprisingly cool-looking dude, with hair of pale ringlets. It was nice of him to turn up, and I told him so.

'One thing you never mentioned in your letter . . .' said the vicar to me. 'Did Martyn have any hobbies or pastimes that he was fond of? Might be nice to give something like that a mention.'

'Drinking,' Allan butted in.

The vicar turned to him.

'He liked going off – usually alone – and drinking in as many pubs as possible. I think Adrian here can confirm that.'

'Actually,' said the vicar, 'I'm not going to speak for long, and I probably have enough as it is.'

The hearse came dawdling through the mist, and we went inside. Carol arrived late. She sat through the vicar's speech (Fortunes of war . . . Life spent in search of a higher truth . . .

Let's hope he's found it now . . . etc.) and walked out in tears. She had taken the precaution of not wearing her contact lenses.

Later, she walked red-eyed and white-faced around the bleak little hospitality room at the crematorium, carrying incongruously stylish nibbles that she'd brought up from London. The place was overheated by a reverberating radiator. Carol's brother was present, for some reason, and two mute crematorium staff.

The sea crashed and banged outside. As the vicar lit his cigarette from a shockingly long-flamed lighter, I began talking to Allan.

'What exactly was The Group for?'

'To me, it was purely a talking shop. You know, sixth-form stuff: the continuities between Hegel's and Marx's notion of alienation; macro-economics from the physiocrats to Keynes via Marx.'

'Eh?'

'Exactly. Very basic stuff.'

'Have you had any trouble from anyone?'

'I suppose I'm on some death list somewhere,' said Allan casually. 'I've had a couple of letters telling me to leave the country, calling me a traitor, that sort of thing. Not because of my beliefs so much as my association with Bilton.'

'Of course, he drank far too much,' I mused.

'Really?' said Allan. 'I never noticed.'

'You amaze me.'

'I'm joking. It went hand-in-hand with the depression he had. But I liked the guy. He believed in something, you see, and it's a rare gift these days: the gift of an opinion. Of course, that's at the heart of this whole hero-worship of Lazenby that now seems to have passed. People can't think, so they cleave to a media icon.'

'But you believe in something as well?'

'That's right,' he said. 'I do.'

We munched in silence for a while.

'What was The Group's line on Zubarov?'

Allan shrugged.

'Complicated. We're still working it out.'

'And the war?'

'That as well.'

'Bilton used to say that the war was inevitable. Something about monopoly capitalism.'

'That's the theory all right,' said Allan.

And now Timm interrupted us. Did I want a lift back to London?

I couldn't talk to Timm. He was too grand; and I didn't much feel like talking anyway. As we swept towards the capital in his silent car, I got sadder and sadder. And I was bloody tired. My mobile phone rang and I turned it off. At least, I thought I'd turned it off, but then it rang again. I turned it off again.

When I got back home, Barnaby was screaming and Eleanor was standing in the hall holding the phone. 'It's Harry Piper,' she said. 'He wants an article on the funeral after all. One thousand words by six o'clock.'

'Tell him to fuck off,' I said.

Now I was doing something in the kitchen, and Eleanor walked in.

'Little Willie Meltchitt is at the door,' she said. 'He wants to talk to you about Bilton.'

I had a cup of coffee in my hand. I walked to the door and threw . . .

'This you?' said Timm. I awoke from my dream to find him looking at me in the rear-view mirror. His girlfriend was turning around in her seat, smiling at me. I looked out and saw that we were driving down my street.

Chapter Twenty-Five

(Two years and eight months after the incident, and still counting . . .)

And on that artfully bathetic note my account might have finished. But four weeks later Allan called me.

'Hello,' he said. 'How are you?'

'Pretty well,' I said. 'And you?'

'Good,' he said. 'It was nice to meet you at the funeral.'

'It was nice to meet you,' I replied.

In my experience, unusually protracted small talk usually heralds significant conversation.

'So you've been well?' Allan went on. 'That's good to hear . . .'

'I've been extremely well,' I replied. 'And you say that you've been well too? That's excellent. How can I help you?'

'Have you ever thought about Bilton's background? Where he came from, I mean?'

I *had* wondered whether there were homes, apart from my own, where his death was sadly resonating.

I recalled that on one of our drunken rambles through London, the fraught question of Bilton's parentage had come up. We were in the City at the time, on an informal tour of the pubs, and I told Allan that I remembered Bilton leaning up against St Paul's, and saying, 'Actually I do know her bloody name. The old lady. It's Lomas, isn't it? Miss Lomas of Orpington and that's all you're getting out of me.'

'But I thought you were born in Greenwich?' I had wailed exasperatedly. He had just laughed, and I had scrawled the name Lomas into my diary at the first opportunity.

There was only one woman in the phone book for Orpington who was so old-fashioned as to identify herself as Miss: a Miss H.B.Y. Lomas. Encouraged by the chintzy initials, I had taken a coffee up to my study and called the number.

'Miss Lomas?'

'Who is that?' said a quavering, elderly female.

'Is that Miss Lomas?'

'No, it certainly is not. Miss Lomas is out on a walk with her pekes, and I'm holding the fort.'

'I may well have the wrong number, but could I just ask one question: does Miss Lomas have any children?'

'No. She's a watchamacallit, spinster.'

'Oh. Thank you then.'

'Why do you ask?'

'I have reason to believe that a woman called Lomas, who lives in this area, was the mother of a friend of mine, Martyn Bilton.'

'Are you suggesting that my best friend was a scarlet woman who's lived a lie and concealed the birth of a bastard?'

'I'm sorry. I don't mean to be rude.'

There was a pause.

'Well, it's not absolutely impossible. Are you anything to do with William?'

'No. Who's William?'

'He's a painter and decorator of sorts,' said the woman. 'Lived in Maidstone. Once I saw him and Jean – Miss Lomas, that is – who, as I say, I always thought was a spinster. I saw them together: they were just talking, but it did make me wonder.'

'What I . . .'

'And now this. Extraordinary. I shan't say anything, of course. Well, not to Miss Lomas herself, but this news will be very interesting to the ladies at St Dunstan's Church. Could you leave a number, and I'll ask her to call you? I shan't say what it's about.'

I told Allan that I had never heard anything more and that, later on, I had wondered whether Lomas had been the name mentioned by Bilton after all. I had also begun to have my doubts about Orpington.

'I see,' said Allan, and then he told me what he had called to say.

The next day I took the tube to Charing Cross and boarded what was optimistically billed as a 'fast train' for Greenwich.

This train banged and clanged along its Dickensian route, seemingly traversing the very back yards of negligible ter- races. At Greenwich I hurried past the colonnaded palaces at the foot of the park and began to climb a steep street of beau- tiful town houses. It was a freezing day with sunshine; behind me, London was a low, grey blur. I passed a church that was ringing its bell; walked past a manor house of sorts, gigantic trees and old walls.

At the top of the hill, I turned into a gravel pathwalk through high, gold-topped gates and entered the shadow of the red-brick mansion. I looked at the stunted forest of chimneypots. There were thirty-six in all. I stood there and counted them. The bell was covered in verdigris and as big as a dinner plate. With two hands I set it clanging.

To the sides of the house and behind were the grounds; to my left and right I could see tennis courts, an ornamental lake and four gardeners, silently toiling, breathing steam, barely within shouting distance of one another. Two were plodding with spades between piles of fertiliser and crescents of soil. Two were sawing branches in disparate high trees, looking like weirdly displaced carpenters.

The massive door juddered open, and a man looked down

at me. He was large, in his seventies, with a good figure, a pile of tousled white hair, and black eyebrows.

'What?' he said.

'Are you Sir Richard Haverstock?'

'I am the butler,' he replied, rather bitterly. 'Sir Richard is in the gazebo.'

'Can I see him?'

This was actually something of a bluff, because I had no idea what a gazebo was. I was vaguely entertaining the idea that it might be a place in Africa rather like The Congo. I hoped not.

'What is it?' drawled a voice to my left. The man wasn't as handsome as his butler. He was slight, wizened, with a narrow arrow of grey hair and a face of unattractive frosted pink. His hands, one of which gripped an effeminate trowel, were swollen and purplish.

'Gentleman wants to see you, sir,' said the butler.

I was out of breath with nervousness.

'I'm sorry to bother you,' I said. 'It's something quite personal.'

The man scratched the back of his left hand with his right hand.

'Talk out here,' he said. 'What is it?'

'Two things: one is that I knew your son; and the second thing – about which I'm very sorry – is that he's dead. But I can't believe you didn't know that; it was in all the papers.'

The man scratched his hand again and looked at me.

'Well, I don't have a son,' he said, 'and I never did.' He was now scratching his chin. 'Which rather puts a spanner in the works, doesn't it?'

'I'm a journalist,' I said. 'I worked with your son on *The New Globe*. With the person I was told was your son. I'm sorry. I seem to have been given the wrong information.'

The man was still scratching his chin.

'Yes, I would say that you had.'

He looked at the butler and smiled slightly. 'Labouring under a delusion, isn't he, Chester?'

'I'm sorry,' I said, and walked back towards the gates.

I proceeded with an insolent slowness born of exultation, and one of the gardeners suddenly dashed in front of me, wheelbarrow bouncing, muttering to himself as though sharing my excitement.

The 'Chester', of course, had clinched it – the name that Bilton had babbled after I'd seen his disastrous Granger interview. But Sir Richard Haverstock had Bilton's purple eyes, and I had fancied there was whisky on his breath. And that garden: that must have been where Bilton learnt about plants.

I considered what Allan had said. Bilton had settled on claiming *petit bourgeois* origins because to claim proletarian ones might have stretched credulity too far. Perhaps he'd been a little over-cautious here; after all, in our relatively egalitarian age, a refined accent would have been his only betrayer, and his wasn't particularly refined.

Bilton had briefly attended Eton, apparently. That rang true. His monomania was a close relation of the confidence which Etonians famously possess. Allan had told me that Bilton's hatred of his father came first and the politics of it all came second. What was it Allan had said? That Bilton's father – a self-made man, incidentally, and no aristocrat – was 'the biggest bastard in England'. The mother was long gone from an untenable marriage. Bilton and his father had disowned each other at approximately the same time, when Bilton was about thirteen. He had then been farmed out to aunts, one of whom had lent him her name.

Bilton had been willing to confess that some of his childhood had been spent in Greenwich because, according to

Allan, 'at least he'd know the area if anybody asked him questions about it'.

'Bilton liked you,' Allan had said. 'He just liked you. But he was never going to tell you the truth. I only found out by accident.'

And now I would tell Carol.

The dauntingly elegant terraces of the downwards-winding street had given way to a low building with frosted glass. I walked inside. It was a café of some sort, all steamed up. It appeared to be run by young people. On the radio was Ornette Coleman. A very fanciable waitress gave me a menu and I sat down and gave her my order. When she came back with my soup, I looked up to thank her, and then I saw Bilton behind the high counter.

It was a picture of him, torn from a magazine, the start of what Harry Piper had predicted would be the biggest cult amongst young people since the one that was the biggest since the one before.

It's thirty-five years since I sat in that café, and even now what I suppose one could call Biltonia has shown no sign of a let-up: the two volumes of collected journalism; the incessant articles and academic essays; the four biographies; the feature film. I prefer not to think of the T-shirts, CD covers and coffee mugs.

Why has it taken me so long to write my own account? At first, I was put off by the hype surrounding his death, which is peculiar, since hype was – as it remains – my profession. And then a subtle combination of sloth and six children intervened.

My long delay in putting pen to paper has at least allowed me to ask Martyn Bilton's son, Willoughby, for permission to go ahead, and this fine young man put no obstacle in my way.

I have added to the canon one revelation – that concerning Bilton's parentage – and, I hope, the perspective of a friend.

I think about him every day.